OUTCASTE

TALES OF TOLARI SPACE
BOOK SIX

CHRISTIE MEIERZ

OUTCASTE

TALES OF TOLARI SPACE
BOOK SIX

Histria SciFi & Fantasy
Las Vegas ◇ Chicago ◇ Palm Beach

Published in the United States of America by
Histria Books
7181 N. Hualapai Way, Ste. 130-86
Las Vegas, NV 89166 USA
HistriaBooks.com

Histria SciFi & Fantasy is an imprint of Histria Books encompassing outstanding, innovative works in the genres of science fiction and fantasy. Titles published under the imprints of Histria Books are distributed worldwide.

Library of Congress Control Number: 2024942604

ISBN 978-1-96151-192-7 (softbound)
ISBN 978-1-96151-191-0 (eBook)

PREFACE

Twelve years ago, while recovering from a near-fatal illness, I sat down at my computer, opened a fresh document in my word processor, and began to write about a little girl splashing her heels in a stream. That little girl was named Kyza, and she was about to undergo Suralia's Great Trial.

The story was almost immediately hijacked by the growing relationship between her father, the Sural, and her tutor, Marianne Woolsey, because while I grew up reading science fiction, I was at the same time sneaking the romance novels out of my mother's book closet and devouring those too. (I don't think she ever figured it out!) It was a given that science fiction and romance would collide in anything I wrote. The result, independently published, became the first novel in the Tales of Tolari Space. A surprise electronic bestseller, it went on to win the 2013 PRISM Award for Futuristic Romance.

The second novel, another bestseller, was really four interleaved stories. I wrote the third intimately informed by my experience of a close family member with a traumatic brain injury that led to memory loss and wild behavior changes. The last scene of that novel demanded that I write the fourth, which set our hero loose in human space and turned out to be my first foray into romantic suspense. The

PREFACE

fifth novel literally came to me in a dream; Bertie wanted the romance I hinted at in *The Fall* and invaded my dreams until I gave it to him.

Throughout these five books, I wrote extensively about Tolari culture in the strongholds and cities of the great provinces of Tolar, where a true empathic society developed and evolved. In this sixth novel of the series, I take a different turn and begin to explore the outcastes who rejected that society or were expelled from it, and how *they* feel about their world and the provincials running it. In the process, I bring in a few new characters to play with the more familiar faces. I hope you enjoy reading their adventures as much as I did writing them.

Christie Meierz, Rochester NY
February 22, 2024

For Kay and Lauretta, with much gratitude

CHAPTER 1

Shock cracked the English loose from Kim's tongue.

"You can't be serious," he said, then gave himself a mental shove and repeated the words in Kekrax First. On any other world, both exclamations would have bounced off the walls and floors of the Six Planets Embassy, but echoes struggled to birth on a Kekrax planet. Instead, his clicks, hisses, and squeaks landed dully and disappeared into the mud coating the marble floor and the accompanying thick layer of fine dust on every horizontal surface. The iconic smell of Kekrax mud pervaded the air in this patently disused room. Housekeeping's efforts to keep ahead of the challenge Kekrax Main presented, even here in the only stone building in a city constructed of brick and thatch, had failed miserably.

That the room they'd put him in *was* disused, Kim reflected, might have been deliberate on the embassy staff's part. They knew the Kekrax judge he'd come to meet was unlikely to see the mud on the floor, since the little aliens were usually covered with it themselves. Come to think of it, nine months on Kekrax Main had changed his own attitude toward mud and dirt, and he seldom noticed the grey streaks on his own bronze skin, although it could be bothersome in his shaggy black curls. Still, he would recognize the conditions in the Embassy, and they knew it.

Now the small reptilian sophont before him bowed her head. The distressed manner in which Nine-Three of Nine-Three Slash First's twin tails twisted around each other, first one way and then the other, telegraphed just how upset she was that her news spelled disaster for Kim.

"Venerated male," Nine-Three hissed in creditable English, a difficult language for Kekrax. "She regrets to say she is most serious."

Kim rocked back on his heels. Carefully, he said, "Honored First, she corrects him if he is mistaken. The research organization he works for sells his contract with *value owed*. They come for him in a week, the debt owners. Does he have that correctly?"

"He does, venerated male. They regret they can do nothing legal to help him, the Kekrax judges."

The wind went out of Kim. He sat down hard on the dusty, mud-stained marble. That brought him more or less eye to eye with Nine-Three, who would have been perhaps a meter tall were she not stooped with age. She laid her first pair of arms on his left shoulder and flicked his cheek with a long, sticky tongue. It was an affectionate gesture from a Kekrax, one they used to calm and give comfort to one another.

Kim offered her a slight smile. Kekrax assigned to interact with humans knew about smiles, but out of consideration he'd cultivated the habit of keeping his lips closed as much as possible, to avoid the alarming show of teeth. Underneath, he felt a little sick. Selling his contract with value owed wasn't legal. It never had been, but Central Command, for reasons a moral person could only guess at, had done nothing to stop the black market in forced indenture. His now-former employer XenoResearch, or more likely its corporate owners, had likely spun the contrived debt out of a vague line in the fine print of his sabbatical contract that got past the University's legal department.

Debt worker. They'd made him into a debt worker. It was tantamount to kidnapping, and Kim had no family to mount a legal effort to stop them. His friends and colleagues back on Tau Ceti Station, who knew how much he valued his independence in the field, were unlikely to notice his disappearance until he failed to return at the end of his sabbatical, three months from now. By then, his location would be untraceable, and he would be remembered only as a cautionary tale to the unwary: never work alone.

"He goes to the hostel and speaks to the First there," Nine-Three said. "He uses the communications grid for the finding of legal representation."

He let out a breath and caught himself before he nodded. It wouldn't do to give what was to a Kekrax a gesture of happy pride, or worse, a slow nod of abiding friendship. "He thanks her, honored Nine-Three of Nine-Three Slash First."

Nine-Three gave his cheek another tongue-flick and turned to scurry away on all eight limbs, looking like nothing so much as a ribbon of green and brown camouflage splattered with grey mud. After she disappeared out the door, he retrieved a handkerchief from his shoulder bag to wipe the sticky dribble from his cheek. It would have devastated the dear old judge to see her saliva wiped away in front of her. The lick was a gift and a kindness, and it wouldn't harm him, since almost nothing on Kekrax Main was toxic to humans. But as much as he enjoyed interacting with the subjects of his research here, he couldn't abide wearing Kekrax spit.

He tucked the handkerchief back into the bag and pulled out his tablet to search his media subscriptions. He didn't read the news every day, or even every week, and apparently he should have. Up to now, he hadn't much cared which large conglomerate owned XenoResearch; they all paid the same rate for a short-term market research contract, and Xeno offered him more freedom than the others. But Nine-Three informed him that it was owned by Di Fata, formerly the largest, wealthiest company in human space, which for its owner-family's sins and many offenses was suffering the same fate as a lion set upon by dogs. The latest pound of flesh the hounds had ripped away and begun to devour was Xeno and its assets, including Kim's contract. That would be merely inconvenient if they'd just demanded a final report based on current data and sent him on his way. He'd

3

have simply returned to his post lecturing at the University sooner than expected. Unfortunately, Di Fata was a consummate corporate predator, and some bean counter had noticed his lack of family and conspicuous solitude on Kekrax Main. According to Nine-Three, they'd declared Kim's contract unfulfilled and Kim liable for an eye-watering balance that represented the entire future marketing potential of his economic and cultural survey of the Kekrax.

Even if he wanted to pay the fictional debt, he couldn't. His wages had gone to purchasing shinies and sparklies in a long-running effort to gain social access to the fantastically rare Kekrax broodmales. Not for the first time, he wished he'd been a bit more far-sighted with respect to saving for the future, although that scarcely mattered now. The amount Di Fata decided he owed them exceeded what he could earn in decades as a professor at Tau Ceti University. He spat and watched the foamy spittle sink into the mud and dust caked on the floor. He'd done the research Xeno asked of him, and now Di Fata held him responsible for the profits their own bankruptcy had erased.

He needed an attorney and fast, before his new *employers* arrived to carry him off. He could end up anywhere: in a toxic industrial hellhole with a faulty breather, or doing hard labor on a colony world that shunned automation, or somewhere along the demarcation line with the Terosha, strapped into an environment pod, sweltering in the stink of his own sweat, scarcely able to move. If he was lucky, for values of *lucky* that included a longer life in servitude, they would assign him to a farm. Fieldwork was backbreaking, but it was safer than being a building inspector on Hlatra, where a steel tool lasted mere days and buildings could fall on you without warning. Either way, he'd never again see his students or an academic paper with his name on it.

He shook himself and hauled himself to his feet. First things first. He should speak to the Six Planets ambassador. Out in the embassy reception area, there was no sign of Nine-Three, but the lobby was lightly populated, mainly by a number of obvious tourists awaiting appointments with Visa Control upstairs. Two men limped heavily as they approached the lifts—victims, no doubt, of Kekrax Main's slippery mud. A few took notice of him as he made his way across the marble floor, shaking their heads or grinning. One huffed and turned away, stiff-backed and offended.

The reason for the various reactions was most likely his attire—or rather, his lack thereof. Kim wore nothing other than the cleated sandals on his feet and a shoulder bag to keep his tablet and research materials clean. On most days, he also wore a smile, but today his face was stripped of that as well.

At the reception desk, a bored-looking woman in Central Security greys sat staring at her tablet, its colors moving across her face. She looked up at his approach, and her gaze turned glacial. The embassy staff didn't appreciate his casual nudity and didn't share his view that clothing was simply too much trouble, given the heat, the omnipresent mud, and the notorious Kekrax curiosity about alien anatomy. He'd dispensed with it mere weeks after his arrival, blessing his grandmothers—one Far Indian, the other New Chin—for a complexion that protected him very well from K'kraxin's equatorial sun. After all, skin was easier to clean than fabric.

The Embassy staff was less than sanguine about his sartorial choice, but Six Planets law protected his right to wear local clothing on an alien planet, even if that meant wearing nothing at all. Their curiosity satisfied now, the locals no longer noticed him. More or less. He didn't give a toss what the staff thought. Prudish Terrans, Central Command's typical hires, the lot of them.

As he walked into the security field, the sounds of conversation and people moving about in the lobby abruptly faded to quiet.

"Professor," the woman at the desk said to a spot in the air somewhere to the west of his left shoulder.

"I need to speak with the ambassador," he said. "XenoResearch sold me into indenture. I need legal help, and I don't have enough in my account to get back to Tau Ceti."

That snapped her gaze to his face. "The ambassador is on station this week."

"There has to be a way to see her. Does she have any open appointments up there?"

5

She poked at the receptionist station. "Her earliest opening is in two days, on Wednesday. Do you want me to book a seat for you on the next shuttle?"

"Please."

More poking. Then, "I'm sorry, Professor, you have insufficient funds for the shuttle fare."

Kim sucked in a breath. "That can't be right. Try my credit line."

"There's nothing to try. Your credit line is closed. Your account balance is zero." She folded her hands on the desk. "Would you like an appointment after she returns? Her first opening is the following Tuesday."

He couldn't breathe. They'd already seized his assets, such as they were. He stared at her, the edges of his vision darkening. "Is there a way to contact her sooner? A conference call? A note? Anything? I'll —" he gulped air "—I'll be gone by Tuesday."

"Good luck, Professor." It was clearly a dismissal.

Perhaps he should have bothered with clothing after all. It might have garnered him some sympathy now. He took a deep breath and planted his hands on the desk, fashionably overlong curls falling into his eyes as he glared into hers.

"Do you understand what's happening here?" he hissed. "If they can grab a *Tau Ceti University professor*—"

"Good luck, Professor," she repeated, comprehensively.

He held her gaze until she lowered hers. Then she raised her eyes again with a look of panic on her face.

"Really, it's just skin," he said, and the disdain he suddenly felt for her lent strength to his voice. "You should try it sometime. You'd be more comfortable in the heat."

She spluttered. He turned and walked out of the security field, into the sound of murmurs from the unwitting audience of human tourists and Embassy officials. In the thoroughly muddy avenue outside, the familiar heat wrapped around him like a blanket. He kept to the shade and turned toward the humans-friendly hostel where he lived, taking a route that wandered, as all Kekrax roads did, through spreading trees and leafy vines that protected low, mud-brick buildings. The

Embassy abutted a commercial area of shops and eateries, but it was a rest day and few Kekrax were out, much to his relief. He didn't feel like talking. A Second—a male—across the avenue performed a human-style wave, and he waved back, but he wasn't close enough to be sure who it was. Seven-Three of Nine-Six, an official of this area's education collective, maybe, but Kekrax mostly did all look alike, even to his practiced eye. They looked even more similar when splattered with mud, as they usually were.

The smell of that mud filled his nostrils, along with floral scents and something reminiscent of fresh-mown grass. He breathed in the fragrance, trying to think and failing miserably. *Damn.* What to do now? At least he knew where to start. He could use the proffered communications grid, first to find out if there were any human attorneys on Kekrax Main's orbital station, and then to send messages to his friends and colleagues on Tau Ceti Station, alerting them to his situation. He stepped up his pace. Realistically, the chances of a human-run legal office on the station were slim to none this far into alien space, but he had to try, because the only other way to avoid his indenture was to run away.

Debt owners typically employed security forces to prevent flight and retrieve reluctant assets. Should Kim fail to report for duty, they would show up in short order, sniffing out his human DNA among the Kekrax with ease. Getting to a human planet where he would be harder to find, by sneaking onto a starliner, required getting to the station, but stowing away on a shuttle to get there would be akin to trying to hide in the back of a rowboat.

There had to be a way out of this.

He was halfway back to the hostel, still keeping to the shade, when a mob of shin-high broodlings pelted out of an alley at high speed and swarmed him. He did a practiced count by tens—progeny were power here—and came up a little short of four. That probably made them the currently celebrated clutch of thirty-seven that included a single precious broodmale, who had been safely left in the nest, of course. His mere existence raised this entire brood's importance despite its small size.

Kim paused to wonder. He'd *never* seen an unaccompanied brood this young. They jumped up and down at and on his feet, making grabs for his hands, squeaking and hissing. One adventurous individual climbed up his leg, leapt onto his arm, and was perched on his shoulder when Four-Three of Eight-One Slash First, their female parent, and Two-Five of Four-Seven Slash Second, one of their male parents, whipped around the corner, hissing and clacking their displeasure, scolding Kekrax-fashion. The little beggars must have run when the First and Second weren't looking.

Up close, both adults were readily recognizable, at least to Kim. More, they were distinguished by the especially vibrant greens and rich browns of their scales, which was due to the fact that they were parents. Well, more accurately, to the fact that they were sexually active, thanks to the adult broodmale who completed their trio. Once they stopped hissing and the brood was mostly quiet, they turned to Kim, tails waving, heads bobbing with pride.

"Honored First," Kim said to Four-Three, in Kekrax First. He bowed, and the enterprising broodling fell off his shoulder to bounce into the mud with a squeak. "Venerated Second! Joy of producing a broodmale for K'kraxin!"

Their heads bobbed faster for a moment, then slowed. Two-Five peered closely at Kim.

"It chases him, an untold," he said to Four-Three. He gestured toward a nearby park, dotted with mud pools where human parks would have placed picnic tables. "He sits with them and talks, the venerated Kim male."

Kim sighed. He didn't want to *talk* about it; he wanted to get started on finding a way out of this mess. But Two-Five and Four-Three were the closest friends he had on this muddy jungle of a planet, and he could certainly spare them a quarter hour. It might help him to gather his wits for the coming ordeal of trying to convince a lawyer on the orbital station above, if there was one, to help him *pro bono*. If there weren't any human attorneys here, maybe someone on Tau Ceti could send help, although that would cut things close. With his funds gone, an L-space link was out of the question, and the K-space message delay to Tau Ceti was two and a half days. Nine-Three had estimated in her careful way that he had perhaps six days' grace. Still, a quarter hour wouldn't hurt.

He followed Two-Five to the nearest pool of warm, slick mud and plopped into it, careful to tuck his more floaty bits between his thighs before the broodlings took the opportunity to explore his alien architecture. All thirty-six little ones splashed in after him—his count was secure with their identity confirmed—and used his head and shoulders as diving platforms until Two-Five and Four-Three settled in and hissed at them. The brood gave up trying to use Kim as a water feature and started swimming through the thin mud like leggy little eels, making warm cross-currents and poking their small noses onto every bit of skin they could reach. Kim aimed a close-lipped smile down at them. Just as human babies popped everything in their mouths, Kekrax babies touched everything with their snouts. Good thing he wasn't ticklish.

"He talks," Two-Five said, with demanding teeth-clacks that were rather imperious for a male. Females tended to assertiveness, not males, who were generally mellow sorts.

Kim talked. The warm mud, the cool shade, the silly antics of the broodlings, the occasional sympathetic tongue-flick from Four-Three, it all combined to relax him, and the whole sorry story came spilling out, from Di Fata's collapse to XenoResearch's sale of his contract to Kim's imminent indenture if he couldn't find an attorney willing to help. Two-Five, an interstellar trader who traveled into human space regularly, knew some of the Di Fata story already, although the nuances probably hadn't made it into the Kekrax media markets, so Kim launched into explaining those as well.

It was the exposure of the Di Fata Johnsons' moral turpitude combined with their status as a Boston-based company that had brought them down, after investigation turned up several illegal psychosexual simulacra imprisoned on Earth by the Di Fata Johnson family. Notably, one represented a deceased daughter of a prominent rival company. Outrage, embargos, and boycotts against Di Fata began on Earth, then erupted across human space. Di Fata and its subsidiaries were falling like a house of cards, with each layer of subsidiaries bringing down the next. XenoResearch was simply the latest card to—ahem—hit the deck.

Unaccountably, he felt better when he stopped talking. Two-Five and Four-Three stared at each other long enough to make Kim wonder what they were doing with their tails, down there under the mud. Their left tails were essentially one big scent gland, although it could also serve as a defensive whip. The other tail was a sex organ, and *that* wasn't widely known offworld. Most humans thought the Kekrax kept their reproductive organs discreetly tucked away like the terrestrial reptiles they resembled. If the hidebound local government in Boston discovered that the little reptilians actually carried their sexual capability high and proud at all times, they'd probably ban the Kekrax from Earth Station Hawking for indecent exposure.

It had taken six months for Kim to realize the relevance of tails to Kekrax reproduction. The humorous byplay in their two languages— he suspected the existence of a third, but wasn't yet able to verify it— contained an endless stream of tail jokes. Biological information was tightly held by most members of the Trade Alliance, and the compact that formed it had ensured its privacy in perpetuity. Kekrax trade with Tau Ceti was steadily increasing, however, so sooner or later Boston would find out about tails and Earth's popular press would tear them apart, but Kim refused to be a party to it. He'd written for the popular press precisely once, interning between semesters in Brazil while out of funds. It was a disaster he refused to repeat, certainly not now. He *liked* the Kekrax. They were highly intelligent, decidedly civilized, and, he now believed, profoundly misunderstood by every other race in the Interstellar Trade Alliance. Most of all, they were deeply kind in a way that made his soul ache. He didn't want to create more obstacles to the respect they so richly deserved and so seldom received.

But he had no idea what the devil Two-Five and Four-Three were doing now, silently staring at one another. Mated Firsts and Seconds sometimes simply stopped, separately or together, for five minutes at a time or even ten. He'd yet to crack the puzzle of what they were doing. Obviously, it was a form of communication, but that was all he could determine. There was nothing he could do to get them talking until they came back to reality. Then, in his experience with this pair, one would make an announcement and both would refuse to talk about anything else. He leaned back against the soft plants lining the edge of the mud pool to wait out the strange interlude.

The broodlings took advantage of the parental distraction to resume using Kim as a diving platform. Their dives mostly ended in awkward belly flops, until one finally jumped far enough to land on Four-Three's head, and that jolted both adults out of their silent communion. Kim clicked his best approximation of Kekrax laughter and made a mental note to drop a broodling on their heads the next time they stared into the void for too long. If there *was* a next time. He frowned. The quarter hour he had allotted to them was long expired.

Four-Three hissed at her broodlings, who settled back into swimming around Kim and chasing each other, while Two-Five said, "He comes to eat a meal with them, the First, the Second, and Two-Three of Three. Consumption of human foods. He comes now."

Kim straightened. Two-Three of Three was their *broodmale*. No wonder the pair had contemplated so long. Despite his situation, an offer of social access to an active adult broodmale represented an opportunity he couldn't pass up, and if it helped him come up with something, anything, in the way of a breakthrough, perhaps he could parlay that into repayment of his contract and convince Di Fata to give him back his life.

Besides, he hadn't yet eaten this morning, and his mouth watered to think what kind of delicacies Two-Five might have brought back from his latest foray into human space.

"He comes," Kim exclaimed. "He comes quickly!"

CHAPTER 2

ay over Sanctuary Aanesh dawned grey as Halla's robe. She picked her way down the defile that led to the beach. *That* beach. The one the others said she should avoid for the memories. It was bad for her, the sanctuary leader said, who left unspoken that she thought Halla's daily journey there was bad for everyone else too. The idea that one must regulate one's emotions for the good of all was a provincial one, yet a current of it ran through all seventeen outcaste sanctuaries. It was strongest here, at Aanesh.

The path was steep, with high rock steps set in at regular intervals. That was no impediment to Halla, who was taller than anyone she had ever met. She could rest her chin on even the tallest person's head. Her legs were adequate for these steps.

Her lover, in contrast, had been tiny. On fair mornings, they had come down to the beach together, and Halla had had to lift Tarasheth down the defile. Then they sat in the sand and talked, practicing the languages they'd learned, keeping them fresh. Each of the seventeen sanctuaries on Tolar had its own tongue, some as different from one another as sunrise from sunset. Their variety and uniqueness had interested Halla, and still did, but they had entirely fascinated

Tarasheth, who set out to learn them all. She loved learning new languages and delighted in the idea of knowing all the words for a thing. During their journey, traveling from one sanctuary to the next all the way around the world, Halla discovered that when she changed the language she spoke, her feelings changed too. She had merely noted it, but Tarasheth, the curious one, the adventurous one, had lived for those changes. She had wanted them all.

Here, on this beach, her journey ended, one sanctuary short of achieving that goal. Halla continued on, alone, to finish it in her honor. At that thought, a sudden fire caught Halla's heart, flaring agony through her chest. She buried her fists in the sand, eyes stinging, barely breathing under the weight of the pain. Sometimes it was not this bad, but it had grown worse with each season that passed. Now it seemed to almost crush the life out of her.

Finally, the agony ebbed. The sound of the crashing waves returned, along with the cries of sea flutters and the smell of the ocean. In the first days of her loss, the pain had not been so intense as to blot out the world around her. Then, she had been able to exist without Tarasheth. She had gone on to the last sanctuary, Kerreth, and learned the language there, though it took longer to learn and become fluent without her love and life-partner. Afterward, she had been unable to make herself return home to Venak alone. Still bereft, still grieving, Halla went back to Aanesh and found a small house near this beach, visiting this spot every day, the last place she saw Tarasheth alive, the place where the other half of her heart had died. *Died*, the way animals did, without walking into the dark. Every day, no matter the weather, Halla came to sit in the sand, speaking slowly and carefully as if to teach her lover the one language she had not learned. Some days, Halla thought she could feel Tarasheth sitting beside her.

Not today. The surf crashed wild and loud today, and beyond the waves, dark clouds threatened the horizon. A storm was coming, or perhaps passing by. She pulled in her senses and gazed at the clouds, trying to determine their direction, if they were blowing west along the equator, or heading south toward the Aanesh peninsula. She failed to sense or hear Varina until the sanctuary leader settled onto the sand beside her.

"You talk to her here?" Varina asked.

Halla shifted her gaze to the rolling waves. "I teach her the language of Sanctuary Kerreth."

"Oh? I was born there."

Halla blinked and looked down at Varina. Upon reflection, she did hear a trace of the accent.

"My mother came here from Kerreth when I was a newling," the woman continued. "After a time, she led Aanesh. Now I do."

Halla returned her gaze to the distant clouds and then peered sidelong at Varina. Parent, then child, leading the same sanctuary. It spoke of ambition of the hereditary sort. Could she be descended from the ruling caste? There was no way to know. When a provincial arrived in a sanctuary, no one asked their caste. Some were obvious, such as those whose muscular bodies and observant manner shouted that they had been provincial guards, but no one, *no one*, spoke of who they had been before. All the sanctuaries had received new exiles from Detralar after its ruler tried to assassinate the Sural's human, and it was whispered that the Detral's young son lived among the outcastes of Sanctuary Triss, trauma-bonded by an advisor who did not wish to walk into the dark for his ruler's crime. More recently, of course, everyone knew the story of Farryn, the former ruler of Monralar, now the shipmaster of the world's trade fleet. His shocking fall into exile was only adverted to through comparisons to other dishonors. No one dared *say* that he had been a member of the provincial ruling caste. Those were whispers, not to be spoken aloud.

In any case, Farryn's and the Detral's scandals were far too recent to explain Varina. Could she descend from one of the ancient, exiled rulers? Unlike Farryn, those rulers had vanished into exile without a trace. No one even knew where they took sanctuary, but once in dishonor, their lines need not have died out. They could have any number of living descendants now, since outcastes engendered as few or as many children as they wished. Some might even know their lineage, passed from parent to child.

But surely no descendent of an exiled ruler was likely to *admit* their ancestry, even if they knew it.

Varina was talking again. "...and Steth brought a message from Suralia's human. It seems she wishes to study us."

That jolted Halla out of her musings. "*Study* us?"

"She does not use that term, of course. The Suralians say they wish to know more of our history and culture, because we too are Tolari."

"How considerate of them to notice," Halla snorted.

Varina pressed her lips together and drew her brows. "The ruling caste's rediscovery of the guide's gift alarmed them, and I suspect they worry over the existence of sensitives they did not train. Or perhaps, now that they have so graciously permitted us a path to 'honor' through the station above us, they believe we might band together to upset their Game. Whatever the reason, they say they wish to...understand us better."

Halla considered that. Provincial fears regarding untrained sensitives were nonsense, but she had spent enough time in each sanctuary to know there was indeed more to learn than merely a unique language. "It might be useful, for us, if anyone will talk to them."

"I cannot envisage many of us talking to a provincial, not for long. Can you?"

"A few might, here and there."

Varina shook her head. "That may be, but it will not be enough to achieve their goal. Of more concern to me is that start where they may, no matter whom they send into the sanctuaries, they will need an interpreter. The Sural could make all our lives uncomfortable if we withhold something he wants." She met Halla's gaze. "If provincials come asking for a translator, will you consider it?"

Mother of All, Halla thought sourly. The sanctuary leaders would remember Tarasheth's unusual quest and they would remember Halla for her remarkable height. How could they not? Of course they would ask her. And yet, Halla had heard no news of a consultation with the other leaders.

"That would get me out of your hair," she said in a flat voice, "and into the Sural's."

Varina remained silent, but even without probing Halla could see the twist in her emotional landscape, like a child caught in a lie, and she gave herself an inner nod. The people of Aanesh had welcomed her return three years ago, but her unrelenting grief for Tarasheth now irritated many, and Varina most of all. Besides, leaving Aanesh was a notion she had already given consideration, and in truth, she would like to meet the Sural. Gossip painted him so tall that he had to bend his neck to walk through a stronghold doorway. If that were true, he was taller than she was, and looking up at another person while standing was something she would like to experience in her lifetime.

On the other hand, she had no inclination to serve him. Would a provincial ruler who was also the leader of his caste settle for less? Doubtful. Best to simply say no, but Varina would only ask again, repeatedly, if she refused now.

Say something true, she thought. That might gain her some time to find reasons for refusal that the sanctuary leader would accept.

"Their proposal has merit," Halla said. "I will give it some thought."

* * *

THE STORM DID INDEED PASS to the north, tracking west along the equator, and the following day the weather cleared. Halla strolled back from the village, the midmorning sun hot on her back, a bag filled with enough rolls and fruit to last the rest of the day slung over her shoulder. The fruit, a coveted treat, came in a recent shipment from Monralar, which possessed vast orchards and, along with Parania, grew most of the fruit eaten in this part of the world. Since summer, that province had grown more generous in its donations, something she particularly appreciated. With more food available, the fact that she ate as much as two people put less of a burden on the sanctuary, where the soil was poor and lack of proper tools forced them to rely on support from the provinces, which outcastes could not enter unless they grew their hair and left everyone they knew and loved, forever. Even speaking with an outcaste brought dishonor to a provincial. The only exceptions were those who left their sanctuaries to serve a province, and those who served Tolar Trade Station.

The fruit in the shipment was varied, fresh, and ripe; Monralar's reputation for generosity was well-earned. She hoped the increase to the Monral's donations shamed other provinces into doing the same, though such hopes were low. There was a chance among Monralar's allies, especially as the Monral's human lover was so outspoken on the matter that even the sanctuaries heard about it.

As a girl, sanctuary-born, she thought she might like living in Monralar, mainly for that reputation of hospitality. Joining the wandering laborers had held appeal for her, as did the assurance of enough food, even for a person of her stature. Then she grew old enough to understand the personal reputation of the Monral his father—of Farryn—and she abandoned that ambition. She cut her own hair. She remained in Sanctuary Venak. She met Tarasheth.

If the Monral his father had had more honor, if she had left the sanctuary and gone provincial, would Tarasheth still live? Would she perhaps have embarked on her language journey without Halla, but been less adventurous and more cautious? Avoided the beach?

Avoided the water?

She would never know. Halla shook her head, heart once more afire and spreading its ache. Tarasheth was gone. Tarasheth still lingered. Some days, Halla could not decide which was true, or which was worse. She breathed into the pain, but it was not as bad this time. The world remained solid around her, filled with the sound of the breeze in the grasses, the faint smell of the sea, the heat of the sun. She adjusted her grip on the bag and strode on.

The cottage where she lived sat tree-shaded amid a garden of flowers and herbs, set well back from the cliff above the beach. Some of the herbs she grew were for cooking and some were for medicine, but by mid-autumn she had already harvested and distributed to the others in the village as much as would not harm the plants. She did pick a few purely decorative autumn flowers on her way to the door, and laid them on the table in the kitchen while she brought out a wide, shallow bowl to fill it with a little water. Then she sat and ate about half the food in her bag while she trimmed off the stems and set the delicate blooms floating. Tarasheth had always loved purple flowers.

A presence approached the cottage. Varina, again. Halla sighed as she began to clean up after her meal and set out mugs for tea. When the sanctuary leader neared the door, Halla called out a greeting that was far more cheerful than she felt, and Varina made her way through the house and into the kitchen.

"Be welcome in my home," Halla said as the woman took a seat at the table. She filled the mugs with fresh tea and set one before her guest, returning to her own chair with the other. "What brings you? Have you news?"

"Yes," Varina said. "After you left the village, Farryn arrived, newly come from the station. He said the provincials seek to engage the services of a human from Outside for their project, who will, of course, need an interpreter. Would you work with such a one?"

Halla stared. She knew little about humans, but the few already on their world had all taken the Jorann's blessing and gone provincial, which some believed said little that was good about them.

"A man trained to rule a province would pay attention to such talk," she said. "Is he certain it is more than mere words?"

Varina shrugged. "Does it matter? But yes, I believe it to be more than mere words. Farryn reports that the Sural consulted the other provincial rulers, great and small alike, and none wished to send any provincial, human or not, into the sanctuaries."

"Of course not." Then a thought occurred to her, and her curiosity caught fire. "Do we know what humans are like before they go provincial? There is one, the new stationmaster. Perhaps I should visit the station one day and discover the answer."

"Doubtless one with your language skills could find work there," Varina said, adopting a carefully neutral expression.

Halla sipped her tea. The sanctuary leader no longer hid her desire to get her out of Aanesh. She considered confronting Varina about that, but a confrontation might be what she wanted. Perhaps if Halla agreed to visit the station, it might satisfy Varina enough to leave her alone for now.

"Doubtless," Halla agreed. "I will travel there at the next opportunity."

"Excellent!" Varina said. "Come back to the village with me. Farryn is holding the shuttle for you."

CHAPTER 3

$\mathcal{K}$im knew better. He told himself that firmly as a wave of punishing hammers pounded the inside of his skull. He knew better than to drink Kekrax wine. Therefore, the fact that he had done so was probably down to Two-Five and Four-Three releasing pheromones that interfered with his good judgment. That—oh damn. That had started with lifting his mood while they were still in the mud pool, hadn't it? No, earlier than that. As soon as he encountered Two-Five and Four-Three on the street. They had *arrived* waving their tails.

Manipulative little lizards.

He had to be honest with himself and admit that maybe he just wanted to drown his woes for a few hours.

His friends had only wanted to help. Of that, he was certain. But Kekrax wine! Jesus. There was a reason Central Command banned it from human-controlled space. He might as well have been drinking straight absinthe, except that he didn't *feel* drunk at the time. Not a good accompaniment to an evening spent conversing with an adult broodmale in his prime, which now—he let out a sigh. The entire interview was a fuzzy blur. If he'd hoped to salvage his situation with fresh information on broodmales, the opportunity had fled. *Damn!* What a waste.

Kim flung an arm over his face, blocking out the tormenting light on the other side of his eyelids, and became aware of warm, pleasant weights pressing him down, weights that wriggled in response to his movement. He lifted his throbbing head to peer one-eyed out from under his elbow and met the drowsy blink of a broodling curled up on his chest. A First, he thought, though it was hard to tell with one so young. It—she—had two tails, so she definitely wasn't the baby broodmale. They had only one.

Kim was fully awake now, unfortunately. He lowered his arm. He was flat on his back in a shallow bed of warm mud, head propped on a sandbag, with Four-Three and Two-Five's current mob curled on top of and around him, most of them asleep. Well, that made sense. Kekrax were warm-blooded, but humans had a higher body temperature. The way all the babies were crowded about him suggested they appreciated his warmth.

Thanks to the wine, however, he remembered nothing at all of how the evening ended. The adults must have herded him into the nursery to sleep it off. Maybe he'd get another chance to interview the broodmale? He'd beg if that's what it took. He got his elbows underneath him, which provoked another round of sleepy wriggling and a series of dull plops as the broodlings on his chest slid off. He looked around, but still didn't see the young broodmale. He would be smaller than his siblings, but piled on as they were, he would be hard to find. Kim started counting.

Hold on. Those weren't mud-brick walls.

This wasn't his friends' house in K'kraxin.

Kim sat up, fully awake. This was a spaceship. Now that he thought about it, the soft hum of a K-space drive sent a slight vibration through his sit bones. It was a spaceship *in flight*. Good lord. Two-Five and Four-Three had kidnapped him.

Aliens. God. Devote your life to learning about them, and you still never really knew what they would do next.

He had a sudden urge to laugh. *They regret they can do nothing legal to help him*, Nine-Three had said. Nothing legal indeed, but it looked as if the Kekrax judges had been willing to venture into less legal approaches. When the company that owned his debt—that owned *him*, when it came down to it—arrived, he wouldn't be there for them to collect.

He'd wanted a way to get off Kekrax Main ahead of his so-called *employers*, hadn't he? It looked as if his friends had given him that way, even if it got him into more legal trouble. A cold chill went through him, along with a sensation of the blood draining from his face. He was a fugitive now. If he couldn't find a way to clear his name, he'd never work or publish in his field again.

That made getting back to Tau Ceti imperative. He could get help there, see this business cleared up, and go back to the University. Likely he'd have to compete for students if he returned while they were still running the holo lectures he'd recorded in order to get an early sabbatical in the first place, but he could contribute something new that he couldn't before he left: a more immediate experience of Kekrax culture and belief systems.

Slowly, Kim eased out of the bed of mud without squashing any broodlings under a knee or stepping on any small limbs with the cleated sandals still on his feet. The little ones rolled into the space he left behind, piled on top of each other like puppies, and stopped moving again. He swiped as much mud off his skin as he could, and was heartened to find his shoulder bag by the door. Perhaps they'd brought his belongings from the hostel as well. He tapped a doorplate placed well out of broodling reach and ventured out.

The air in the hall was comfortable and only a little cooler than in the nursery. As the door closed behind him, a blast of warm air combined with a sonic cleanser turned the mud on his skin into a mound of dust around his feet. Then even the dust was gone, sucked down through small holes that opened in the floor plating and closed again. That was impressive. He'd never been in a Kekrax ship before, having arrived at their planet on a human tourister. He'd occasionally wondered how the mud-loving reptilians dealt with it on a ship. He could still smell the mud, but he couldn't see a trace of it. He ran his hands through his hair. Some dehydrated clots remained, but it wasn't his hosts' fault they weren't equipped to remove every bit of mud from a mammal. The rest of him was clean. That was good enough.

Kim looked around. His duffle leaned against the wall by the nursery door, neatly packed, by the smooth lines of it. His hosts, or perhaps the First who ran the hostel, must have rummaged through his rooms for his stuff, but where did naked reptilians learn how to pack clothing? He shook his head. It wasn't hard to find good instructional recordings if you had access to human social media markets. Which the hostel did, and which a trader like Two-Five very well might.

Right. Next thing. He left the duffle where it was and stopped to think. Now that the broodlings were old enough to leave Two-Three's nest, Two-Five and Four-Three would be raising them, all of them but for the baby broodmale, who would stay with Two-Three. So the adults had to be around here somewhere. He'd wander about until he found one of them.

The nursery door stood at one end of an *extensive* hall that probably ran a fair fraction of the ship's length. A number of doors, all plated-over, dotted the hall at regular intervals, right up to the single exit at the end. At least there was no doubt as to which direction to start his search. Two clacking, slipping strides later, he detached the cleats from his sandals, stuffed them into his bag, and blinked. He looked up. The overhead was a good twenty centimeters above him, sufficient head room for even a tall human but far too much for a Kekrax.

Oh, right. Two-Five had purchased the ship from a retired A'aan' trader. He knew that; Four-Three had told him. *Christ* he was thick this…morning? How long had he slept? He shook his head, provoking the hammers into renewed activity. He groaned. Kekrax wine. *Never* again.

The door at the end of the hall led onto a corner of the bridge. As the door shut behind him, Two-Five, the sole occupant of the room, began to bob his head and wave his tails, dark gold eyes gleaming. His scales appeared even more vibrantly green and richly brown than

Kim had ever seen, the camouflage patterns clear without their usual splotches and streaks of mud, and he was the very picture of a proud and happy Kekrax.

"Look at you," Kim muttered. *Stay calm*, he told himself. Kekrax sprayed pheromones when confronted by large, angry animals, and he'd had quite enough sedation for one day—or days, or whatever time period it had been. Conversationally, he said, "What does he plan? He needs to reach Tau Ceti, this male. If he cannot get help, they will alert Trade Alliance authorities, the debt owners. Then he is arrested when he leaves this ship."

Two-Five clicked Kekrax laughter.

"He is very pleased to see his friend," the little reptilian said, by way of confirming that he was, indeed, very proud of himself. "They go to Tolar."

"You're taking me to Tolar?" Kim exclaimed in English, too startled to form a suitably elliptical phrase in Kekrax Second. "I can't go there. Humans are banned, forbidden, unacceptable at any time."

That wasn't quite accurate. *Six Planets citizens* were banned. It amounted to mostly the same thing, unless you were a Freebooter or a Sayyar. Which meant that Tolar was precisely where his debt owners wouldn't think to look for him.

Kim wondered what his IQ was this morning.

"Aye." Two-Five clicked more laughter, because *that* word, in Kekrax Second, was a double entendre having to do with assent and ascent of tails, and it dovetailed nicely with English to form a salacious pun in both languages at the same time.

Kim snorted.

"Well," he said, collecting himself. Two-Five was clearly in high spirits. If Kim wanted information, he'd best be as direct as their indirect languages allowed. "He stays on the ship, and the Tolari stationmaster never knows he is there? What does he do? Does he take this male to Tau Ceti at all? Where do they go next?"

"Tolar." More clicking.

Kim sighed. This was familiar behavior. Two-Five wasn't going to be more forthcoming, at least not yet. Kim would have to try again later, because further questions now would only amuse the little alien into more and more oblique answers. Well, if Kim was about to violate the Tolari interdict, he might as well know more about the people into whose territory he would trespass.

"Will he allow this male to use the data station?" Kim asked, inwardly bracing himself for a difficult negotiation. An interstellar trader would want to protect his data, after all, not that Kim would know a trade secret if it crawled into his ear and shouted.

Two-Five flicked some fingers toward a right-hand panel in Kekrax-style assent while simultaneously tapping at the control arm on his chair with a middle hand. Setting permissions, Kim thought, his eyebrows rising of their own accord. Well. That was easy. He hoped Two-Five wasn't so trusting with everyone.

He went to the data station and pondered the tiny, backless chair in front of it. As he watched, it descended until the cushion was flush with the floor. He made a gesture of thanks, something resembling a tongue-flick done with one hand, and settled in.

Kekrax didn't use a written language, holding as an article of faith that such things got in the way of experiencing reality. On the other hand, they were savvy enough to realize that reality was complicated and multifaceted, and that was probably why they developed two, or possibly three, distinct languages. Kekrax First was objective, dogmatic, and clear, while Kekrax Second was opinionated, witty, subtle and, at least to Kim's mind, more catty than not.

He'd not used a Kekrax data terminal in months, but this one was practically identical to the system he'd trained on when he arrived. As the display came to life, he beheld a single Kekrax female, tilting her head at him quizzically, while another Kekrax, smaller and male, peered in at the side of the display frame, then made himself scarce.

"Tell me about Tolar," he enunciated as carefully as he could, shading the vowels in the way Three-Four and Two-Five had taught him to do when embarking on a new subject.

And they were off and running.

A single speaker—the female, of course—and perhaps twenty minutes was sufficient to cover what was for Kekrax "the news of today," everything the data terminal thought was immediately relevant based on the fluency of his Kekrax First and his current location aboard a full-time trading starship in flight. She began with a monologue on the physical characteristics of Beta Hydri and its planetary system, including the fourth principal planet, Tolar, a metal-poor world with relatively small land masses just coming out of a prolonged glacial period for perhaps the first time. Two or three times the male peeked in as if to check on the validity of the information, but stayed blessedly silent. The lecture concluded with a balance-of-goods statement, a list of notable debts—the ledger was even, presently—and a summary of the relevant trading equity regulations.

Kim waited. Finally, the First got to the part he needed right now: something about the *inhabitants* of Beta Hydri IV. Kim reached behind him for his tablet and, without looking away from the data terminal, set it up to record. With that in hand, he settled in to listen to the First, only to find a great deal more in the details than he thought anyone could reasonably know just twenty years after the Tolari had emerged from their self-imposed isolation.

As a freshman at Tau Ceti University, he'd been fascinated when news broke of a human-looking race of aliens, whose ability to disappear from sight and to form empathic bonds with one another marked them as quite distinct from any branch of humanity. The stories had to have been exaggerated and, he thought, distorted a good bit by entertainment media and the propagandists of Central Command. The Kekrax version was more prosaic and, to a professional xenologist, much more interesting.

According to the First on the terminal, the Tolari had a caste structure with at least a dozen groupings, all vocational in nature, identified by the color of their clothing. Political power was exercised by a single caste, or possibly a pair of castes, who had adopted a separate scheme of colors that distinguished their many provinces from each other. Violence was endemic to these two castes but seemed otherwise rare. The ruling caste had come together to build an orbital station a number of years back, but that was as far as cooperation seemed to go. It was very Dolphi, class 5, in structure, and most likely served to allocate the labor and skills of a relatively small population across a planet which was becoming increasingly hospitable to warm-blooded life. He could imagine the pleasure of his committee chair, Dr. Kuan, if he had lived to see these details. The old man's social paradigms remained surprisingly applicable, twenty years on.

Still, this wouldn't get him any closer to Tau Ceti and safety from his new owners. On the display screen the First paused, in response to a particularly obnoxious wisecrack from her Second about the Tolari tendency to have single offspring instead of broods, and he managed to get in the question he had been saving for this moment.

"What actual legal authority do they have on Tolar, the Trade Alliance," he asked in Second. "Do they yet have any extradition treaties in place with them, the Tolari?"

The First assured him that such existed. The A'aan' sponsorship of the Tolari was *grub rich*, the Kekrax way of saying it was a profitable arrangement for all concerned parties, and so of course the Tolari would honor their legal obligations. The Second made as if to interject, but then relapsed into silence as the First whipped her left tail in his direction. She continued that they placed a premium on social honor, did the Tolari, even going to war or committing suicide over it, and that this had been their way for at least a thousand Judgeships on the homeworld of the Kekrax, and possibly more. Kim repeated that last phrase back to her, including the final triple click, and paused. A judge's term on Kekrax Main was about four standard years, which meant the span of a thousand was simply ridiculous. The Kekrax had been a star-faring race for a few centuries, not four millennia.

Apparently there was doubt in his voice he hadn't meant to put there, and it was enough of a challenge that the First and Second on the screen held a hurried consultation. He heard an alarm go off somewhere to his left, and craned his head around to see Two-Five tapping on his control arm without a word, authorizing more permissions. Kim could only wonder what he had done to earn such trust.

The lecture began again, somewhat less guarded this time and with frequent interruptions from the male at the display's edge, with a statement that was common knowledge: a mysterious and long-disappeared benefactor race had snatched the Tolari's ancestors from Earth, six millennia ago. That such a race existed had come out during the early years of Marianne Woolsey's tenure as the first human allowed to live on Tolar. That it had disappeared wasn't admitted until later, when the Tolari petitioned to join the Trade Alliance and revealed that these so-called Benefactors had left them a vast store of technology, which they had been building on ever since. That much data on the early history of Tolar was documented at Tau Ceti University, but the Kekrax also traced Tolar's first two thousand standard years, a time when the Tolari were a spacefaring culture. Except that back then, the Kekrax were almost as primitive as Earth had been, so how could they know such things?

According to the lecturing First, the Tolari fleet had been extensive and consisted of massive sentient ships, bred for exploration and cargo-handling. Something about their neighbors, or the distance from their homeworld, or both, had troubled the Tolari and led to massive social strife on Tolar itself. They withdrew from space and isolated themselves, concealing their technology as, one by one, the trading races of the time moved on or disappeared.

Some three hundred standard years ago, soon after the Kekrax went into space, they found their reclusive neighbors and initiated trade with them. The Tolari, it seemed, were willing to accept Kekrax trade missions as long as they remained on their ships in orbit, exchanging Kekrax raw materials for exquisite Tolari artwork of various kinds. They were content to delegate all the lifting to Kekrax transport drones.

The Kekrax had been damned clever, it turned out. They had put fairly sophisticated monitoring devices on their drones, and learned far more from the Tolari than the latter might have intended. Kekrax color vision, Kim already knew, was extraordinary, and that was how they made their breakthrough: the colors worn by the Tolari, particularly the bright yellow of the medical caste, were simply too consistent to come from anything other than advanced manufactories. With this knowledge in hand, the Kekrax had gone to the Tolari and bargained with them for bits of the Benefactors' technology to enhance life on their own homeworld. Meanwhile, neighboring races like the V'kri and Terosha warned humanity and other newcomers to the Alliance that the Tolari should be left alone, as their system and the whole Drift around it were dangerous territory, where ships tended to disappear. The Kekrax kept their own knowledge of the Tolari to themselves. It was, for them, a useful and grub-rich arrangement.

Even the bare bones of the tale were enthralling, despite the interjected comments of the Second questioning the truth of practically every claim. The Tolari would eventually open up further, Kim guessed, since they were on the twenty-year plan to have their ruling caste exchange ambassadors formally with the Trade Alliance races. Cultural changes on Tolar were sure to follow as a result, and those would bear watching. But in any case, whoever chanced to study the Tolari would be someone quite a lot more senior than a lowly tenure-track professor like Kim, even if he was good enough to win a position at Tau Ceti, the premier university in human space. He wished luck to whoever got the post, but right now he was focused on getting back to Tau Ceti as quickly as possible and somehow finding a way to settle his stupid problem with his contract employer. Or rather, his now-*former* contract employer, XenoResearch, which apparently was just another way of saying Di Fata.

"Venerable Kim male?" said Four-Three.

Kim glanced at his tablet. He'd been rooting around in the Kekrax data archive on Tolar for more than four hours, apparently absorbed enough to miss a change in the watch.

"He needs food and drink," Four-Three said, in emphatic Kekrax First.

Kim took a breath. He did need it. He wasn't sure how his uneasy stomach would react to the typical Kekrax fare of bugs and grubs, but water would definitely help his headache. He made a gesture of assent, shut off his tablet, and got to his feet.

"He thanks her, Four-Three of Eight-One Slash First."

CHAPTER 4

"*D*o you speak English?" Farryn asked, in the language of Aanesh.

The lavender-robed Monrali guard next to him at the front of the shuttle ignored them, eyes ahead and hands moving deftly over the controls. That *somewhat* reduced the itch of being in the presence of a provincial guard. Halla eyed him for a moment before turning her attention on the man's former ruler, who wore tanned animal skins, dyed outcaste grey. She could smell them. It was a strange, alien odor that overpowered the oddly scented air inside the shuttle. She could not say whether the smell came from the skins, the dye, or the man himself after living several years Outside.

"No," she replied, wrinkling her nose.

"We launch," the guard said. "Take hold. And…now."

A mild heaviness came over her as she gripped the armrests, and she wondered at the strange lack of any sense of movement as the ground fell away. In moments, she could see the blue-green waters that surrounded the Aanesh peninsula and outlined the coasts of nearby provincial lands. Swirling patterns marked the decoratively cultivated hills of Parania and Monralar, which abutted the ancient, crumbling, and tree-covered mountains of Nalevia. Tarasheth's beach mercifully disappeared quickly from sight.

When the heaviness eased, Farryn rotated his shuttle seat all the way around to face her. "If you intend to spend any time aboard the station, you would be well-advised to learn both English and Suralian," he continued. "English is used as a neutral trade language among the staff, who represent every sanctuary on our world."

"*And* Suralian?" Here she was on dangerous ground. The language of the current leader of the ruling caste was the language of trade and diplomacy in the provinces, and the Sural of Suralia had held that leadership for as long as almost everyone alive could remember. Clearly it nettled Farryn, but she was still angry at Varina for tricking her into giving her word, and she cared little for the effect her jibe might have.

She met Farryn's gaze. His eyes were pale, almost gold, and gossip said the Monral his son had those same eyes. Not unattractive, but not trustworthy, either. She considered a moment, then said, "I speak Suralian, but I hardly need it. I can speak with any outcaste."

An eyebrow lifted. "Oh indeed? And how if you address station staff from different sanctuaries when they are gathered together?"

She gave him a tight smile. She had never spoken directly with Farryn until Varina took her to the shuttle, although she had observed him often enough. The man used words like snares, but she was chary now and possessed no desire to fall into one of his verbal traps. If he wanted to trick her any further than Varina had done, he needed to try harder.

He seemed to realize it. With a slight nod, he rotated his chair forward and left her to the view. She would enjoy what she could of the journey to the station, keep her word to Varina as principle required, and work her passage back down to the planet. There would be no need for new languages this day.

The view *was* breathtaking. The shuttle was heading toward Tolar's night side, and the line between day and night fast approached. On the other side of that line, mats of phosphorescent plant-creatures dotted the darkened seas, and a splash of light sat on the horizon.

What city that was, she could not say. While she could name every one of the seventeen outcaste sanctuaries that girdled the planet and describe the route she and Tarasheth had taken to travel from each to the next, she had only the most rudimentary knowledge of the provinces, having never bothered to learn more than the names of the few near Aanesh and Kerreth and her home sanctuary of Venak.

No moon graced the sky. Perhaps the world's bulk obscured it, or perhaps it was behind the shuttle; Halla did not know. She watched land and sea become a globe beneath them, the yellow of mid-autumn in what she could see of the south, verdant at the equator, and lush in the north, right up to the edge of the polar icecap. Tarasheth would have loved this. The thought brought up the familiar urge to tell her lover about it, and she clamped her barriers closed before she could broadcast the pain that always accompanied such thoughts. It took conscious effort to keep the words behind her teeth and not describe the view aloud. Farryn would think her mad.

Too much time alone on the beach in Aanesh, perhaps. She lost herself too easily in her musings with Tarasheth. And the darkness was always there, pulling at her.

A different, tangible darkness lay below them now, and the dayside was waning into a crescent. Ahead, something she assumed was the station twinkled, and beyond it, the moon finally peeked out from behind the world's rim, half-full. It was painful, seeing so much that was new and wonderful without her Tarasheth. Nevertheless, she spent long moments examining the airless, battered moon before fixing her gaze closer, on the slow-flashing lights of the trade station.

Tarasheth once complained that the world belonged to the provinces. Yet the trade fleet crews came entirely from the sanctuaries, which had kept alive the old knowledge of the guide caste and helped Farryn to recover and seize the ancient trade fleet for himself. Tarasheth's words had been tinged with bitterness when she said it, but it seemed to be coming true: "The world belongs to the provincials, but at least space belongs to us."

Halla comforted herself with that thought while she watched the

station grow closer, until Farryn once more rotated his seat to
face her.

"I advise you to reconsider your stance on English," he said. "You
will need it if you are to work with the human coming in. He will
arrive within days, and while we expect him to learn Suralian, it
would be best if you spoke his language as well."

Halla stared at him.

"That is *not* why I am here," she said, voice tight. She knew the
anger showed, and for the first time in her life, she wished for a
provincial's physical discipline.

Farryn lifted an eyebrow. "Oh? Then why did you request
transport?"

"Is that what Varina told you? That *I* had requested it?"

No surprise colored Farryn's presence. He had conspired with the
Aanesh leader—of course he had. Varina *must* have descended from
the ruling caste, because colluding with Farryn to trick Halla onto
Tolar Trade Station was a tactic provincial rulers would use. Proper
sanctuary leaders *asked*. Directly. Without resorting to trickery when
the answer was other than they liked.

And Halla, the careful one, had suspected nothing. Fury bubbled
up. She should have mistrusted Varina's cheerful cooperation for the
ruse it was and not happiness at finally ridding the sanctuary of her,
although in retrospect, it was probably both. Halla pointedly looked
away from Farryn and crossed her arms.

Farryn rotated to face forward as the shuttle entered a bay in the
station spire, and after it stopped with a soft scrape, he turned again
to indicate the back hatch with one arm.

She continued to stare at the back of the pilot's chair. The air
hummed with unsaid words.

Farryn uttered a soft chuckle and exited.

The pilot made some final passes at the controls and swiveled his
seat to face her. His attention itched, but it was balm compared to
Farryn's imitation of friendliness.

"I beg your indulgence," he said, and there was no animosity in his
voice, which helped her hold fast to the shreds of her temper. "You

33

cannot remain in the shuttle, as it requires maintenance. Will you allow me to take you to Command and Control? It is night shift, but I am willing to summon the stationmaster from her rest to settle this matter."

Halla took a breath, doubting her own hearing, and kept her barriers tightly closed. Why would a provincial—why would a *guard* offer aid to *her*, an outcaste? Her first instinct was to reject his help, but no. His face was clear, although that meant nothing in one of his caste, whose training required them to appear impassive at all times. Yet it was surely worth the risk if he meant it. She nodded, and he tapped a spot behind one ear and spent some few moments subvocalizing before gesturing toward the hatch.

The shuttle bay doors had already closed when she stepped out, and the station air, cooler than Halla would have liked, held an odd, perhaps metallic edge. She took a deep breath, then turned to follow the guard pilot through metal corridors and up shadowed floors in lifts that ascended silently by themselves. It was well that she had a guide; she could never have found the place called Command and Control on her own.

The stationmaster's office was a large space focused on a sizeable desk covered in green things growing from ceramic pots, with a central seating area where Farryn was already sprawled across a divan as if to declare it his own. The pilot excused himself with a bow and left. Drawing a deep breath to quell a fresh surge of fury, Halla turned her back on Farryn in time to see a woman swathed in grey rush through the door. The newcomer skidded to a halt in front of her. Her robe, a little disheveled, was of an unfamiliar style that covered her head and left only her eyes and hands showing.

The eyes, large, brown, and puffy from interrupted sleep, made a quick survey of Halla. The hands, as dark as those of any Tolari, spread palms forward as she made an outcaste's slight bow.

"Finally!" she said in strongly accented Suralian, as she straightened. The fabric covering her face puffed as she breathed hard to catch her breath. "Someone who can reach the high shelves! It is unfortunate that we will have you such a short time. I am Aafreen, the stationmaster. Be welcome to Tolar Trade Station."

So this was a human untouched by the Jorann's blessing. Even Halla's fury could not fully quell her curiosity, and she stretched out her senses. The woman was blissfully free of a province's prickling entanglements. Of course it would be so, she told herself.

Halla felt Farryn's eyes on her, caught herself, and glowered.

"I am Halla," she replied, in her lowest, flattest voice.

Behind her, Farryn chuckled. Aafreen's eyes widened and fixed on him.

"Merciful Allah, did you bring the translator *unwilling?*" she demanded.

"She requested transport," he drawled. "I offered her a seat on the shuttle."

Aafreen stared at Farryn, looked up at Halla, and then returned her gaze to Farryn, eyes narrowing. She crossed her arms. "You misled her, then."

"I? No."

That was true, strictly speaking, Halla thought. It was *Varina* who had misled her. Farryn, however, had certainly participated in Varina's scheme. That was what rulers did, was it not? Plot, connive, scheme together, and let others suffer the consequences. Halla felt her glower settle into a scowl and did nothing to stop it. Sanctuary leaders, ruling caste, *former* ruling caste. None of them could be trusted. The sanctuaries were meant to be free of the provincial rulers' Great Game. Farryn's exile had clearly put an end to that.

"I would return to the planet," she said. "Any sanctuary but Aanesh."

Aafreen nodded, grim-eyed. "I can arrange that." She tapped her head behind one fabric-covered ear, as the guard had, but unlike him, she continued to speak aloud. "Command." A pause. "Send Aran to my office. Control." Another pause. "Make a list of the next few shuttles going into the sanctuaries, or which can reasonably detour past one, and send it to my tablet."

While she was still speaking, an outcaste arrived behind Aafreen.

He looked in his middle years, with lines creasing the corners of very dark eyes and a few strands of white in his close-cropped hair, and his expression as he stepped into her view was one of pleasant anticipation.

"Stationmaster?" he said.

"Aran. This is Halla. She is here by mistake."

Aran frowned. "By—"

"By mistake," Aafreen repeated. "Take her to the cafeteria for a meal while I make arrangements for her return to the planet below. Halla, this is Aran, my deputy. He will take good care of you while I fix this."

Halla eyed them, her back still turned to Farryn, who like her had his barriers up. She *looked* past them anyway, a daring provocation to such a dangerous man as well as rude. But she could conceal herself and her senses from almost anyone if she wished, and only a sensitive would be able to see what she was doing. *If* they were looking.

No one in the room was a sensitive. No one here could perceive her rudeness. She looked at will.

Farryn was in a state of annoyed perplexity. Well, if this meeting had not gone as he expected, she was glad of it. It was no matter that he once ruled a large and flourishing province. He was an outcaste now. He should learn to negotiate like one—frankly, openly, treating other outcastes with respect, and not the way the ruling caste treated others, as pieces on a game board to place as they wished. She was glad to have frustrated Varina's scheme with him, if it taught them both that.

She was also glad to have seen the world from orbit. That was a memory she would share with Tarasheth the moment she had time to herself. Her heart slid down its familiar path, forcing her to concentrate on quelling the grief. But she was not in Aanesh, and no one here was likely to notice her grief, or even care. Let it be.

"I promise you," Aafreen added, when she did not reply, "I will return you to Tolar as soon as it is possible to do so. I took no part in bringing you here, and I *will* have a conversation with Farryn on the matter." A rustle behind Halla prompted Aafreen to level a glare past her. Then she continued, "Halla. Forgive me. I will do what I can do, but this station runs on a schedule, and there are no shuttles heading downworld until next shift. If you would like to sleep or take some rest until then, I can arrange that."

Halla took a breath and said, "My thanks, stationmaster. It was midday when I left Aanesh, so I have no need of sleep, but I would welcome the meal you offer."

She bowed to Aran. He returned it with a smile, which lit his face with humor and good nature. Despite herself, Halla warmed to him. He gestured toward the open doorway.

"This way," he said.

*　*　*

THE *CAFETERIA*—NO Suralian word, that—was a few levels up from C&C. It was built to human design, Aran told her, and resembled neither a provincial refectory nor a village communal table. That had been a deliberate compromise made to keep provincials and outcastes at peace with one another, as both groups could grumble about the unfamiliar arrangement equally. It possessed the additional virtue of being efficient at dispensing vast amounts of food to large numbers of people during times of peak activity. According to Aran, humans had a considerable talent for efficiency.

Because it was deep into station night, the place was almost empty. A pair of yellow-robed apothecaries sat together at a small table with a lavender-robed Monrali guard, the provincials perhaps taking comfort in each other's company as they ate. A small number of outcaste staff were scattered more widely about the room. Aran led her to a long, sculptured bench covered with food of all sorts, and took only tea as she filled a tray with as much as she thought she could eat.

She refused to feel guilt for taking so much. It was well-known that every province sent food and supplies to the station. No one here would suffer any lack.

"Individuals of your height are exceedingly rare," Aran said, after they settled at a table. "Are you a Grandchild?"

Halla grimaced as she tore a roll in half, and would have turned to spit had she been in her own garden. *Grandchild of the Jorann.* The tallest of the tall and the rarest of the rare, whom crisis could trigger into even more strength and speed than they already had. Untriggered as she was, she merely possessed strength proportionate to her size. Despite the usefulness of that and the accompanying reach, the amount of food she required made her a liability in most sanctuaries. She had long since decided never to engender a child, to avoid passing on the trait.

"Probably," she said, biting into the roll. It was rich and herby, and she had never tasted the like. The provincials sent no such grain to any sanctuary. "I have never yet met anyone as tall as I, but I have never been in the provinces, only the sanctuaries."

"Every sanctuary, as I understand it."

"Yes."

"I find that astonishing. What led you to undertake such a journey?"

"My..." She took a breath, heart starting its slide. "My life-partner."

His eyebrows went up and then pinched downward as he sensed the pain she was unable to hide quickly enough. She cursed herself for lowering her guard and letting her barriers loosen.

"My heart grieves for your pain," he said, and genuine compassion colored his voice and lit the glow of his emotional presence.

It had been long since she elicited that response in another person. She nodded, and bit into the roll, eyes stinging a little.

"How long has it been?" he asked carefully.

He had no right to ask. He did *not.* Yet the kindness and concern in him was real. It shamed her to admit it even to herself, but she *wanted* that, wanted her grief seen and not disdained, even by a stranger.

"Three years," she said, in a hoarse whisper.

He nodded, the look in his eyes sad, and gentle, and accepting.

"I have seen this before," he said. "It is very rare, but I know of it because my brother experienced the grief that would not subside, and the darkness that comes with it, after he lost his life-partner. The provincials have an idea about the cause, if you can hear it."

She met his gaze. Did she want to know what provincials thought about anything?

What if it could help?

Not trusting her voice, she nodded.

"Provincials know pair-bonds far better than we do," he said. "Perhaps if more of us formed them, we ourselves might notice that some pairs are more attuned than others and can more easily blend their hearts, even without conscious volition. When I sought aid for my brother, the apothecaries here told me they think it a kind of partial bonding, and that there is help when such a bond is…disrupted."

Partial bonding. Halla thought about that, blinking rapidly to hold back tears. She had thought that she and Tarasheth were closer than a typical pair of life-partners. It stirred her to her depths to think it might actually have been true, though it appalled her at the same time. Bonded pairs walked into the dark together, and if one died by misadventure, the other usually followed soon after. She opened her mouth, but her throat was completely dry, so she took a bite of ripe redfruit, with its crisp skin and juicy flesh. She chewed. Swallowed.

"Tarasheth," she whispered, and could say no more.

"If your experience is like my brother's, she took part of you with her," he said. "And part of her remained with you."

She nodded.

"Do you ever talk to her?"

The question jolted Halla. She took a breath, looking at her hands, and found her voice again. "I teach her the language of Sanctuary Kerreth." She glanced up, expecting derision, but a gentle smile curved his lips.

"My brother speaks often to his lost love. He never lost that sense of her presence. Halla, hear me." Aran laid a hand over his heart, a commitment to the truth at any cost, a truth and a caution together. "There is someone who can help."

The words stopped her breath. "Who?" she asked, on an exhale.

"The Jorann. The provincials forget that we have as much right to see her as they do, as almost none of us try the opportunity. If you choose to go, she can perhaps ease your pain as she did for my brother. If you wish, as deputy stationmaster I can contact Suralia and make arrangements on your behalf. As you are arguably a Grandchild, the Sural, who all know is one himself, will surely desire to meet you. Only make the request, and I will see to it."

* * *

IT WOULD BE THREE DAYS, Aafreen said when informed of Halla's change of plans, until a direct shuttle would leave for Suralia, but a smaller shuttle was due to depart at the beginning of station day. It was bound for a series of sanctuaries, one of which was as close as she could hope to get to Suralia until then. That route might take longer, if there were no transport pods available at the sanctuary, but Halla decided it was better than waiting on the station and enduring the inevitable attempts to sway her decision. She took the opportunity to rest a little and to eat more before it was time to board.

Eight other passengers filled the shuttle, three of them traveling to Halla's destination of Sanctuary Sacaea, and there was only room for her because Aafreen convinced the pilot to allow her the copilot's seat. That was a little uncomfortable, as sitting so close to the Monrali guard disturbed her mood, but it also allowed her to keep to herself. The rest of the passengers, outcastes like herself, chatted amicably with each other in both their various tongues and one that sounded like nothing Halla had ever heard. That was surely the human language, English. Interest stirred within her, unbidden. She leaned back in her seat and listened to the sound of it until flames licked the viewports and a tornado roar filled the cabin, consuming all conversation. Halla murmured to Tarasheth while the shuttle thundered its way into the atmosphere and no one could hear.

There is help, she whispered, over and over. *There is help for us.*

CHAPTER 5

Sacaea lay farther from the equator than most sanctuaries, on a large island in the midst of the northern sea. The air was fresh and the wind cold, just as it had been years ago when she arrived here with Tarasheth. The sanctuary leader, an old, old man who called himself Sandbird and who apparently knew she was coming, greeted her with a warm smile and a thick robe as she unfolded herself out the shuttle hatch.

She took the robe gratefully, throwing it on over the loose, equatorial-style one she wore. It was almost long enough for her.

Sandbird's brows quirked together as the shuttle hatch closed. "And where is your—" he began, and stopped as the needles jabbed her heart and the pain returned once more.

She had not expected the question he nearly asked. She should have, but as time passed, she simply failed more and more to think of ordinary things.

"Forgive me," he said, and bowed carefully, as old ones often did. "My heart grieves for your pain. How can Sanctuary Sacaea assist you?"

It was the same question he asked when she and Tarasheth first

41

arrived in an old, battered pod from Sanctuary Iraaz, all those years ago. *We wish to learn your language* had been the answer then, from Tarasheth's lips. Her lover, eager to learn new words, had ever been the first to declare their intention.

We will gladly help with the work, Halla always added, with a fond, happy smile for the woman who owned her heart.

"I seek passage to Suralia," Halla said now. "I intend to see the Jorann."

Sandbird's brows tried to meet his hairline.

"That is," he said, and paused to think. His white brows descended into a furl. "An unusual quest." He gestured vaguely at the clear horizon, where the sun sat, newly risen. "And it is, as you can see, quite early in the day. Come to my home. Raasa will find something for you to eat while I discover where our pods are this morning."

A weight lifted at his words. She had not realized how afraid she was that Sandbird would deny or delay her, or express disapproval, or be uncooperative in other, more subtle ways. That was unfair of her, perhaps. She was too accustomed to Varina's censure. Sandbird had been kind during the time she and Tarasheth lived in Sacaea, and there was no reason to think he would have changed. Another thing she should have remembered and considered.

There was so much that no longer came to her mind. It was a troubling thought. *I am more clever than this.*

Or I was.

"My gratitude," she said, and followed him into the village, to a house set a little apart, as all the others were set apart, amid a garden full of herbs, half-grown because it was a cold mid-spring here in the north, surrounded by the sea.

Raasa, Sandbird's life-partner, was as old and as kind as Halla remembered. She settled Halla in their kitchen and proceeded to put large quantities of food in front of her, rolls and more rolls, roasted nuts and baked roots and dried fruit, more than even Halla could eat. Seeing her so well supplied, Sandbird left on his errand, muttering as he disappeared out the door about the inconvenient habits of people who exercise too much. Raasa chuckled at his back.

What would it be like to live so long with the love of one's heart, Halla wondered. Would she and Tarasheth have lived their way into such an easy, affectionate way of relating to one another? A sharp ache, worse than usual, took her by surprise before she could close her barriers.

Raasa's head came up sharply, and she set down the two steaming mugs of tea she carried, waiting to speak until the pain had ebbed.

"My dear child," she said, when Halla could once more hear. "My heart grieves for your pain."

"I regret," Halla replied, voice hoarse. She picked up a roll and tore it in half. "I do not mean to burden you, but it—" She swallowed. "I cannot seem to heal."

"Burden me?" Raasa lowered herself carefully into a chair, radiating surprise.

"Is it not a burden?" Halla asked, and because she was *so* lonely and too tired to care how Raasa received the words, she went on, "My grief, on and on, day after day? Which I do not *regulate* for the good of my community? For *three years?*"

The surprise turned to shock. "Who dares to say this? Who has treated you so?"

"It is a current in every sanctuary, this provincial belief that we must moderate ourselves for the good of everyone. I have sensed it in *every* sanctuary, even here. You must see it, Raasa. You *must.*"

Raasa gazed at her steadily. "There are the normal displeasures of life, the normal disagreements among members of a community—and then there is losing the other half of your heart. Each parting and each life is different, but treating you as if such a loss can compare to daily displeasures, that is—" She let out a breath. "I cannot think of a word for such behavior toward a bereft life-partner. Where did this happen, Halla?"

Halla took a breath and did not look up. "Aanesh."

"Ah. That one." Heavy disapproval colored Raasa's voice. "Varina."

Halla bit into the roll to avoid responding. She chewed, unable to taste it.

"She has a reputation among the sanctuary leaders," Raasa continued. "Too ambitious, too much like a provincial ruler. Is Aanesh where you lost your Tarasheth?"

She nodded and kept eating. Her body needed the food, even if her heart did not want it.

"That you experienced this kind of grief— Even as long as I have lived, I have seen it before only twice, but Halla, my dear child, both ended in tragedy. That her loss did this to you is no surprise. All of us saw how you and Tarasheth were."

Halla swallowed a mouthful. "On the station, I was told that the apothecaries there say we had a kind of partial bonding, that when she —that she took part of me—" She took a bite and chewed savagely.

"And the apothecaries told you to go to the Jorann?"

"No," Halla said around a mouthful of food. "The deputy station-master. He is one of us. He told me that his brother experienced the same kind of grief, and that the Jorann eased his pain."

"Child, it would be known if she could do such a thing."

"Would it? I sensed no lie in the deputy's words."

"Of course they—" Raasa interrupted herself, and then frowned, nodding. "No. We cannot assume provincials would tell us, can we? She— Well. Perhaps she can. For your sake, I hope so. For now, you are too thin to convince me that Aanesh fed you properly. You will eat, and you will tell me about your travels while we wait for Sandbird to return with a transport pod."

* * *

FULLY HALF RAASA'S sitting room was taken up with row upon row of small plant starts in cups made of cora paper, basking in the light from the large front window. The furniture, including several comfortable woven chairs, clustered on the other side, providing a cozy space for conversation, to which they retreated after Halla finished her meal. She was deeply into the story of a time after she and Tarasheth left Sacaea, in which they fell into a crate of fabric while helping unload a shipment, when Sandbird appeared in the doorway. He waited patiently while his life-partner wiped away tears of laughter and calmed herself, then allowed his face to wrinkle into a triumphant smile. Raasa responded with a happy smile of her own and stood to take his hand in hers.

Halla's giggles abruptly turned to weeping at the sight. She and Tarasheth had been so *happy* then. The journey, the learning, the companionship, the heart she had felt beating with her own. Halla pushed down the grief that had ambushed her and took deep breaths until they stopped turning into sobs.

"Forgive me." She gulped down a last hiccough and wiped her face. From the corner of her eye, she saw Sandbird cast a troubled glance at Raasa. Raasa shook her head.

"I have prevailed," Sandbird announced then, with forced glee in his voice, "over those who condition their bodies rather than do an *honest* day's work."

Halla snorted. He said it with a twinkle in his eye, but Halla knew from experience in many sanctuaries that those who had once been provincial guards did indeed spend a great deal of time exercising, together and separately. And still Sandbird had never named their former caste.

"I have come away," he continued, "with a small transport pod and someone willing to guide it to Suralia for you. You may leave at any time."

"My gratitude," she replied, her voice thick from weeping, try as she might to smooth it. She stood. "My gratitude for your hospitality, truly, but I wish to leave now if I may."

Raasa nodded. "Of course, child. We understand." She laid a gnarled hand on Halla's arm. Care flowed from her fingers, warm and maternal.

"My thanks," Halla whispered. She bowed, shouldered her bag, and made her way outside to blink at the midmorning sun. A two-person transport pod sat outside the garden, the smallest she had ever seen, a crystalline ovoid hovering a hand-width above the groundcover. It was none too clear, but it looked serviceable, and she could sense a willingness to serve and a desire for speed.

She touched its side, and it made an opening for her. The young man inside, well-built and certainly muscular enough to be a guard, grinned as she folded herself into the second seat. She looked around and found the space behind them occupied by a net bag full of rolls and dried fruit, small pouches of nuts, and a pair of water containers.

"So it must be the sea route from here. How deep do you want to go?" he asked, eyes sparkling.

"As shallow as possible," she replied, and watched with some amusement as the grin slid off his face and he wilted dramatically. The journey from sanctuary to sanctuary was nearly always by sea, and Halla was as averse to that as anyone, but this young man appeared to feel otherwise. How bad could it be? "Or perhaps as deep as you like."

He straightened, and the grin returned.

"Excellent!" he exclaimed. "I am Finnic, and you are Halla, and we are—" he paused to give the pod a nudge with his senses, and it headed toward the space between two nearby houses "—on our way to Suralia!"

The pod dropped over a cliff, and despite herself, Halla screamed.

* * *

SOME PEOPLE ENJOYED THE SEA, Halla thought, with some asperity. Not many, perhaps not one in a ten of thousands of Tolari, surely. But her initial impression was right. Finnic was clearly one of them.

He whooped as the pod dove into the surging waves, his empathic presence flaring with fierce joy. Halla gripped the armrests the pod formed of its own body and wished with all her heart that the sanctuaries had access to the deep transport tunnels used by the provinces. Then at least they could travel cleanly, through the stable land rather than the treacherous, roiling ocean. She gritted her teeth as the pod skimmed the sea floor. The light faded until it was dark enough for her to pretend she was in a closet back in her cottage on Aanesh.

Then it grew darker still, too dark to see Finnic, too dark to see anything, and strangely, Halla began to relax.

"Good," Finnic said, with a smile in his voice.

Halla closed in on herself, shutting her barriers completely, shutting *him* out.

"Are you a sensitive?" she demanded. That would be *just* like a sanctuary leader, she thought, prying while they still could, testing her, probing her for more than she wanted to share. Her mood soured. She had thought Sandbird better than that.

"Yes," he replied, "but I am not here to read you. Which I cannot, at present. You are very good, you know, very subtle. That takes a great deal of time and practice, as my mentor taught me. If I could not hear you breathing, I would not know you were there."

"Why *are* you here, then? Why you and not another?"

"I know where to take you, where to come out of the water, and how to approach the Suralians. They have had a little time to become accustomed to occasional visits by outcastes, but it is still best to treat with as few of them as possible."

"You have gone to their stronghold?"

"Many times."

Halla frowned. What kind of outcaste was this that Sandbird had entrusted her to?

Finnic laughed. "Are you glowering at me?"

Her lips twitched. "Yes."

He laughed again and said, "To answer the question you are not asking, the Suralian sensitive, Storaas, is teaching me. I am not exceptionally gifted, as sensitives go, but I have a very large range, and that can be overwhelming. So he is training me in his own fashion, when we have the opportunity—not as often as either of us might wish, and it has been half a season since my last visit. Bringing you to see the Jorann gave me a convenient excuse to return for more instruction."

"Does he not think it dishonorable to teach you?" she asked.

"Oh no, not at all. The Sural knows and he approves, but many Suralians wish he did not, and some prefer to pretend we do not exist. We try to keep my visits quiet for the present, to avoid any public disapproval should they become known."

Halla grunted. "Provincials treat us as if we are a contagion of dishonor."

"What do you expect? They are taught that our mere existence is dishonor, and that to so much as speak to us spreads it to them."

She opened her mouth. That was true. "The ruling caste could change that."

"They could," he replied equably. "And my Suralian mentor has told me there is a move in the ruling caste to do so. If and until they do, however, tell yourself it is not a sign of animosity but of fear when a Suralian turns her back on you. Ah. Here we are."

"Already?"

"Not Suralia. Open your barriers—I will not look, my word on it. Open and *feel*."

Halla pressed her lips together. Nothing could be worth that kind of trust.

"You will not wish to miss this," he said.

"Miss what?"

"This place. We call it the Deep. I believe that is how the hevalra themselves regard it. I promise that you are safe. Just *feel* it."

She eased her barriers a bit—and then dropped them in wonder. She floated in tranquility, immersed in it as in the waters of the warm salt springs of Sanctuary Iraaz. Deeper down, at the farthest reach of her senses, she perceived four great leviathans of the sea, hevalra, moving slowly in concert. It *was* a concert, she thought. A symphony of peace and serenity, of abundance and humor and vast stretches of time.

"Oh," she said. "How did you know to come here?"

"We Sacaeans know of this place. I wish we could go closer, but this is as deep as a pod can safely go. There is a basin, farther down, where they gather. Someday I would like to join them, somehow. Perhaps one of the great living ships could dive so deep and not be crushed. Or a shuttle. There must surely be a means to do it."

Halla shook her head, and Finnic fell silent. All too soon, the pod left the hevalra and their sea of calm behind, but the tranquility stayed with her for most of the morning. Neither of them spoke much, until the sea began to lighten. Halla gripped the armrests, stomach once more tight.

"We near Suralia's city now," Finnic said, in a quiet voice. "The path we take is the way Storaas brought me in after a shuttle pilot discovered my talent—a tunnel from the sea which leads directly into the stronghold. I am enjoined to show it to no one nor even to speak of it, but I am confident they would make an exception for you."

"Me? Why?"

He looked her up and down. "Can you not guess?"

"Because I am a Grandchild?" The hevalra-induced serenity fled, and she scoffed. "That says nothing of my character. I could be a criminal and be a Grandchild."

"True. But you are who you *are*, and not one to depart her own principles."

She shook her head as the pod nosed under a rock to find an opening. Eagerly, it emerged from the water and sped up the smooth floor of a tunnel.

"They will have detected us," Finnic said. "Guards, very *alert* guards, will be waiting. Make no sudden moves and try not to be alarmed. They know that I sometimes arrive unannounced."

Halla nodded, stomach uneasy. She disliked the feel of this place, and the farther up the tunnel they progressed, the more it stabbed at her. There was danger here.

"I feel it too," he added.

She threw up her barriers and glared at Finnic, but he only responded with a lopsided grin.

Then they were at the top of a shaft, in a brightly lit room of dark stone floored with dark tile in subtle patterns. As predicted, guards dropped out of camouflage all around them. *Ten* prickly and pricking provincial guards surrounded the pod, which was simply an absurd response to a mere two visitors, however unexpected. Halla could not suppress a shudder, though the skin of the pod stood safely between her and the drugged needles glinting on their fingertips.

Then the large double doors on one side of the room opened on the tallest man Halla had ever seen, wearing the pale blue of Suralia, the intricately braided hair of the ruling caste, and the collar-to-hem embroidery that marked him as not only the ruler of Suralia but leader of the ruling caste. The Sural.

Beside him walked a normal-sized woman, a human with pale skin and impossibly blue eyes, also wearing a Suralian robe. With the bright white ruling caste embroidery marking collar and cuffs and her golden brown hair plaited into a somewhat simpler version of the Sural's braids and twists, she could only be the Marann, his storied human bond-partner. Behind them came an apothecary and a scholar. They all stopped a few paces from the pod, just beyond the guards.

Halla stared at the two high ones. *Bond-partners*. Bonded pairs were so rare in the sanctuaries that she could not recall ever seeing any side by side. There was something flowing between these two, a connection just beyond her ability to sense. They felt—they *felt* like one person in two bodies.

From behind her, Finnic touched her shoulder. Hastily, she patted the side of the pod. An opening appeared, large enough to step through, and she managed to go through it with enough grace to avoid embarrassing herself before it sealed behind them.

Finnic turned to the Sural and gave him an outcaste's bow, but the ruler's gaze was on Halla as he acknowledged Finnic with a hand gesture. She imitated Finnic and bowed like the outcaste she was, feeling a little defiant. Abruptly, an amused sparkle appeared in the scholar's eyes. Halla hissed in a breath and tightened her barriers. A sensitive? If not, he was intrusively observant. She glanced at Finnic in time to see him give the man a nod. The Storaas he had mentioned. Of course. This Suralian sensitive would bear watching.

The Sural gestured to the guards, all of whom camouflaged and left. It became a little easier to breathe.

"I am the Sural," he said in his own language, when the last guard's glow had disappeared into the hall. He indicated the woman beside him with a gesture of the hand. "My beloved, the Marann."

"I am Finnic," her companion replied promptly.

Provincial manners, Halla thought, annoyed. The highest rank always spoke first, and in their own tongue unless they wished to grant an honor. She should have introduced herself at once, though she doubted any high one would know the language of Sanctuary Venak. Halla reached out with her senses, to read what she may, but the Sural was an inscrutable empathic emptiness.

Well, and so was she, when she chose. She lifted her chin and looked *up* to meet his gaze, and that was as strange as she had imagined it would be. Only then did she reply in reluctant Suralian, "I am Halla."

The Sural lifted a hand, palm up, and indicated the room. "Be welcome in my stronghold."

Halla's jaw went slack. "Welcome?" she said, before she could stop herself.

"Yes," said the Marann, with genuine friendliness, but Halla was still too much on guard to warm to her. The woman continued, with a faint, strange accent, "You are expected and welcome."

Expected. Of course. The station must have contacted them, not the Sacaeans, because Finnic had clearly believed they were unannounced. Tarasheth's resentment of provincials and their ruling caste bubbled up and flared out as she swung to face the Sural.

"So an outcaste is only welcome when expected? Or is it only *we* two, because we are *useful* pieces that you can manipulate as you like in your Game? Is this Farryn's doing? Or the Marann's? Or yours?"

It was rude, unconscionably so. Halla knew that and could not care, though Finnic drew a sharp breath and radiated shock. The Marann's eyes went wide for a moment before her face returned to a neutral expression.

The Sural, unexpectedly, burst into a hearty laugh. "You are very like I was in my youth."

"Really?" said the Marann, eyebrows raised.

"Yes, beloved," he said, smiling—a Suralian, actually smiling—down at his bond-partner. He returned his gaze to Halla, and his face did not lose its cordiality. "We understand your suspicion, after such treatment as you recently experienced. Come, share a meal with us."

It was almost a command, and it was *hard* to turn down food. Still, she wanted to be out of this prickling, dangerous stronghold and on her way. "I came to see the Jorann."

"The way to her dwelling lies through my stronghold, but she is occupied at present," the Sural replied. "I believe she will be free within the day, but she is extremely difficult to predict. I beg your patience. Until then, come, eat with us."

Halla squinted. He had not opened his barriers so much as a crack since her arrival, but nothing in his posture told of deceit. Then again, nothing in Farryn's posture had told of *his* deceit either, nor Varina's of hers. *You cannot trust what high ones or leaders say*, Tarasheth's voice whispered in her memory. *They are trained to lie.* Halla braced herself, glad her barriers were already closed. The pain that always followed such memories would remain private, concealed. Her own.

The Sural waited, serene, a mild, expectant look on his handsome face. The Suralian sensitive behind him—the renowned Storaas, for certain—stirred as the ache in her chest surged and then tapered away. *Mother of All*, she thought. *He must be* very *strong*. She wished him anywhere but here.

Then her stomach sank. If the Jorann could heal her heart, then that healing lay in the Sural's hands. She had little choice other than to do as he bid.

"Very well," she said.

"Excellent!" he replied, and it took her a moment to realize he had used the Venaki word. He smiled, not unkindly, and half turned, sweeping a long arm toward the hall. "This way."

She balked. "You speak my language?"

"Only a little," the Marann answered for him, in Suralian. "We do what we can, but we have few records, fewer recordings, and no living voices. I have extensive training in many languages, both Earth's and Tolar's, but it only covers provincial languages. It is difficult for us to learn anything from the sanctuaries."

Halla looked from one blue robe to the other, then glanced at the scholar and the apothecary. Those two watched with the impassive, emotionless expression she would expect from Suralians, given their reputation. *As cold as Suralia's glaciers*, the saying went. Even in the sanctuaries, the Sural had a long reputation for it, but here, now, he was almost warm, like his Marann.

"You are not what I expected," Halla said.

The Marann burst into laughter.

CHAPTER 6

$\mathcal{A}$fter days in K-space, Kim was glad to see stars again. And ships. And a planet. And anything other than a sucking black void, really. Even Tolar Trade Station was a welcome sight, despite his legal concerns. It was a small station, as orbitals went, and he recognized the design, the Den's classic double ring around an elegant spire. Each end of the spire flared into a wall of windows—twin observation decks, a nice touch. The Den did good work.

Kim gazed at the main bridge monitor as tugs maneuvered the ship toward its assigned dock, which happened to be close to the restricted section where a Tolari tradeship was visible. The Kekrax files indicated those ships swam through K-space in all shapes and sizes, and the images had resembled giant deep-sea nightmares. This one was a huge, spherical specimen, opaque, devoid of color, and covered with spikes and waving tendrils. On the sunward side, a dark membrane stretched taut over the spikes. The Kekrax had no information on what they actually did for a creature that lived in hard vacuum, but then the Tolari ships didn't make sense to the Kekrax in the first place. They simply could not imagine a creature that never touched the ground, or more specifically, mud.

Very little about the Tolari made sense to Kim, for that matter. The empathy might; animal communication on Earth could serve as a model for that. But disappearing from sight, clothing and all? It seemed far-fetched, unless their technology was unbelievably sophisticated. Asked about that, Two-Five performed the sequential hand lifts of a Kekrax shrug, as if to say that it was just how Tolari were. It wasn't his business when opportunities for trade were on offer.

It wasn't Kim's business, either. His task focused on convincing his friendly kidnappers to take him to Tau Ceti post-haste, please and thank you. Yet his arguments not only went exactly nowhere, they turned into cultural discussions. He would always regret not finishing his research on Kekrax Main, certainly, but this was absurd. His priority needed to be staying ahead of his new owners, finding a lawyer, and praying he could stay a free man long enough to regain the protection of the University.

It had been several days since Two-Five spirited him off Kekrax Main. Word of his flight would be all over the sector by now. He could imagine the notices: HAVE YOU SEEN THIS MAN below one of his professional University headshots. The compact required every Trade Alliance station to watch for fugitives of any member race. Tolar was not yet a member, but it was far enough along the membership process to have put extradition treaties in place. They'd arrest him on sight.

He supposed he could always take refuge with the Den. They couldn't distinguish human faces—although they could certainly see skin and hair color, and the DNA problem remained. Hiding among the Den wouldn't work either. Damn.

A soft bump reverberated through the floor plates. The station tugs had docked the ship while Kim was lost in thought, and the bridge monitor now offered a spectacular view of the planet below. Jewel tones of blue-green, brown, yellow, and white rotated against the black of space, not much different from the view of Britannia from Tau Ceti Station, except that Tolar possessed a sizable polar icecap. Sure enough, breaks in the cloud cover revealed land coated in a solid layer of white.

Two-Five's data archive indicated that Tolar, a world the size of

Britannia, hosted a population of a mere 40 million, with six millennia of history. Four thousand years ago, they had turned their backs on the stars. Why? And why return now?

Loud clangs announced the docking clamps connecting to the ship's airlock, followed by softer thumps and scrapes that were supply lines attaching to their respective ports along the hull. Two-Five gestured toward the floor plating with both left arms.

"They speak with her, the stationmaster," he said.

"They—" Kim sputtered, but Two-Five's eyes were glittering. Uh oh. What in the name of little green apples had the little lizard done this time? He pinched the skin between his eyebrows, shook his head, and dropped his hand. Two-Five had spoken in *First*, in the indicative, with markers for collective planning, confirming what Kim's neatly packed bag suggested. Two-Five, Four-Three, Nine-Three of Nine-Three, and possibly the entire raft of current Kekrax judges had colluded with the stationmaster, if not the Tolari ruling caste itself, to deliver the hapless and unfortunate Kim to Tolar Trade Station. No wonder Two-Five had been so tight-lipped, despite days of prying. "What? How? What does he do?"

"He understands the plan when he speaks with her." Two-Five had lapsed back into Second, but his hiss was firm.

"He gets arrested as soon as he leaves the ship and never reaches her office."

Clicks of laughter. "No fears of arresting, no fears. He trusts Two-Five of Four-Seven Slash Second."

Kim grumbled. "He trusts him, the abductor," he hissed, lacing the words with as much irony as Second could give them, which was enough to fill a Liaoning operetta on Boxing Day.

Two-Five lowered his head, suddenly sobered. "He understands the doubting." He closed the distance between them and leaned his two pairs of arms against Kim's thigh, looking straight up in that peculiar, neck-disappearing way his race had. "He trusts him, this male."

Kim stared down at the little upward-pointing snout. Two-Five had better be right. If the Tolari arrested him, either for his fugitive status or for breaking their interdict against Six Planets citizens, he'd never make it to Tau Ceti, and he'd have years added to his indenture, no question.

"All right," he said in English, and then looked down at himself. "He gets dressed."

* * *

KIM STEPPED out the airlock and into the station's outer docking ring, with its familiar smells of canned air and burnt space, and shifted his shoulders. He wasn't used to clothing anymore. The blousy shirt felt too loose, the form-fitting breeches too tight, and the knee-high boots pinched his feet. He was sure they fit the last time he wore them, but perhaps nine months of wearing nothing but sandals had made his feet spread. Every bit of his clothing felt too intrusively *there*. To distract himself, he combed his loose curls with his fingers to make sure they held no lingering clots of mud, and breathed in the crisp, familiar scent of station air.

"You're very lively for a dead man," said a woman who came to stand in front of him. She was covered head to toe in dove grey fabric, with dark and slanted Sayyar eyes showing through a niqab and only her bronze hands uncovered. "I'm Aafreen, the stationmaster. And you, my piratical-looking friend, must be Dr. Storm-Gale."

"Just call me—" The usual exhortation stuttered to a halt as her words hit home. "Did you say *dead man*?"

Aafreen laughed merrily. "Oh yes, but actually, dead is overstating it. For the present, you are missing." She rolled her eyes and placed a dramatic hand against the fabric covering her forehead. "According to the Kekrax, you received devastating news and disappeared, presumably into the jungle. The judges of Kekrax Main fear for your life." She straightened and continued in a bright tone, "Would you care to come with me to C&C and talk about it?"

"Y-yes," Kim said, and paused to glare down at Two-Five. "What did he do?"

Two-Five bobbed his head a few times and said nothing. Blasted little lizard.

"He's really very clever even for a Kekrax, and that's saying something considering how smart they are," Aafreen commented, as she turned and headed for the nearest spoke, a few docks down the ring. Kim stared wide-eyed at her back. He wasn't sure he'd ever heard another human compliment a Kekrax. "It's probably one of the reasons his broodmale chose him," she added over her shoulder.

Kim hurried after her, gazing all around him as he did. The docks looked typical for a nonhuman station. An assortment of aliens populated the outer ring, mostly the vaguely humanoid Den, naked in their iridescent and mobile scales, some with tool belts slung over slender shoulders. Grey-robed, shorthaired Tolari were everywhere, driving cargo carriers and tending the docks. These were obviously the outcastes he'd read about, but there were also two black-robed Tolari in sight, both with ankle-length hair done into braids and twists, strolling hand-in-hand down the middle of the torus like tourists. A lavender-robed man with equally long hair stood near the corridor into the station's central spire, speaking into an acoustic annunciator that looked like a Den antique.

At the corridor, Aafreen ushered them into a tram beside a slideway. Two-Five's head was *still* bobbing from the compliment she'd given him. The way to a Second's heart was through his broodmale, apparently. He pulled out his tablet to make a note of that.

He shoved the tablet back into his shoulder bag and said, "Living or dead, if I can't get to Tau Ceti soon I'll never be able to leave Two-Five's ship again, much less do any research." He took a seat as the tram began to move toward the spire.

"It's not so bad as all that," Aafreen said. "But let's get to C&C before we say anything more. Tolar Trade Station has good security, but you never know."

Kim blew an exasperated puff of air in no particular direction. Two-Five hissed an acknowledgment and nodded. He was proud of himself again, and that hadn't ended well for Kim last time, for values of *ending well* that excluded kidnapping. Blasted little alien. If he weren't so likeable, Kim could be properly angry with him.

On the other hand, his own placid acceptance of the situation could be a result of Kekrax pheromones. It stood to reason that Two-Five and Four-Three might not want to risk a large, angry mammal near their brood. He scrubbed his face with his hands. Those two had probably kept Kim sedated since the mud pool. He should have wondered why his situation didn't bother him very much. He dropped his hands and turned a glare on the little trader. Two-Five clicked.

"You look like a Sayyar," Aafreen said, apparently by way of trying to distract him.

Kim shrugged. He'd heard that before. The stationer children in the crèche had bullied him about his looks, saying that since Sayyar were subversive and weren't allowed on Tau Ceti Station, he didn't belong there either. He'd been immensely grateful, for that reason, that he didn't achieve his full adult height of 178 centimeters until after he left for University. It could be coincidence, of course, since that was well inside human averages, but it was also the exact height of every adult male Sayyar.

Aafreen was right. He *did* look like a Sayyar, if a clean-faced one.

But the evidence was against it. On his eighteenth birthday the crèche had handed him a birth certificate showing he'd been born on Tau Ceti Station, and two death certificates indicating his parents had died in a shuttle accident when he was a few months old. He'd kept that date as an anniversary ever since, as he had nothing else of them but a few images.

The crèche also informed him that both his grandfathers, long dead, were local stationers who had married while traveling, one to a Far Indian woman and the other to a New Chin, also long dead. He wished he'd known that when he defended himself from the crèche bullies, because the certificates indicated that both marriages were performed planetside, proving he couldn't be Sayyar; their beliefs forbade them setting foot on a planet.

The genetic analysis included with the birth certificate showed few matches in Central Command's DNA archive, none closer than fourth cousin and none who looked anything like him. Further, the documentation noted that he'd been placed in Tau Ceti's government crèche after no one showed up to claim him from Station Rescue. Armed with that information, his choice was simple: he'd accepted Six Planets citizenship before the day was over, along with the full ride at Tau Ceti University his academic scores earned for him. Then during his freshman year, news of Tolar's discovery broke, and he chose then and there to study xenology and how human and alien cultures interacted, rather than seek out relatives who obviously didn't want him.

He told Aafreen all that and watched her eyes sadden.

"And now I'm breaking your interdict just sitting here," Kim finished just as the tram arrived at the spire and interrupted the conversation.

Then it was into a lift, down a hall, into another lift, and through a door that opened on Tolar Trade Station's Command and Control, a large space filled with the smell of coffee and populated by data stations busy with Tolari in gray, with dark hair no more than shoulder length. None glanced Kim's way. Aafreen led the way into a spacious private office with a large, plant-covered desk and a sizable seating area across from it, where a young and handsome man with a blond ponytail, dressed in a loose, pale lavender robe, sat sporting a toothy grin on a face so fair that it could only come from Britannia's North Isles.

It was to Two-Five's credit that he didn't turn and run at the sight of so many teeth. Then again, he was an experienced trader with souvenirs from all over human space. He was probably accustomed to smiles by now.

"Bertie!" Aafreen cried. "What are you doing away from your caliph? Did he run out of grapes to feed you?" Then she squinted, but her body language remained relaxed. "Or are you checking up on me?"

Kim looked from one to the other. On the ship, swapping tall tales, Two-Five had mentioned a human friend named Albert Rembrandt who had overseen the construction of this station for the Tolari. But this man certainly wasn't old enough to have governed an orbital station for—what was it, five years? Six?

"The Monral sent me up on short notice," the young man said in a crisp accent that was *pure* upper class Britannic. He stood, proving to be half a head taller than Kim.

"*Ekh.*" Aafreen twitched a hand. "I can probably use the help. You can explain the planetside portion better than I can."

"Of course." Bertie offered Kim a warmer, less blinding smile. "You must be Dr. Storm-Gale. A pleasure to meet you. Bertie Rembrandt, at your service. I am, as you have probably surmised, Aafreen's predecessor in this office, hence the taunt."

Bertie stuck out a hand. Aafreen ducked in front of Kim, arms out, before he could grasp it.

"Put that hand away. You're an empath now. Shame on you!"

Kim blinked. An empath, after the Tolari fashion? But the man was obviously Britannic, and with an aristocrat's accent as well. With that surname, he might even be a member of the ducal family that owned Di Fata's major pharmaceuticals competitor. If he was here to pump Kim for information on Di Fata, they would have small satisfaction out of him. Still...an empath?

Bertie pursed his lips. "I don't pry."

"You don't have to."

"I won't pick up anything unless he has something to hide." He quirked one golden eyebrow upward and his accent thickened into the Britannic king's drawl. "*Do* you have something to hide?"

"Bertie!" Aafreen sounded genuinely outraged now.

"Very well, very well, I'll behave," Bertie sighed, and now his accent was definitely North Isles. He threw himself back onto the divan.

"Thank you," Aafreen said, twitching her shoulders. She turned, indicating the seating with a gesture that encompassed Kim and Two-Five. "Please, have a seat." As Two-Five scrambled onto the other divan and Kim took a chair not too near a man who might be close kin to a fabulously wealthy and powerful duke, she went on, "This scoundrel is Lord Albert St. John Rembrandt, the first—and probably last—Earl Whitdon."

"Ouch," Bertie said. "I suppose I deserved that."

"Yes, you do, *Lord Albert*." Aafreen emphasized the title, and Bertie winced. "What's gotten into you?" Aafreen flopped into a chair. "Shaking hands! Merciful Allah. But anyway. We already know Two-Five, of course, and yes, this is Dr. Kimberly Storm-Gale, a cultural xenologist from Tau Ceti University, formerly under a sabbatical contract with XenoResearch."

Kim groaned. "It's just Kim. Anything else turns me into a living example of why some people shouldn't be allowed to marry each other."

Blissfully, no one laughed. Bertie's lips were twitching, but only sympathy lit his sky-blue eyes. Kim heaved an inner sigh of relief.

"Kim," Bertie said. "Trust me when I say that you're unlikely to meet a Tolari who can determine the risibility of a human name. But back to cases, my understanding is that Di Fata dissolved XenoResearch and sold its employees' contracts, value-owed if they thought they could get away with it, which they appear to believe in your case."

"Yes," Kim replied. "And I'm not sure that Two-Five and Four-Three didn't make things worse by bringing me here. I'll have runaway debtor charges against me now, and that will lengthen the indenture."

"Do you have anyone back home to stand up for you?"

Kim pressed his lips tight and shook his head. "Probably not. I have maybe a couple of days left to get a Tau Ceti lawyer before the debt owners show up on Kekrax Main and don't find me. The University might help, but only if I'm on the premises and back on the payroll."

"Typical. Well. What did you do to brass off Di Fata?"

Kim considered the question. "Any number of things, but it's probably that I refused to change my data or my conclusions to suit Xeno's mistaken view of the Kekrax."

Bertie gave him a measuring look. "Almost everyone underestimates the Kekrax. Do you actually believe what you just said, or are you merely saying it for effect? I'm an attorney, if you didn't know."

"Ask Two-Five, if you don't believe me," Kim snapped. *God!* Had

Two-Five brought him all this way for nothing? He shot the little reptilian a glance, but then Bertie's serious expression transformed into a toothy grin.

"Good man! In fact, that's just the sort of sentiment I wanted to hear. How do you feel about gathering cultural data here on Tolar, of, for, and to the benefit of the Tolari? Would such a project interest you?"

CHAPTER 7

*K*im straightened, and looked at Two-Five, whose head was bobbing up and down like a toy, very, *very* pleased with himself now. Kim opened his mouth, shut it, and leaned forward, turning to Bertie. He'd speak with Two-Five later.

He took a breath to speak—and let it out. "But there's no *time* for me to do it. Even if I could get this ridiculous debt cleared tomorrow, I've only got three months left on my sabbatical."

"We thought of that," Bertie said. "Do you truly believe Tau Ceti University will say no if a legal representative of Tolar—that would be me—requests one of their xenologists for a long-term research contract and insists that no one will do but you?"

Kim blinked. "I—" Then it hit him, and the air left the room.

The first social scientist on Tolar. He'd be *the first.* He reminded himself to breathe.

"Please, tell me more," he said. "Milord. Or is it Your Lordship?"

"God no, neither," Bertie said, pale eyes filled with horror, and his hands came up as if to ward Kim off. "I'm not even a stationmaster anymore. Call me *Lord* anything and I might just have to go so Britannic noble on you that you shrivel up like a low-quality raisin. I'm a guard of Monralar, that's all, and a low-ranking one at that.

Although I'm really quite good at the fighting-other-guards part, so who knows if I might rise through the ranks, as it were."

He cleared his throat, sobering. "Before you make any kind of decision, you need to know what you're walking into. The original plan was for Aafreen to tell you all this, and there's a delegation from the leader of the ruling caste coming up from the planet tomorrow with a firm proposal, but the Monral—that's the ruler of Monralar— *he* sent me up, and since I'm here..."

Aafreen rolled her eyes, which only added weight to Kim's impression that she and Bertie were old friends. "What he's not telling you is that he and the ruler of Monralar are lovers, and that makes him more than *just a low-ranking guard.*"

"Aafreen."

"Merciful Allah, Bertie, everyone knows he proposed the night after he poisoned you. It was a nine days' wonder. Do you think a man who collects stories for a living won't hear about the Monral and his human life-partner? Even on station I hear about the way the pair of you make eyes at each other—"

"The sanctuaries don't care about how the ruling caste carries on."

"Yes, they do." Aafreen nodded at Kim. "And that's why we need you, Kim. Because the likes of him don't know anything about what outcastes really care about."

Kim's head was spinning, now. "So I'm to study the outcastes?"

Bertie uttered a strangled sound. "You're getting ahead of the thing, Aafreen. But yes, Kim, the outcastes. Marianne—that's Marianne Woolsey, you may have heard of her?"

"Who hasn't?" The change in topic helped him collect his wits. Kim had watched the entire drama series about Marianne Carter Woolsey in one go and had paid twice for tickets to the award-winning musical. It was *The King and I* in space, featuring a brilliant schoolteacher from Earth and a primitive Tolari monarch, spun as a cautionary tale spiced with treason, betrayal, and even murder. It had been wildly popular when he was in graduate school, back when everyone who was anyone believed the Tolari were pre-tech agriculturalists.

"She's decided the ruling caste's not-so-benign neglect has gone on long enough, and she has the right of it on that. When we recovered our trade fleet, the provinces discovered the hard way that they need the sanctuaries, because the ships require guides with a particular talent, and every guide we have is outcaste-born. After more than five years of searching, we've still not found a single individual with the gift in any province. We were damned lucky that a few guide families in the sanctuaries still retained and passed down their traditions after two local millennia of planet-bound isolation, but it occurred to Marianne recently to ask what else we don't know about them. And the answer is," and he stopped to take a breath, "almost everything. We don't know how they govern themselves, or how they educate their children, or even what kind of tea they drink, and the outcastes themselves aren't likely to tell us. This trade station aside—it's a special case—provincials and outcastes get on like oxidizer and aluminium. Very unstable."

"And so you're proposing a human researcher? An outsider?" Kim asked.

Aafreen nodded. "The outcastes talk to me, but I'm Sayyar and planets are *haram*. Besides, I'm busy training my deputy until he has enough experience to take my job away."

"You *could* stay," Bertie said.

"Not without my people. And you know how that feels."

Bertie cleared his throat. "Indeed. Well. To continue, there aren't many humans on Tolar, but we all have ties to the provinces. *Strong* ties. Any outcaste can sense that, and it sets their teeth on edge. And apart from that, none of us have the right academic training. So that's where you come in. You have the skills for the task, and with care, you can earn their trust. Unfortunately, there are catches. Chief among them is the fact that Tolar is rich in heavy metals, mainly arsenic, with significant traces of other toxins, such as cyanide. Humans living on the planet's surface need to be exquisitely careful. It *can* be done—Marianne proved that over the course of her first eight years here—but it requires steadfast resolution and constant attention."

Kim tilted his head. "Sir—" he started.

Bertie glared from under his eyebrows. "Don't call me *sir*. I work for a living."

Aafreen uttered a high-pitched squeak and clamped her hand over her mouth through the niqab.

"As I was saying," Bertie drawled in Aafreen's direction, sounding again like Britannia's King Henry. Then he continued in his previous manner, "Tolar is a dangerous place for humans. And it's not just the food and drink. There's no privacy, in any sense of the word. This is a planet of empaths, after all, but the ruling caste is a collection of quarrelling Nosy Parkers with a positively lethal sense of honor who spy on everyone, although you can't tell *them* that's what they're doing. They call it *surveillance*, which is not, repeat *not*, the despicable practice of espionage, thank you very much." He rolled his eyes. "Nevertheless, all Tolari can sense how you feel, and if you're *very* loud about it, they'll sense what you feel whether they want to or not. We call that broadcasting, by the way, and most humans do a lot of it, since they've no need to rein it in."

"Do I?" Kim asked. "Broadcast, I mean?"

Bertie blinked. "Not since you walked into this office," he said. "You might just be one of the lucky ones. Marianne was one of those. Somewhat introverted and rarely broadcasts anything, so those around her had to *look* to know how she felt, at least from farther than a few paces away. Considering you've just spent nine months mostly alone on Kekrax Main without going stark raving mad, I'll guess you're similar."

"Well, I did go starkers," Kim said. "And I'm sure the folks at the embassy thought I was mad, but really, between the mud and the heat, clothing was a bad idea unless you enjoy doing laundry every three hours."

Aafreen exploded. She laughed, and laughed, and gasped, holding her sides with one arm, pounding the arm of the chair with the other. Bertie shook his head at her, a slight smile on his patrician face. Finally, she straightened, wiping at her eyes, and squeaked, "Thank you. I needed that."

"Glad to be of service," Kim replied, with a grin. "But as intriguing as the project sounds, with the risk of heavy metal poisoning, it sounds like a bad idea for a human to participate directly."

"It would be, if the Tolari didn't have a way to deal with that," Bertie said, spreading his arms along the back of the divan and crossing his long legs at the ankle. "Fortunately, they do. There are two options on offer. Firstly, we can give you a food scanner to detect what you can and cannot safely eat or drink, and provide nutritional supplements to make up any lack in your diet—which will be boring, I warn you. But that worked for Marianne for her first eight years onworld, and it worked for me for seven years. The second is less an option than a life choice, and it's irreversible. You could become Tolari."

Kim blinked. The words *you're an empath now* came back in a rush, as well as Bertie's use of *we* when referring to what the ruling caste knew. "What do you mean, *become* Tolari?"

"I mean it literally, and this is where I am obliged to pry a non-disclosure agreement out of you before we go any further." He pulled out a tablet and proffered it.

"I—"

"It's nothing sinister. No one's committing any crimes, at least not on Tolar or this space station. But Tolari are *of great interest* to Central Command, and it's in our best interest to prevent them getting their hands on our persons."

"Ah," Kim said. Growing up on Tau Ceti Station, the seat of Earth Central Command, he knew the government's reputation too well to miss the implication woven into Bertie's words. He ventured a guess. "Medical experiments?"

Bertie's eyebrows lifted. "Yes. And we can't allow them to happen again."

Again? No wonder Bertie was asking for confidence.

"All right then." Kim took the tablet and read the agreement displayed on its screen. It covered only what Bertie said in this office from the time Kim signed it until the moment Bertie walked out the door. That seemed an acceptable risk. He pressed his thumb on the signature pad and handed it back.

"Thank you, Kim," Bertie said, pocketing the tablet. He took a breath. "Right then. It's already known that the Tolari are genetically engineered humans. The secret is in the nature of their gen mod. They call it the Jorann's blessing, and it's essentially a cellular reset that can heal a Tolari or turn a human into one. That's what it did for me after I was poisoned. A human with the gen mod gains Tolari empathy and their ability to shed the toxins in the food here, among other things."

Kim took a breath. "You were poisoned despite scanning the food?"

"It wasn't the food," Aafreen murmured.

Bertie shot her a pointed glare. "Aafreen!"

"He's going to find out. Everyone knows what you and the Monral were doing that night."

Realization dawned. *Tolari shed toxins. Bertie and the Monral are lovers.*

"No need to explain," Kim put in, before Bertie could respond. "So the gen mod. You were saying?"

Bertie shifted his shoulders as if unruffling feathers. "The blessing has a number of other benefits in addition to granting you the ability to eat the food, such as increased strength, keener sight and hearing, faster reflexes and the like. However, the legal ramifications might be of specific interest to you: taking the blessing grants permanent residency here. It's a change the ruling caste made, and a hard-fought one on the Sural's part, who pushed it through to shield Marianne from Central Command's efforts to prise her out of Suralia. Particularly, it means you'd no longer be breaking the interdict, Six Planets citizen or not. Once we claim you, Central Command will no longer have sole authority over you, regardless of what they say on the matter. That's Trade Alliance law when genetic modification is involved. The significant drawback is that once Central Security realizes you're here, you'd be ill-advised to leave before we get this debt matter settled. Even the station might not be safe enough if the Chairman's head of security makes another play for one of us."

"Oh," said Kim. "But hold on. What about my debt? My *so-called* debt."

Bertie grinned toothily. "As I said, I'm an attorney, among other things. I can't practice laws in human space, but I have access to solicitors who can. I'll put them onto it. It won't be a quick or easy task, but we can get you sorted."

"And if I turn down your offer?"

"I don't recommend it. I doubt the Duke will allow me to call down the wrath of the Rembrandt Pharmaceuticals legal department unless you're working for me. However, it does look as if Di Fata's troubles were an opportunity the indenture lobby couldn't and didn't pass up, and several hundred souls just fell into your same situation, poor sods. Some of *them* might be former Rembrandt employees. If I can access Rembrandt resources on their behalf, I can fold you into that case along with the rest, and we'll strike a blow against debt slavery at the same time. That's not a guarantee of success, but I'll try. Or, finally, we could take you into nonhuman space on one of our tradeships and drop you off outside Six Planets territory."

"Whose tradeships do you mean? Rembrandt's?"

"Tolar's."

One of Tolar's tradeships, the living vessels he'd seen docked near Two-Five's ship. It would be amazing to travel in one.

"Be advised there's no guarantee you'd be safe. I was on Capella Free Station when Central Security assassinated a Tolari apothecary accompanying the Monrali embassy."

"Christ."

"Indeed."

And, Kim thought sourly, he'd be on the run for the rest of his life, dodging a debt owner's security forces. He frowned. No.

"A bit much to take in at once, isn't it? Well. It did take *me* seven years to decide. I can hardly expect a snap decision from anyone else. You've time to give it thought, since we're still looking for a suitable interpreter. We *thought* we had one—"

"No use crying over spilt milk," Aafreen said, with a tone in her voice that caught Kim's attention.

Bertie huffed. "Farryn did us no favors by getting involved."

"I thought he wanted this project to go forward," Aafreen muttered.

"He does, but he's never learnt that people other than himself are individuals with minds and lives of their own, rather than resources to be used as he pleases." He grimaced and turned back to Kim. "So. That's the offer made. How would you like the cook's tour of Tolar Trade Station while you consider it?"

* * *

KIM LISTENED with half an ear as Bertie, nattering cheerfully, led him about the spire and showed off parts of the station that tourists never saw. The pilots' gym. The maintenance closet that had served as Bertie's office during construction. Stationer that he was, Kim smiled and murmured and paid no attention to it, focusing instead on the problem of what to do next.

Item. Bertie said he could get the illegal debt cleared. If he succeeded, then Kim could find a way to get back to the University and get on with his life.

Item. Kim could stay on as the first xenologist to study the Tolari. That would get his name, ridiculous as it was, into the textbooks, if not the history books. No sane researcher would turn down professional notoriety of that order, and he should jump at the opportunity. Once he published, he'd get offers of tenure from every major university in human space, including Tau Ceti. But that branch on the decision tree also involved either taking a significant risk of disabling, possibly fatal exposure to heavy metals, or accepting a form of genetic modification he'd never heard of. He didn't object to getting a gen mod, per se, but throw in his inability to speak any language on the planet along with gaining Tolari citizenship under a ruling caste willing to kill for honor, and it was one hell of a choice.

He glanced at Bertie as he chattered on. The man was as fair as a Britannic could get, and the Tolari Kim had seen were all about as dark-skinned as he was himself, so whatever the blessing was, it clearly hadn't changed Bertie in any visible way.

"This gen mod," Kim said, as Bertie led him into a lift and gave it a command. "The blessing. It didn't change your appearance that I can tell. What did it change?"

"My feet."

Kim opened his mouth and found he had nothing to say.

Bertie's grin could have lit a small city. "The look on your face!"

"I didn't expect that answer, no. What happened to your feet? And will it happen to mine?"

"My toes are fusing together, and yes, it will. I took the blessing only a season ago, which is six months, more or less. The change is still in progress, and my feet itch like blazes. They'll finish as a flap, quite useful for swimming, which oddly enough Tolari won't do. The less noticeable change is a slight thickening of the skin on my forehead, but other than that, the differences aren't visible. Strength, reflexes, all that. Oh, and I forgot to mention sense of smell. Much keener."

Kim sniffed at himself and winced.

"You smell of mud, yes."

"Two-Five only has sonic cleansers on his ship, I'm afraid."

"Typical for an interstellar trader. It's not offensive, so don't give it any thought. Ah, here we are." The lift door whooshed open, and Bertie swept a hand toward the enormous circular room around them. "The observation deck. After you."

Kim stepped onto gleaming black flooring that reflected the view. Tolar rotated like a jewel against the black, mainly blue ocean and white polar cap giving way to a bluish shade of green in whichever part of the planet currently presented itself to the station.

"It's mid-spring in the north," Bertie said, as they reached the windows. "It's still cold enough to snow in the inhabited areas, because this planet hasn't finished coming out of an ice age. It's quite pleasant in Monralar just now, however. That's in the southern hemisphere, near the equator. Home for me, now."

"Where do the outcastes live?"

"In sanctuaries along the equator, mainly on large islands and peninsulas. There are seventeen of them, scattered more or less evenly around the planet. The provinces take up the habitable areas of the two big continents. They've had six thousand standard years to spread out and settle."

"That's a long time."

Bertie nodded. "Six millennia of advanced technological civilization. Earth can't say the same."

"No," Kim murmured. "But why did they hide it? Why even now live so primitively when they don't have to?"

"In many ways they don't. They strike quite a remarkable balance."

"I'd like to see that."

A bright smile lit Bertie's face. "Does that mean you'll take the post?"

Kim hesitated for a moment, but the allure of all that research and the professional notoriety he'd gain from publishing it was just too strong.

"Yes. I'm in."

* * *

THE FOUR OF them reconvened in Aafreen's office. Before Two-Five could scramble onto the furniture, Kim stooped down to sit eye to eye with him on the floor. Two-Five's eyes were gleaming, and a small bag now hung from one small shoulder. Kim put two fingers of his left hand on that shoulder, in his best approximation of the Kekrax gesture of friendship, and leaned forward to lick his face.

"He pleases this male," Kim said.

Two-Five nodded gently, once, twice, three times. Kim's heart clenched.

"He has a gift for his friend," Two-Five replied, reaching into the bag. He brought out a clear red data crystal and dropped it into Kim's right palm. "He speaks with the broodmale, the venerated Kim male. They record the interview, the First and Second."

Kim stared at the crystal, then closed his fingers around it and looked back up at Two-Five, eyes misting. The interview with Two-Three hadn't been lost after all. He'd have something tangible to show for his time on Kekrax Main, something that Di Fata couldn't claim.

"This means a lot to me," Kim managed past the lump in his throat, when no Kekrax phrase for what he felt came to mind. He collected himself. "He thanks him, his kindest friend."

Two-Five returned the lick with a tongue-flick to Kim's cheek, then turned and scurried out on all eight, whipping out the door like a ribbon. Kim stared after him, shaking his head, then opened his fingers and gazed down at the data crystal in his hand. Saliva dribbled down his face, but somehow, this one time, it was comforting.

A sniffle came from above him. Aafreen stood frozen, gazing out the door, eyes glistening. Bertie had taken a seat on a divan and was also staring out the door, stilled, lips parted.

Kim hauled himself to his feet and took a deep breath. "Well," he said, and took another breath to clear his lungs of any lingering pheromones. "I knew Two-Five was fond of me, but... Well. All right. What's next?"

His companions seemed to come back to life and took deep breaths themselves. Aafreen flopped onto the other divan, and Kim took a chair across from both.

"Have you made a decision about the Jorann's blessing?" Bertie asked.

"I have," he said. "I want to be safe from poisoning. I'll do no good to anyone if I'm *more* than theoretically dead. And I see no downside to taking it, all things considered and given my current options."

Bertie nodded. "Then the next step is to take you down to the planet and administer it to you. The apothecaries up here do keep a small supply, but they need to reserve it for serious injury, which does unfortunately happen, space stations being what they are. In any event, we need to get you safely onworld. If the human authorities work out where you are ahead of schedule, Aafreen needs plausible deniability so they can chalk everything up to Tolari inscrutability. I'm inclined to take you to *warm, sunny* Monralar, but *cold, wintry* Suralia is also an option. Do you have a preference?"

"It sounds as if I'm meant to choose Monralar," Kim said, "but I've no idea what sort of politics might be involved. According to the Kekrax, the Tolari have a confusing and shifting system of alliances and enmities. I wouldn't want to step on any toes right off."

"They don't have toes." Bertie winked, then continued, "But Monralar and Suralia are allies, so you're unlikely to start a war or anything of that sort. The ruler of Suralia is also the leader of the ruling caste, so he sticks his fingers into everyone's pies. But this project was Marianne's idea, and she brought me into it for the legalities involved in hiring a human, so you're working for me as least as much as for her, if not more. I'm inclined to continue your orientation in Monralar, where you might also have the opportunity to meet two of the other humans on the planet, but it's really up to you."

Kim blinked. "What other two? You and Marianne Woolsey are the only humans on Tolar."

"As far as the media markets know. There are actually five of us."

"Five!"

"Bertie," Aafreen said, breaking into the conversation. "You *do* remember that a delegation from Suralia is coming up tomorrow to collect him? He needs to make an *informed* choice if you're going to improvise alterations to the plan."

Kim jolted. "*Collect* me?" he exclaimed.

"Not like that," she continued. "But my concern is that you're an adult Sayyar, even if you don't acknowledge it and you've chosen to live..." she paused, considering "...planet-bound. The only person who should have a say in where you go is you."

"I'm a Six Planets citizen," Kim said. "Not a Sayyar."

"If you're not one of us, then I'm a custard tart."

Bertie sniffed. "That's my line."

"Hold on," Kim said, blowing a loud huff of air. "Let me think."

Bertie and Aafreen subsided.

Kim took yet another deep breath and considered.

"Honestly," he continued, thinking aloud, "I prefer warm weather. Whether or not I'm Sayyar, I did grow up on a space station, where it was the same comfortable temperature all the time, with only short trips downworld to Britannia. My internships were on Earth in the

Amazon and my post-doc was on a V'kri station, which was warmer than ours. The only other time I've ever spent more than a week onworld was my sabbatical on Kekrax Main, and I loved the heat there. You said Monralar is on Tolar's equator?"

"I did," Bertie replied. "If the equator were marked with a visible line, you'd see it from the stronghold. It's directly offshore."

"I'll go there then."

"Good enough," Aafreen said, with a note of deep satisfaction in her voice. Bertie lifted an eyebrow at her. "I just want him to make his own decisions, not get bullied into what a certain Britannic lord wants."

"You're a custard tart, Aafreen."

"I can't be a custard tart. You loathe them."

Bertie chuckled, then caught Kim's eye. "She has a point. My apologies in advance if necessary. During my years as stationmaster, I learnt to be overbearing at need."

Aafreen choked. Bertie effected not to hear it.

"Your legal...shall we call it a dilemma? It came at a perfect moment for us. Now that you're hired, we need to get you off the station and safely lost on Tolar before I set Rembrandt's legal department loose on your debt owners. That's another reason Monralar is the better choice. It's *not* the seat of the current titular ruler, which is the first place the human authorities will call to ask questions, assuming they figure out you're here. Which they might not do, but Monralar gives the Sural as much plausible deniability as it does to Aafreen."

One particular word stuck out at Kim. "Hired?"

"Oh yes!" Bertie grinned. "We've yet to negotiate your contract with the University, of course, but you'll find the salary generous and all expenses covered. Tolar operates on a barter economy at every level, so there's nowhere to actually spend your salary here. However, if you want to grow your savings against future difficulties, I can help you there. And don't forget that after you take the blessing, you've a right to live on the planet or on the station, or both by turns, your choice. And...right, here's another thing I forgot to tell you. The blessing will give you a Tolari lifespan."

Kim flinched, almost afraid to know, but he had to ask. "Is it much shorter than I could normally expect to live, given good health?"

"Oh no, quite the opposite. It's about three centuries Earth standard, give or take."

Kim felt his jaw slacken and was unable to stop his mouth from literally dropping open. He couldn't breathe. "Three hundred...?" he said, faintly.

"Too much? Not everyone wants to imitate Methuselah, to be sure. You're free to change your mind at any time before you actually consume it, but it's not a reversible mod. After you take it, there's no going back."

"No," he replied, still having trouble getting enough air into his lungs to speak properly. "It's fine. It's just... I don't know what to say. Three hundred years? Are you certain of that?"

"Quite."

Kim slumped in his chair. "Three hundred *years*. Think of all the papers I could write."

CHAPTER 8

The Jorann lived deep under the mountain just north of the Sural's stronghold. So said the Marann, as she gave Halla a thermal winter robe, outcaste grey and heavier even than the one Sandbird had given her. Halla fingered the material, wondering whether it came from outcaste or provincial hands. Would a Suralian feel dishonor, crafting such fine clothing in grey?

She folded the robe from Sacaea away in her bag and donned the new. It fit without binding about her shoulders, and more, it was the correct length, just touching the top of her slippers. Someone had adjusted this robe for *her*. A lump rose in her throat, and she could only nod her thanks.

The Marann's presence glowed with kindliness. "The Jorann will challenge you when you arrive," she said. "You need only state that you bring her no harm."

"My thanks," Halla said. "I will remember." She turned toward the spiral stair, then turned back. "Will you answer a question?"

Brown eyebrows lifted. "If I can."

"Why did you laugh when I told the Sural he was not what I expected?"

The Marann smiled. "Because I said nearly the same thing to him the day I arrived to teach his daughter the languages of Earth."

The words startled a laugh out of her. "Truly?"

"Truly." The Marann's smile broadened. "Is there anything else?"

Halla shook her head, and on second thought, offered a bow. "No. Again, my thanks."

The Marann nodded as Halla turned once more to begin the descent and called, "Fair journey."

The steep steps wound down into darkness. Lamps came on at her approach, flickering out as she left them behind. She was to descend to the bottom, enter and traverse the tunnel she found there, and take the stairs up from the tunnel's end. There was no other path. She could not lose her way. Step after jarring step, down, and down, and down. She could not decide if it would be more jolting to individuals of normal height, or less. And always a bubble of light surrounded her, holding the darkness away, until, after such a long time that Halla thought she must surely be in the heart of the world, the next light illuminated a floor.

She sat heavily on the last steps at the base of the stair, knees and peds aching from the unnatural rhythm of the descent. The air here smelled of dust and was chill enough to sting her face. She was very grateful now for the thermal robe the Marann had given her as she dug into her shoulder bag for the water sack included with her provisions. She uncapped it and took a long drink.

"We are almost there, my love," she murmured to Tarasheth after she satisfied her thirst. "We are almost there."

She heaved herself up, shouldered the bag, and walked, appreciative of the smooth, flat surface beneath her, hard stone though it was. It was a moderately long tunnel, but she had walked paths longer than this every day of her life, regardless the sanctuary. As her legs recovered from the descent, she settled into her normal, ground-eating stride. Soon enough, she reached the tunnel's other end. The next stair greeted her there, this one wider, shallower, and more gently curving. She started up.

It was not nearly so long as the spiral stair down. After only one full curve, it opened on a huge cavern, longer than it was wide, its walls and ceiling glistening with frost. In the middle sat a platform of rock and ice, roughly circular, about as wide as Halla was tall. On the near edge of the platform sat the Jorann.

The Mother of All looked as every story described her: pale of skin, yellow of hair, wearing a white, sleeveless robe in the bitter cold, and when she stood, she was very tall.

"Come, child," she said, in a soft voice that nevertheless carried across the cavern. "Sit with me."

Halla crossed the distance between them. A white blanket lay across the platform where the Jorann had sat, and more blankets covered the floor at its base. As Halla reached the platform, she noticed two things at the same time: that the Jorann's eyes were the color of the sea before a storm, and that the two of them stood eye to eye, each as tall as the other.

"Oh," Halla said, because words fled from her mind.

The Jorann's lips curved in a warm smile. "Granddaughter," she said, and returned to her seat on the edge of the platform, posture relaxed and at the same time welcoming, hands resting lightly to each side. No trace of her presence showed. She was as unreadable as if she were not there. "Sit, child."

Halla lowered herself to the blankets at her peds, thoughts spinning. *She called me granddaughter.* Then memory sparked, and she lifted her eyes to meet the gaze of her own ancient ancestor.

"You did not challenge me."

"No, granddaughter," she replied, and her words were those of Sanctuary Venak. "I do not challenge those whose hearts bleed as does yours. There can be only one reason you sought me."

A sudden welling of emotion clogged Halla's throat and filled her eyes, to hear her own language fall from the lips of the Mother of All, and she could only nod.

"I can heal you," the Jorann said, still in the words of Venak. "But not without pain. Are you willing to bear it?"

Halla could imagine nothing she would not endure if it put an end to the long years of anguish. She nodded.

"What was her name?"

"Tarasheth," Halla whispered.

"Tarasheth." The Mother of All seemed to roll the name around her mouth, tasting it. "Tell me about Tarasheth."

CHAPTER 9

$\mathcal{K}$im had steeled himself to endure the surgical coldness of a phase platform, but to his unqualified relief, Aafreen informed him that phase tech was antithetical to Tolari instrumentation and Kim would have to take the long way down. Fortunately it turned out that Bertie was a qualified shuttle pilot. His hands moved with reassuring ease over the controls of what looked like a refurbished A'aan' short-hauler, while Kim occupied the co-pilot's seat. Two provincial Tolari, both women in lavender robes like Bertie's, sat in the back looking unconcerned and chatting in a language Kim couldn't understand. Monrali, he assumed, based on the color of their robes.

The project still needed to do something about the language problem. The Kekrax information he'd downloaded to his tablet indicated that Tolar boasted more than a hundred languages, divided into several families, and those were just the official provincial languages. Bertie further informed him that the inhabitants of the seventeen sanctuaries each spoke a distinct argot that was usually but not always a mix of the nearby provincial tongues. Kim would need an interpreter for some time to come—or more likely several. That was less than ideal, if he intended to really make sense of the cultural gestalt of the societies before him.

He stared out the forward windows, considering which Tolari language to study first. His native English was, ironically, the official lingua franca of the station. For the planet, however, Suralian served the same purpose, at least in the provinces, so perhaps that was the best place to start. He leaned back. The planet, its moon, and all the stars in Tolar's heavens spread out before him. He savored the view until the shuttle juddered into the atmosphere and the roar and the flames began. The noise washed over him and subsided ten or so minutes later, and then they were streaking across the northern coast of the southern continent at night. As they descended, a splash of light ahead resolved into the outline of a city stretched along the shore of the sea.

"*Oînops póntos,*" Bertie said, hands busy on the control panel. He pointed with his chin. "The wine-dark sea. I never tire of this view. It's Monralar's city, where most of the population lives. The scholar's tower is in the southwest quarter. By Tolari lights, that's where you would lodge if you weren't guesting at the stronghold."

"*Monralar's city,* you called it. Does it have a name?"

"Not really. Names are funny things on Tolar. Rulers are stripped of them at the moment of his or her rise to power, and from their founding the cities never had any. As for the people, well, they have names, but when and how they use them can be tricky, and the outcastes are yet a different kettle of popcorn. But I expect you'll pick up the knack of it before long."

As they approached, a brightly lit building, or perhaps it was a complex of buildings, resolved as its own set of discrete lights, inland and uphill of the city. The structure was only three stories tall, but it was a vast rectangular fortress, encompassing acres of land within its walls. The shuttle slowed and headed directly for it.

"And that's the stronghold," Bertie said. Then, more softly, "Home."

A Tolari with harshly blunt features, his ankle-length hair plaited into fantastically complicated braids and twists, waited in a corner of the roof as Bertie manually landed the shuttle. The man had the build of a rugby player, and his lavender robe sported bright white embroidery from collar to waist. That was a sign of the ruling caste, Kim had read, so this must be the Monral—Bertie's *caliph*, as Aafreen called him. Bertie touched a control, with a light in his eyes that hadn't been there before, and the rear hatch opened. Warm air wafted in, fragrant with flowers and an alien tang that Kim guessed came from the nearby ocean.

"After you," Bertie said, gesturing toward the now-open hatch.

Kim followed the lavender-robed women out. He stepped onto the white stone roof in time to see them bow deeply to the Monral. The Tolari ruler was about Kim's own height, and after dismissing the women, he turned striking amber eyes on him. Not knowing what else to do, Kim bowed, imitating the way the women had held their hands, palms forward, as they bent. Bertie climbed out of the shuttle behind him as he straightened.

The Monral favored Bertie with a long look and a smile that softened his harsh features.

"Welcome home, my love," he said in English, in an accent at once Nordic and Chin. Then he turned his attention back to Kim. "I am the Monral," he continued, and gazed into Kim's face with an expectant look.

While Kim hesitated, Bertie strode forward to take the Monral's hand. "You're meant to introduce yourself," he said. "My apologies, I should have gone over some basic points of etiquette with you. The proper form of address for any member of the ruling caste is *high one*. They use other titles amongst themselves, but stick clear of those. Oh, and the usual procedure with a high one is *don't speak until spoken to*."

The Monral elbowed Bertie without letting go of his hand. "Monralar does not stand on ceremony, as humans say, but should you find yourself facing an unfamiliar member of my caste, yes, waiting for the invitation to speak is the safest path."

Kim took a breath. "My name is Kimberly Storm-Gale. I'm a cultural xenologist with—" he hesitated. The University might well not take him back. "Bertie hired me to conduct research for his project with Marianne Woolsey."

"Be welcome in my stronghold, Dr. Storm-Gale. Follow me." He gestured toward the corner of the roof, and from this angle, Kim could see stairs leading down. "I will show you to the guest wing. The servants have already prepared a room for your use. You will have come from station day, but I suggest you take what rest you can until our local morning."

"Thank you, sir—uh, high one," he said. "And please, it's just Kim."

The Monral's eyebrows went up. "This way, Kim," he said, indicating the stairs.

* * *

THE MONRAL CALLED IT A ROOM. Kim called it a suite. The door in the guest wing opened by itself on a spacious, brightly lit room, its white stone floor—marble?—polished to a high gloss and laid with ornate carpets very like those woven on New Arabia. Tolari culture, or at least that of Monralar, had embraced the concept of chairs and tables, but Kim wasn't convinced even the richest of the rich in human space possessed designs like these. What looked like conspicuously padded runner carpets, formed into chairs. Semi-circular divans. Small tables carved from—and Kim was guessing here—a single, possibly purpose-grown tree branch. Paintings graced the walls, but none of the exquisitely carved frames were square. In one corner stood three bookshelves designed for interlocking diagonal piles of books. Windows of more familiar design separated the room from a balcony overlooking a garden, which glimmered under a setting half-moon. It was obviously a space designed to allow its occupant to relax, alone or in company, and to converse, or read, or do any of a number of other quiet activities.

The Monral excused himself and left Bertie to explain the amenities of the sleeping room and bathing area. Kim's bags were somehow already unpacked, with one wardrobe door in the sleeping room left open to show his shirts and trousers, neatly folded on a shelf.

"Really," Kim said, once he had a grasp of how the plumbing

worked. "A room with a bed, a desk, a chair, and a refresher would have done well enough for me."

"Oh no, that would never do," Bertie said. He led Kim back to the sitting room and dropped into a chair, tapping on a tablet before stuffing it into a pocket of his robe. "Monralar is renowned for his hospitality, and to offer you less than his best would do violence to that reputation."

"Monralar? Or the Monral?"

"It's confusing, I know, but it's both. You'll understand better once you've taken the blessing, but the Monral is both himself and, in a very real way, his province, at the same time."

"And nameless you said."

"He *had* a name." Bertie's tone was wistful. "As with every ruler, it was taken away when he came to power."

"Well that's certainly a new twist on the royal We," Kim murmured.

Bertie chuckled.

Kim took a chair, which as strange as it looked, was remarkably comfortable. On the small table next to it, a hand-sized stone statue sat, carved into something that could be a whale, if whales possessed six flippers, twin blow holes, and a long, bladed tail.

The door to the hall opened, this time on a black-robed servant bearing what was unmistakably a tea service on a tray. He placed it on a long, low table that resembled nothing so much as two branches reaching for each other, and poured a steaming, honey-colored liquid into elegant mugs with iridescent glazes before leaving them alone again.

"It's safe," Bertie said, taking one of the mugs and gesturing to the other. "It's Suralian tea flower. The servants here are well aware of what's safe for humans to consume, so you can trust anything they give you, but you needn't concern yourself that anyone will try to harm you. You're a scholar by Tolari definitions, and that caste is strictly noncombatant, so it's just not done. But I thought I might answer one or a few of your questions, before we each toddle off to our rest."

"You'd be all night answering everything," Kim said. He took a moment to consider his mental list, sipping at the tea. The flavor spread over his tongue, at once floral and faintly sweet. He liked it instantly, and took another, larger sip. Then he said, "First, how do we stand for interpreters, and second, what's my brief, precisely?"

"Yes, I thought the language matter might concern you. As I mentioned on the station, we did have a top-notch translator lined up. Unfortunately, the leader of her sanctuary, combined with our ship-master Farryn and his ruling caste proclivities, bungled the invitation badly. Terrible idea adding him into it, rather like shooting at gnats with a blunderbuss, and in this case, the gnat dodged and fled. So now we're searching for a suitable replacement, or rather replacements." He emphasized the final *S*. "Meanwhile, the Monral would like to offer you a language implant to get you started, assuming you've no prior one. Suralian is the obvious choice, unless you're completely tone deaf. In that case, we'd recommend Monrali, because Suralian is a tonal language. Are you tone deaf? Or have you had a previous implant?"

"No to both," Kim said, shaking his head and stifling a laugh. The cost of an implant was well above what an academic could afford. "I'm no caruso, but I can carry a tune well enough."

"You've the advantage of me there." Bertie's expression turned sheepish. "I can't carry a tune in a bucket. But I can tell higher from lower, so I've no trouble with Suralian."

"Well, that's good. An implant will save time."

"Considerable time. It's a difficult language." Bertie drew out his tablet again and worked at it for a few seconds. "Right then. That's sorted. It will take the apothecaries several days to prepare the implant, and they'll wish to scan your head with their various arcane medical devices. Nothing intrusive. Anything else?"

"So far, you've all been very vague on details—unless you want me to serve as the team lead as well as chief investigator. I can do both if necessary, but I'll need more information. Deadlines, schedules, accommodations, means of transportation, communications, just to name a few. After that, methodology, depth of cultural inquiry, confidence levels for the final report, and the size of the gestalt matrix you want—to put it bluntly, how many of these local cultures are expected to come together at one time, so we can gauge the complexity of social cohesion and dispersion."

Bertie sucked in a breath. "Well," he said, after a moment. "One might notice that none of us here are social scientists. I have to admit none of that occurred to me, but Marianne might have thought of some of it. I'll give her a call before I turn in."

"Who am I working for, by the way? Specifically."

"That's...that's a sticky question. Tolari don't think of work in those terms. Legally, from the human perspective, you work for me, and to a similar extent Marianne, as she's my partner in the endeavor. From a Tolari perspective, the situation is much broader. By their lights, you will have the honor of serving Tolar. The Sural *might* view the project as serving the ruling caste, since Marianne had the original idea and she's his bond-partner, but we can probably nip that off before it grows into a Venus flytrap. I will definitely have a talk with her after I leave you.

"Meanwhile, there's no reason not to give you the blessing as soon as the head apothecary is up and about in the morning, if that sounds acceptable. She wants to supervise, though there's scarcely anything *to* supervise. You take the blessing, you fall asleep, you wake up and you're one of us. It really is as simple as that."

Kim thought about that, sipping at the excellent tea. He'd already consumed half of it without noticing. "How long will I sleep?"

"Six to eight hours, to judge by most of us. A good night's sleep, in other words. We'll feed you up and get plenty of fluids into you first. That's, ah, part of the point of the tea, so drink up."

Kim took a mouthful, swallowed, and squinted. "*Most* of you?"

Bertie lifted a golden eyebrow. "You're a clever one. We may have chosen luckier than we knew. Yes, four of us had no difficulty at all with the transition. One, however..." He paused, eyes flicking while he thought. "Her identity is deeply hush-hush, but she's just next door in Parania, our western neighbor. She had rather a bumpy ride when she took the blessing and ended up an empathic sensitive."

"I'm sorry, but isn't that what *all* of you are? Empaths of some sort?"

Bertie grinned. "Our friend is *extra* sensitive. A few Tolari are. They're rare and treasured by their provinces because they just *know* things. I'm assured it's not telepathy, but it looks damned close to that from here."

Here being Bertie's level of empathy, Kim supposed. Well, if it was that rare, he probably had no need to worry about it. He finished off the tea in one large gulp and said, "Oh, one more thing. I surprised the Monral up there, didn't I? When I told him to call me Kim."

Bertie leaned forward. "That's a point, and yes, you did. The way you phrased it could be construed as correcting a high one, and *that's* not done. The Sural is likely to ignore any missteps as well, but it's not a good habit to get into with the ruling caste if you can avoid it. They're not all so forgiving."

"I see, and thanks for the warning." Kim stifled a yawn. "Well. I'm actually tired. I should try to sleep. It sounds as if tomorrow will be an eventful day."

"Indeed," Bertie said, standing and heading toward the door. "I'll see you in the morning." He halted and turned. "Oh, almost forgot. We'll be having a sort of banquet in the morning in your honor. I can ask the cooks to prepare something extra fiery for you, if you like."

"Please don't. I'd be indisposed for a week."

Bertie physically started at that. "What, really? Aafreen must be mistaken about your lineage, then. You can't be a station rat if you can't eat spicy food."

"Sayyar," Kim corrected, but he wondered about that himself sometimes, because he'd have the iconic Sayyar beard, thick and luxurious, if he let it grow. It had taken three applications of nanites to finally eradicate the stubborn thing.

Bertie cleared his throat. "Yes. Sayyar. My apologies. In my defense, Aafreen never corrected me, although why not is something I should ask her." He huffed. "Back to cases. I'll tell the kitchen to bake the mild bread for you, then. You'll breathe fire if you eat what Tolari consider *herby*."

Kim laughed. "Thank you."

After Bertie disappeared out the door, Kim went into the sleeping room and stripped, told the lights to darken, and crawled under the blanket. The mat was surprisingly comfortable, despite the absence of anything resembling a pillow. He'd long since developed the ability to fall asleep anywhere and in almost any position. He only needed to stop moving. Usually. Tired as he was, he found himself staring into the dark, musing on his recent changes of fortune, from academic research to looming indenture to the opportunity of a lifetime.

He, Kim, without money or influential backing, would conduct research among the Tolari, the most recently discovered civilization in the Orion Arm. That was worth something. Not only that, but the research itself would end up in the history books. *He* would write the foundational texts. And he'd get it all by doing what he loved best: collecting stories, conducting interviews, working to put it all together into an understandable whole. *Seventeen* linked cultures, interacting with scores of surrounding provinces. It would take years, a prospect that was daunting and exciting at the same time. Of *course* he couldn't sleep. He was strongly tempted to pull out his recording of the Kekrax data feed and make some preliminary notes before Bertie or Marianne Woolsey or anyone else snared him with their own preconceived notions of what he might find.

And also—was fame and, well, not necessarily fortune—was *this project* worth an irreversible gen mod? It made sense to take advantage of a language implant if he was blazing a trail. But *genetic modification?* He had Bertie's word, yet he had to admit in the privacy of his own thoughts that he really didn't know the man.

Just the fact that he was too excited to sleep meant, really, that he'd already made his choice. It was either accept the irreversible gen mod or scan everything he put in his mouth for the rest of his time on the planet, and that didn't account for substances that absorbed through the skin. Nothing Bertie had described about the physical aspects of the gen mod would make any real difference to his research, except for granting him a longer life in which to do it. The empathy might even be useful from time to time. No, this "Jorann's blessing" was the safest choice. He'd prefer not to end up *more* than theoretically dead.

It was quite a leap into the dark, especially since thus far, he'd not actually interviewed any Tolari. His ideas of them could well be wildly romanticized along the lines of what they still called "orientalism" in the trade, even though the Pan-Arabs were now more technologically minded and prosaic than Saint Edward Said could have imagined. The usual dangers of any kind of planetary field work ran up against the potential research benefits of Tolari empathy. But it was a singular opportunity, one that would both win him recognition and keep him out of a debt owner's clutches. He shook himself mentally. Let it be.

He took some deep breaths, methodically relaxed his muscles, and finally fell asleep.

* * *

HE WAS IN A CAVE. No, a cavern, a *grand* cavern, even larger than the Vaults on New Arabia, boasting frost-covered walls and a round platform of ice and rock two meters across in its center. At the foot of the platform, a shorthaired Tolari woman in a grey robe sat on a pile of white blankets, conversing with a long-haired blonde woman in white in voices too low for him to make out the words. The blonde lifted her gaze, smiled at him, and returned to nodding encouragingly at the other woman.

Then he was awake, and it was dim predawn in Monralar. In the wan, early light, the garden outside his suite appeared lushly asleep, its flowers closed from the night and its foliage just a little blue. Did the arsenic do that? He shrugged and went into the bathing area to wash, then dressed in fresh clothes that smelled of Kekrax mud even to him. He paced into the sitting room. Experimentally, he called out, "Servant?"

The door opened on emptiness. Then a black-robed man popped into existence in front of Kim, and he literally jumped. God! How did they do that? What was the trick?

"Fair morning, scholar," the man said in heavily accented English. "How may I serve you?"

Kim patted his chest and tried to catch his breath. "Would you please show me to the dining hall?" he asked.

"Dining." The man blinked a few times, then nodded to himself. "The refectory, yes scholar. Follow me."

Refectory. He wondered how the Tolari had settled on that word in their English repertoire. Perhaps that was how they thought of it: a place of refreshment. It wasn't particularly a place of comfort, he decided when he arrived there, though it certainly smelled wonderful, something like warm bread and seasonings. Tables and unpadded chairs of a square style that wouldn't look out of place in a human lay-by restaurant were organized in sections around the room, which was busy even at this early hour, populated by long-haired Tolari in a rainbow of deep-toned robes. He mentally reviewed the caste colors the Kekrax had identified: purple for the arts, blue for scholars, green for laborers, brown for the sciences, mauve for musicians, and more. The only pale colors represented were Monrali lavender—lots of lavender—and the bright yellow of the healers. The only lavender-clad person in evidence with the bright white ruling caste embroidery on his robe was the Monral, whose blunt features seemed less homely this morning as he smiled and conversed, comfortably in his element. He sat in a carved, throne-like chair at the head of the longest table in the room. He beckoned to Kim.

Bertie sat in the first chair down on the left, and a little girl wearing a plain lavender robe, who couldn't be more than five or six years old, sat to the right. Then the child turned her face toward him, and her amber eyes were a perfect match to those of the Monral. She was a pretty little thing, and didn't look at all like him otherwise, but those eyes couldn't be a coincidence. Every other Tolari he'd seen so far had eyes of medium to dark brown. The Monral, it seemed, had a daughter.

Two men in dark blue, one of them old and white-haired, the other just beginning to grey, sat to the little girl's right, and next to them sat a hard-faced woman in lavender. Bertie patted the back of the empty chair at his own left. Kim took it and found a steaming mug on the table in front of him along with a tray holding hand-sized rolls of bread and fruits of various colors, red and orange and one that was dark green. Most of the table's occupants held steaming bowls or some variation of bread and fruit. Or perhaps they were vegetables, although that distinction might not even apply on this planet, for all he knew. At least they didn't wriggle or squirm, unlike Kekrax fare.

"Good morning," Bertie said. "The food on the tray is perfectly safe for you. Eat up."

"Good morning!" the little girl chirped in almost unaccented English. She was on her knees on her chair now, leaning her elbows on the table. "I am Farryneth, daughter to Monralar."

Kim did his best to perform a seated bow. "Pleased to meet you. I'm Kim. I'm a cultural xenologist."

"I am very pleased to meet you! Are you the one who came to talk to the outcastes?"

"I am, yes."

"Daughter." The Monral waited until she looked at him and smiled gently when she did. "Allow our guest to take his meal."

"Okay!" Farryneth sat back. She was clearly eager to pump Kim for information, but she seemed able to hold it in. For now.

Kim shot her a grin and looked around the room. Bertie was sipping from his bowl, rather than spooning the steaming contents into his mouth, but since no one offered Kim any of the soup, he supposed it was toxic for him. There were no plates or silverware in evidence, and everyone seemed to be eating with their fingers. Well, fingers were washable, and after all, who was he to criticize an entire culture for their table habits after he'd spent nine months in the nude just to avoid doing laundry?

He chose a roll off the tray. Imitating the way others around the room were handling theirs, he tore it in half and started in on one piece. It was still warm and fragrant, and delicious, and his appetite took over. He devoured it, and another, and then he picked up a red fruit to take an experimental bite. The skin was crisp as an apple, but the flesh inside had the texture of a peach, sweet and tangy. He ate most of the food on the tray, while Bertie and the Monral and even little Farryneth kept up a patter of light conversation about the weather, this year's crops, and something about gemstone mining that sounded as if it doubled as a teaching exercise for the girl. Eventually, Kim sat back and sighed, sipping tea and feeling comfortably full. Aside from his recent evening with Two-Three of Three, he couldn't remember the last time he'd eaten a meal that didn't include bugs, grubs, or worms. Or all three.

Meanwhile, the white-haired old man sat looking as if he'd just eaten a bad pickle, and then as one, he and the other blue-robed man and the woman in lavender rose from their seats and left. When they had disappeared out the door, Kim took a stab at testing the limits of inquiry here while assessing social relations at the same time. Addressing no one in particular, he asked, "What's with the old man?"

Bertie snorted.

"He is my chief advisor," the Monral said. "Unfortunately, he cares little for humans."

"Really? He dislikes humans?" Kim glanced at the now-empty doorway, then back at Bertie. "Aren't you two engaged or something like that?" A thousand thousand patterns, old Kuan had said, but humans had some form of marriage in all of them.

"Something like," Bertie said, lips twitching.

"That must stick in his craw then."

Bertie rolled his eyes. "You've *no* idea," he drawled.

The Monral laughed. It was a good laugh, rich, whole-hearted, and full of good humor. Probably nothing could make the man handsome, but his laugh lit his eyes and softened the harsh angles of his face, rendering him much less homely. When it subsided, he fixed his amber gaze on Kim.

"Are you ready to visit the apothecaries?" he asked.

Kim's breath caught. It was time to face his decision, for good or ill.

"Yes, high one. I'd like to get this done."

CHAPTER 10

*I*t required time for Halla to tell the Jorann the whole of her life with Tarasheth, but there was nothing other than time in this place. It seemed almost to revolve around them, as if the cavern were the center of the world, or the center of the universe itself. She spoke the words and told the stories, and with them came tears, of the pain and sorrow of losing Tarasheth but also of the joy and laughter of their years together. Above, through the untold weight of the mountain's rock and ice and snow, the sun descended a Suralian sky that Halla could not see, as the Mother of All asked questions when Halla needed them in order to find the words, or sat in silence with her when speaking was too much to bear. Once, only once, the Jorann laid a warm hand on Halla's head, and a riffling sensation went through her, not unpleasant, as if the Jorann leafed through her as she would the pages of a book.

Time circled, and Halla realized she was thirsty. To her astonishment, a *servant* came in with tea. Seated, Halla could not say if they were of the same height, but the black-robed woman was certainly tall enough to be a Grandchild, and her robe, shockingly, bore white embroidery at the collar and cuffs. The mug she offered Halla steamed in the frigid air. The mug she offered the Jorann did not.

The Jorann murmured an acknowledgment, or perhaps a thanks, in what sounded much like the tongue of Sanctuary Lespeni. It might have been Paranian. Halla stared as she cupped her hands around the steaming mug to warm them. It had never occurred to her that the Mother of All needed to *drink*.

But of course she did, and she needed to eat, too, because next the servant brought food, a great deal of it, trays of bread and fruit, vegetables and nuts, roots of many different kinds. Some trays she laid near Halla, while she placed others on the platform near the Jorann. As before, much of what she offered Halla steamed in the frigid air, and none of what she offered the Jorann did. The trays near Halla were themselves almost too hot to touch.

"Eat," said the Jorann, as the servant left them to their meal. "You need warmth and nourishment."

She did. The cold troubled her very little, as the robe the Marann had given her was very effective in countering it, but she was hungry. Halla tore into a roll, relishing the hot bread, gulping it down as if she were a ravenous child instead of a grown woman. Then she turned to the fresh fruit, which was a treat in most sanctuaries. She devoured them all, and began on the roots, choosing one that was an unfamiliar deep blue. Crisp skin gave way to a richly flavored and smooth interior.

When she could eat no more, she leaned back, suddenly embarrassed, but there was only compassion in the Jorann's expression. The servant returned and took away the now mostly empty trays.

"Rest now," the Jorann said, and she smiled. "This is delicate work, as demanding for me as it is painful for you."

"What—" Halla stopped herself. How could she question the Mother of All?

The Jorann, astoundingly, replied to her unvoiced question. "You and your life-partner formed a bond, a strong one. Her death ruptured it. Your heart is torn and bleeding, granddaughter, and draining your life away. You have survived as long as you have only because you are one of my Grandchildren. Had you not come to me, you would have followed your lost love into the dark, soon or late, with or without conscious volition."

Without conscious volition. She could have died *like an animal.* Halla took a shaky breath and said, "The deputy on the station said we might have had a kind of partial pair-bond."

"No. The kind of bond you had was more common in the early days than it is now, but it is a distinct and permanent bond, gentler and less exclusive than a pair-bond. I am closing the wound its rupture made to your heart and spirit, and I am sealing in the part of Tarasheth that she left behind so that it can merge into you, but child —granddaughter—she took with her the part of you that could pair-bond as others do. That is no longer possible for you."

Halla took a breath, nodding. "I never wished to bond, not in that way."

The Jorann smiled. "There is more to the heart than bonding, and no, not all my children wish their hearts bonded. A heart that *cannot* bond is still a gift, the more precious for its wound, and Tarasheth will always be part of yours. You can still love, and you can once more thrive."

* * *

HALLA BURROWED into the blankets after the Jorann left her to herself. It was cold enough that she threw them over her head, though she disliked stale air, and was pleasantly surprised to find the air under the covers remained fresh. There were no blankets like *these* in any sanctuary.

The Jorann's words had been both alarming and profoundly comforting. She closed her eyes and found a smile on her lips at the idea that Tarasheth would become a part of her, truly with her always. Yet she could have *died*, and without conscious volition. No descent into the dark, no honor in a life-ending. *Like an animal.* She shuddered.

She would send Aran a gift of thanks. He had literally saved her life.

It was pleasant under the blankets, and light from their whiteness, and she could not say when the white of the blankets became a white stone wall and then a room with white stone walls and long windows looking out upon a lush garden. A provincial in lavender trod a wandering path past its blooms and bushes and small trees. She could feel the warmth in the air.

Monralar. Lavender was the color of Monralar, one of the few she knew. It was real, and it prickled about her, as Suralia had done the entire time she remained in the stronghold. But how was she here?

She turned. A young man in the embroidered lavender robe of Monralar's ruler occupied an elegant desk of dark wood. In a chair before that desk sat a human, just as young and dressed as a Monrali guard, with hair and skin even paler than the Jorann's, and eyes like the sky on a summer day. *The Monral and his human.* They could be no one else. Neither man took notice of her.

"I found inconsistencies in his documentation," the human said, in a language that sounded like English, yet which she somehow understood. *"They wouldn't fool Central Security—or the Rembrandt legal department—but they're so subtle that it's not surprising his University didn't catch them."*

"He believes he is who he says he is," said the Monral. *"And his interest in your project is sincere."*

"Yes. I wouldn't have brought him downworld if I'd sensed otherwise. His education and awarded degrees check out, too. He did that work, and he's published in professional journals too. I asked a staff xenologist at Rembrandt to look those over, and she said they're remarkable. He's a qualified cultural xenologist, no question. The inconsistencies are farther back. They're in the records from the government crèche where he grew up."

"Ah."

The human nodded. *"Yes. Ah."*

CHAPTER 11

Kim was fairly sure that *this* wasn't supposed to happen. Bertie and the Monral had led him to an infirmary, bright, airy, and odd-smelling, but not unpleasantly so. There, a yellow-robed apothecary with strongly accented English had taken him to a small room with a large window and a lovely view of fields and orchards and distant mountains and directed him to lie on the bed. Then she offered him a small crystal box containing a little milky cube. He'd picked up the cube and popped it in his mouth, and the next thing he knew, he was floating near the ceiling, looking down at his own body. It didn't feel as if any time had passed, but clearly it had, because the light was different. Bertie was still here, and so was the apothecary, but the Monral was gone and now a young woman in dark blue bent over his body, holding one of his hands in both of hers.

"He is not here," she said, speaking the language he'd heard in the refectory. He couldn't understand Monrali, but here, now, he could understand this woman speaking it.

"Yes I am," Kim blurted, somehow, though he had no mouth.

The woman dropped his hand and pivoted to look straight up at him. A smile of relief broke over her youthful features.

"Oh!" she said. "There you are!"

On the other side of the bed, Bertie and the apothecary looked at one another.

"Jeryneth?" Bertie asked. Confusion and concern warred in equal measure across his face.

"He is spirit walking," she said, still speaking probably Monrali. "He must be lost."

"I don't remember getting lost. I don't remember anything after I took the blessing."

At the same time, Bertie said, "Spirit walking?" as if he hadn't heard, and Kim understood him just as easily. "I thought that only the strongest sensitives could do that."

"Yes," she said, "and he is strong, but not strong enough, so this is not good. I wish Laura were here." She turned her attention back to Kim. "Kim, my name is Jeryneth. The Monral called me here when you failed to wake. I am a sensitive studying with the stronghold's political scholars. You should come back to your body now. Will you do that for us?"

"Happily," he said. How was he talking, anyway? For that matter, he didn't seem to be breathing, either. Down on the bed his chest rose and fell evenly, so that was good. He wasn't dead yet. He looked down at his own sleeping face. *Not bad,* he thought, taking a last look. *Peaceful.*

And...wait. How was he meant to return to his body? He was up *here*, and it was down *there*.

"Tell me how?" he asked.

The young woman smiled. "Open your eyes."

Oh. It really was that simple. He opened his eyes, and there was a wrenching disorientation as he suddenly wasn't floating near the ceiling. Gravity pressed him into the bed, and he was looking up rather than down into Jeryneth's sparkling, deep brown eyes. He took a moment to enjoy the sensation of air moving through his lungs as he breathed and reflected that this student sensitive couldn't be older than mid-twenties. She smiled at him, and that removed a few more years.

Kim looked past her. Everything glowed. He closed his eyes again, and he could still see the glows as shapes. Of people. And things. And trails on the floor.

So this is empathy?

"Kim!"

He opened his eyes, somehow knowing that Jeryneth didn't want him to fall out of his body again, not so soon. She spoke once more, and he didn't understand it this time. That was disappointing.

Jeryneth frowned and said in English, "You seemed to understand Monrali, just then."

"He can't possibly yet," said Bertie. "He's only just arrived." Bertie was a study in puzzlement, and Kim felt driven to reassure him.

"But I did understand," he croaked, and abruptly realized that he was parched. "Water. Please."

"I'll fetch it," Bertie said. His thoughts were moving quickly now, out of Kim's reach, but the feelings flowed in and out of Kim's mind like an audio system with most of the frequencies at full volume. "What did you hear?"

Kim struggled to remember exactly. "You talked about spirit walking and said you thought only the strongest sensitives could do that."

Bertie froze in the middle of filling a mug from a pitcher. "Yes."

"Please don't stop," Kim urged, when he didn't immediately continue pouring the water.

"Right, sorry."

Bertie topped up the mug and handed it to him. Kim got it to his lips and swallowed the cool water in long gulps. It flowed down his throat like life.

"Slow down," Bertie said, his glow gleaming in a sparky kind of way. That was alarm, maybe, to judge by the look on his face. Kim struggled to match the not-vision with what his eyes saw. "You'll make yourself sick."

Kim disregarded that and drained the mug. "More," he gasped, handing it back.

As Bertie took the mug, the apothecary shook her head.

"Not yet," she said.

Kim frowned, but her tone brooked no argument. At least the thirst was less urgent. "How long was I out?" he asked, in lieu of begging for more.

"A day and a bit," Bertie said. "It's early afternoon now, and you took the blessing yesterday just after breakfast. We weren't sure you would wake up. We weren't sure you could do."

That was truth. He heard it. He saw it. He *felt* it. His words resonated through the apothecary, too; she agreed with him. An odd woman, that, with a hard shell around her, but she cared about her patients with all her heart.

How did he know these things? Kim rubbed his forehead the way he usually did when he was trying to think, and the sensation of his fingertips pressing into the skin felt very much like an electric shock. He yelped and jerked his hand away.

"Don't do that," Bertie said, with a sympathetic grin. His glow brightened again, though Kim couldn't have said with what. "You've nerves generating there now. The skin will thicken to protect them, but you'll still have to remember not to press into them."

"Those nerves will be very delicate, as sensitive as you are," the young Jeryneth said. "Definitely you are stronger than I am. You might rival Storaas."

"Who?"

"The Sural's chief advisor," Bertie replied. "He's one of the most powerful sensitives on Tolar."

"Wait, what? Me? A sensitive? Powerful?" Kim said. "That wasn't supposed to happen."

"No, we didn't see it coming. We'll have to revise our theory of how to predict sensitives."

Kim frowned. "Yes, perhaps you should."

Bertie aimed a light swat at Kim's shoulder, and—oh. A mercifully brief wave of sexual satiety flowed over Kim with the contact. He truly didn't want to know anything about Bertie's intimate life.

"As a practical matter," Jeryneth said, with a pointed glance at Bertie, "do not touch anyone for now, nor allow anyone to touch you.

You are far too sensitive for casual physical contact. I can teach you techniques to make life more comfortable for you, beginning today with barriers. You will need those in order to sleep."

"Thank you," Kim replied. "I don't even know what I need to know." His stomach interrupted with a loud wamble. "But I do know that I'm starving."

* * *

THEY FED him savory bread and what looked like vegetable soup in a small refectory within the infirmary itself, and he felt the better for it, much to his relief. Afterwards, the crusty apothecary examined every inch of him, performed a sensory and balance check, and cleared him for whatever he felt equal to doing. That, he decided, was a walk in the gardens, away from all these people, where he could sort out this new empathy—and its implications for his work. Knowing *this* keenly how his subjects felt could very well inhibit the objectivity he needed to be professional. He wasn't sure what he thought being an empath would be like, but this was certainly not what he'd imagined. He needed time to think.

When he headed for the door to the outside, however, Bertie followed, and beside that the gardens weren't as empty as he'd hoped —at regular intervals, individuals in green robes tended to the plants. But the sun shone down from most of the way up a clear sky, and it was pleasantly warm. A light breeze carried the tang he'd noticed last night, along with a scent that reminded him of the honeysuckle in Tau Ceti's glassed-in botanical gardens. Along the walls, in shaded areas, stood person-shaped glows he couldn't see with his physical eyes. He stopped, staring.

A flash of something came from Bertie. It might have been realization. This was going to take some getting used to. He just *knew* some things and not others, but why? Of course, he'd only been awake in this new world for seventy-seven minutes, and how he knew *that* was anyone's guess.

Bertie nodded toward the shade. "What you *sense* are guards," he said. "Camouflaged and focusing on intent more than anything else. We'll both be able to camouflage someday, supposedly, but none of us converted humans have worked it out quite yet, so far as I know."

"I read what the Kekrax have to say about Tolari camouflage, but I thought it was some kind of trick. That's…" Kim shaded his eyes with a hand and peered at the closest invisible glow. "That's real. How is he doing that?"

Bertie shrugged. "Good question. Tolari figure it out as small children, and perhaps that's why it's eluding us. Children try whatever occurs to them. We adults are limited by what we *think* will work."

Kim laughed. Maybe he should try to figure out camouflage for himself. He could think of a few good uses for an invisible researcher, and not just in the field.

Bertie snorted. "Me too," he said, as if reading his mind, and then he broke into a toothy grin that made him look like a teenager.

"You look so young," Kim said. "It's hard to believe you're old enough to have been a stationmaster for seven years."

"I was a bit young for it, but not very. I'm forty now. The blessing includes somatic regeneration. And that's another thing we neglected to tell you." Bertie covered his face with a hand. "We should draw up a checklist of all the things our hapless victims need to know before they make a decision, so we don't forget to tell them."

"Mentioning regeneration would seem pretty important. How old do I look now?"

Bertie gave him a quick glance up and down. "No different than you did when you arrived. Change will take a bit of time. You'll likely end up looking, oh, twenty-five or so. You'll age from there. As I'm doing."

Bertie definitely looked younger than twenty-five, and Kim frowned, not liking the implications. It was hard enough at thirty-eight to coax respect out of his older colleagues, particularly the ones who had actually lived through the Second Corporate War and the purges that followed. Looking like a grad student again was the last thing he needed, but there was no help for it now. His work here would just have to speak for itself, and he could refrain from having any new professional headshots taken for a good long while. That would have to do.

CHAPTER 12

The servant returned as Halla was waking. She beckoned wordlessly as Halla stood, then showed her to a place in the wall where a deep shadow hid a dark, heavy curtain. Behind the curtain was another, and beyond that was a small cavern, furnished as a sitting room at one end and a refectory with a kitchen at the other. It was *warm* and smelled of vegetables simmering and bread baking.

Halla stood motionless for a moment, appreciating the warmth, wondering why she was left to sleep in the cold—although, she admitted to herself, the blankets had kept her marvelously comfortable. Perhaps this provincial Grandchild did not want an outcaste for company.

Well, what a provincial thought of her scarcely mattered. The servant, who was perhaps a finger's width shorter than Halla, swept an arm toward a door set in the cave wall, and then turned to open it.

Halla considered a moment, decided the silence was unnecessary, and said in Suralian, "I speak Suralian, if you can understand me."

The woman started and whirled. "Oh!" she exclaimed, and a wide grin bloomed on her face. "Forgive me! The necessary is through this door. The next door leads to the bathing area. I put out toweling and a fresh robe for you."

Words escaped Halla's lips despite herself. "Why would you do that?" *A little like Tarasheth*, she thought. Since that day on the beach she *had* become a little like Tarasheth, who had sometimes been more spontaneous than was convenient.

It was deeply reassuring.

The servant smiled. "She is the Mother of *All*." She bowed as to an equal. "I am Tyrana. Be welcome in my home."

* * *

WHEN HALLA EMERGED from the bathing area, clean and damp-haired and wearing a fresh, perfectly fitting robe, Tyrana was setting food on the table at the kitchen end of the cavern.

"Eat," she said, as Halla approached. "The Jorann will see you when you are finished. But be sure your hair is dry before you leave these quarters or it will suck the heat from your body."

Halla nodded and took a seat, and only then noticed that the table and the chairs were built for individuals her size. *Their* size. For a moment, she thought Tyrana might join her, but the woman smiled and bowed and camouflaged, concealing herself so thoroughly that Halla could not make out her presence. It gave her a distinct impression of being alone. She was entirely uncertain whether that was true.

When she camouflaged, did she do so as thoroughly as Tyrana had just done? If she did, it explained why Varina had asked her to do it as little as possible. Tarasheth had never commented on it, but Tarasheth had always, always known where she was. So also did Halla know Tarasheth's location at all times, regardless of what her eyes or even her *senses* told her. She pondered that as she ate to a comfortable fullness. After finishing, she saw to drying her hair before letting herself into the bitter cold on the other side of the curtain, where the Jorann waited, perched on the edge of the platform.

"Granddaughter," she said, with a warm smile. She gestured at the blankets where Halla had slept, now neatly arranged.

Halla knelt to sit on them. "Mother of All," she replied, not knowing what else to say. Or rather, refusing to call the Jorann *highest*, as the provincials did, as if rank applied to her or even had meaning. "Fair morning," she added. That was safe. She knew it to be morning outside, above the mountain. Her sense of time seemed sharper and more magnified in this place.

For a second time, the Jorann reached down to lay a hand on Halla's hair. This time she left it there and closed her eyes, and once more it was as if time revolved around them. "Tell me how you met your Tarasheth," she murmured.

She left the hand in place as Halla described the day that Tarasheth and her mother arrived from Sanctuary Kenakei, soon after Halla had cut her own hair. The memory was vivid. Halla could smell the ocean, see the way the sun glinted off the waves as the transport pod came ashore, hear the sea flutters calling, and as she ran an assessing gaze over the newcomers she felt the sand crawler scuttle over her bare peds. That had startled an exclamation out of her, drawing attention. Tarasheth's approval at the sight of that short hair had flowed over her like a warm, fragrant breeze, and as their gazes locked, she knew. *They* knew.

Their mothers, both their mothers, said they were too young to know their own hearts. They were scarcely past the age of consent. They looked ridiculous, others said, the tallest and the smallest together. They were mismatched. Tarasheth did not even know the language of Venak. That was certainly true at first, but it had not mattered to either of them. Halla heard the song of Tarasheth's heart and wanted it, and to her undiluted joy, Tarasheth wanted hers. They were so young. They were so *certain*. When Tarasheth, fresh from what was to her the delight of mastering Venaki, decided she would travel to every sanctuary and learn every outcaste tongue, there was never any doubt but that Halla would go with her.

Nothing could stop them.

Until the riptide.

Halla sobbed. The grief was so sudden and so intense that every part of her body ached and every nerve set aflame. The Jorann had said it would be painful. Halla had not imagined *this*. She struggled to keep the sobs from turning to screams.

Somehow, the Jorann sat on the blankets with her now, stroking her hair, murmuring nonsense syllables as a parent does to a crying child. Gradually, the syllables took on a rhythm that Halla could hear even through the grief and the tears. As the tide of anguish finally started to turn and the pain to ebb, the Jorann began to sing, softly, gently, in a rich voice that was low for a woman. The words were not from any language Halla knew, nor did they sound like the English of the station. The lilting song caught her, held her, slowed her sobs, steadied her breathing.

After a time, the Jorann fell silent. Halla lay limp and exhausted next to her, curled around herself, shaken by an occasional hiccough.

"Now, granddaughter," the Jorann said. "Now you can heal."

Halla fell asleep.

* * *

SHE WAS in the white stone stronghold again, on a balcony overlooking its garden. The feel was familiar: Monralar again. Why Monralar? It had seemed an intriguing option during her youth, to go provincial here, but not so much that it should invade her dreams, or that she should invade it. It felt so *real*.

A soft sigh came from behind her. She turned.

A human, not the Monral's human but a darker one, wearing a strange form of dress, leaned on the balcony railing, half-facing away from her, gazing out into the garden, watching the sunset. He had not noticed her yet, but the other two men had not seen her either, so she studied him. She told herself she did it to learn whatever it was she was meant to learn here, but in truth, she felt curiously drawn to look at him. His hair was short as an outcaste's, and black as a Tolari's, but it fell in loose curls rather than hanging straight or in waves. His skin was as brown as her own, in contrast to the Monral's human, whose skin was so pale that his veins showed through in places. This one wore what seemed to be a white half-robe with billowing sleeves, tucked into snug brown trousers, and a kind of open slipper on his...feet. He had feet. With toes. She had heard about human feet. How did they walk without tripping over their toes?

The visible corner of his mouth lifted, and she sensed amusement.

"I know you're there," he said. It sounded like English. He straightened and turned to face her. And froze, staring wide-eyed.

Halla stared back.

"I know you," he said. "I dreamed about you."

Halla's stomach turned to ice. "No," she replied. "No. No. This is a dream."

She fled.

She woke.

It was morning again. Someone—the Jorann? Tyrana?—had pulled the blankets over her to keep her warm. She yawned and stretched and pushed them back from her face, blinking at the frosted ceiling of the cavern with gritty eyes that felt swollen. And certainly they might be. She had not wept so long or so hard in, well. Not ever. Not even when Tarasheth disappeared beneath the waves. She had screamed then, but had not truly wept, not even when someone missed them at the evening meal and came looking. They found Halla slumped in the sand, silently staring at the sea with eyes dripping of their own accord.

Varina was sympathetic at first. Especially after Halla decided to leave for Kerreth and learn the language on Tarasheth's behalf, to finish her journey. Varina was less sympathetic when Halla returned and stayed, and grew less so as season after season passed and Halla's grief did not subside.

She should be angry about that, Halla thought. Instead, she pitied the Aanesh leader's failings, along with outcaste ignorance of a bond they could unwittingly form. If Aran's brother had shared what he learned of his own ruptured bond, the knowledge had not spread. It needed to.

Halla could do that. She could take advantage of the provincials to circle the world again, interpreting for the human they wanted to send into the sanctuaries. The dream came to mind, and she frowned. Dreams were tricky, and some people walked in the dreams of others, but this had been her own. Or had it? Had it been real? That human, was he the one they planned to send? She would like to see him face-to-face rather than in a dream, if the encounter had indeed been real.

A rustle from the shadows interrupted her thoughts, Tyrana pushing through the curtains. Halla sat up as she approached and realized she was famished. This time, after she emerged from the bathing area, the servant sat at the table, and there was food enough on the table for both of them.

"Fair morning," Tyrana said.

"Fair morning," Halla replied as she took a seat. She tore into a roll, again eating like a starving child.

Tyrana ate more moderately, but with every evidence of enjoyment.

When the hunger had subsided a little, Halla said, "Why are you eating with me? Will it not dishonor you?"

"I serve the Jorann," Tyrana said. "I wished to share a meal with another Grandchild. It has been many a year since such an opportunity arose."

"But I am outcaste, and you are provincial."

Tyrana gave her a brief smile and took a sip of tea. "There was a time when the laws against interacting with outcastes were not so strict as they are now. Those are the laws I follow, with the blessing of the Mother of All."

"But that was—" Halla gasped. *Before the fall of Lynadria.* That could not be. It had been two thousands of years since that ancient province had fallen into dishonor and been absorbed by its neighbors, when the sanctuaries were officially established, and the laws affecting them set down. "How long have you served her?"

"Long enough." She smiled again, with a gleam of mischief in her dark eyes.

Halla stared. "Then...how did you come to take service here?"

"I came to see her, as so many do, with ambition riding on my shoulder, wishing her to make me leader of my caste, of all the servants in...the place whence I came. She asked for my service instead." She waved at the embroidery on her robe and grinned. "She enjoys seeing me wear this robe. I wanted to lead my caste. Now I am the leader of the Jorann's servant caste. I am in charge of myself."

Tyrana laughed, and Halla could not help but join her.

"What will you do when you leave this place?" Tyrana asked, when she sobered again. "You look as if you can *do* things, now. As if you can *live*. You did not, before."

Halla took a bite of bread. Chewed. Going along with the ruling caste's project was very tempting, but she had no way to know if the offer was still open, or if the man in her dream was the human they wanted to send. He had intrigued her. She wanted to meet him.

Tyrana was waiting for her answer, amusement still glinting in her presence.

"How did I look before?" Halla asked.

"As if your life was draining away."

She grabbed a handful of nuts. "It was. The Jorann said I can heal now, and—I already feel a little more alive."

"The power of her," Tyrana said, shaking her head. "What she can do. We cannot even know if she might be here, now, listening to us."

"She is," said the Jorann's voice, from behind Tyrana. Then an outline of her shape appeared, colorless and transparent. "Tell my grandson," she continued, addressing Tyrana, "that he might gain an interpreter if he can earn her approval."

CHAPTER 13

A poker-faced Monral and a sour-looking Bertie greeted Kim at the breakfast table. The refectory was loud with conversation and fairly bustled with people coming and going, but little Farryneth was nowhere to be seen. Beneath the impassive expression, the Monral was mildly irritated, though it was impossible to know at what. Perhaps it was Bertie. *He* fairly roiled with annoyance. Had they quarreled? But no, Kim had the sense that Bertie was too well-bred to put something so personal on display.

Kim took the chair next to his fellow human. "What happened?"

"The Sural happened," Bertie groused. "I should have expected as much. I *did* expect as much, but I'd hoped Marianne could hold him off."

"What does he want?"

The Monral answered first. "The Sural requests that we send you to Suralia for your language implant, citing the benefits of immediate immersion. His reasoning does have virtue, and his head apothecary is acknowledged the best on Tolar."

"He's the Sural. Of *course* his reasoning has virtue." Bertie's voice rang with exasperation. "And I shouldn't be surprised, but I had hoped to give Kim more time to acclimate before sending him into the lion's den."

"It is a request," the Monral said, biting each word. His irritation looked very focused, to Kim's new sight, and also somewhat frustrated. If the Sural had foiled his plans to keep Kim here, as Bertie's words seemed to imply, that would make sense.

"What are my options, then?" Kim asked, and dipped the torn end of a half roll into a bowl of soup, prepared to listen.

Bertie took a breath to speak, but expelled it when the Monral touched his wrist.

"You would be ill-advised to remain in Monralar if you wish the Sural's approval," the Monral said. "My apothecaries are of course capable of giving you the implant, and many in my stronghold speak Suralian fluently, including Bertie and myself, but the Sural indeed makes a valid point. I am the only individual here who speaks Suralian without an accent. All others possess one to varying degrees. That might make a difference in your travels. Language, and how you speak it, can determine how others treat you."

Bertie grumbled. The Monral caught his hand and laced their fingers together. For a moment, their gazes locked, and Kim could... almost...see their senses swirling together. Then Bertie sighed, and the Monral continued.

"In my judgment, it would be best for you to go to Suralia and receive the implant there. Certainly the Marann is eager to meet with you and discuss the project."

"The Marann..." Kim frowned. "Marianne Woolsey?"

"Yes," Bertie put in. "The servants dubbed her that after she took the blessing, and it stuck because Tolari prefer to use titles. It's the servants who really run this planet, you know. His sort," Bertie jerked his chin toward the Monral, "only think they do."

"I cannot disagree," the Monral said, with a chuckle. "To continue, traveling to Suralia is the only option compatible with your current plans, as I understand them."

"He could jump into the sea, but that wouldn't help anything," Bertie said, with a toothy grin that Kim had come to recognize as something of a trademark. The roiling annoyance in the man had begun to subside.

Kim laughed and leaned over the bowl to bite into the soup-soaked end of his roll. He really wanted something meaty, but the Tolari diet didn't seem to include meat of any kind. Still, bread and vegetable soup made for a pleasant change from Kekrax Main's grubs, bugs, and, lord help him, worms. He couldn't find it in himself to complain about food that *didn't* move under its own power.

"Did you know that your stronghold is haunted?" Kim said.

Bertie stopped mid-bite, staring at him over a piece of fruit.

The Monral remained unruffled. "Did you encounter Laura wandering about outside her body?" he asked.

"I shouldn't be surprised if she wanted to get a look at you," Bertie added.

"Is that the human sensitive you mentioned? This wasn't a human. It was someone else, definitely Tolari. A *very* tall woman with short hair, wearing a grey robe. Isn't that the garb of an outcaste? But she was a ghost. I could see right through her."

"I say," Bertie said, with his mouth full. He swallowed and caught the Monral's eye. "Do you suppose...?"

The Monral only lifted an eyebrow.

"I've dreamed about this woman before," Kim said. "She was in a cave, talking to a blonde woman in a white robe."

"The Jorann," the Monral said, with utter certainty. "Anything is possible if she has taken an interest in Halla."

"Uh oh," said Bertie. "If the Jorann has an interest in her, we'd best tread carefully."

"Who? What?"

"The Jorann," Bertie replied, "is one of the original children taken from Earth by the Benefactors. Every living Tolari is descended from all of them, but she's the only one left."

"That's not possible. No one could live—what is it, six thousand years?"

Bertie shrugged. "Tell *her* that. She's the most powerful empath on the planet by orders of magnitude and she outranks even the leader of the ruling caste, although it's my understanding she doesn't interfere much in how he governs. I wouldn't want to anger her."

"It was just a dream!"

"There's no such thing on this planet." There was a sardonic edge to Bertie's voice now. "Empaths, you see. They have a sort of shared awareness when they're unconscious and their guard is down. Tolari call it the far shores of sleep."

Kim grunted. "Well, I hope the woman I saw is real, because she was magnificent. The tallest woman I've ever seen, more than two meters tall. Unless there was some sort of perspective thing going on. Or perhaps she was magnified?"

Bertie and the Monral looked at each other again. The hairs went up on the back of Kim's neck. *That* was from the Monral. He was... doing something, though not conscious that he did it.

"Do we have a dreamwalker on our hands?" Bertie murmured.

"Likely, but the question is which one of them it is," the Monral said, finally.

"Both?"

The Monral lifted a shoulder. A Tolari shrug, that was. At Kim's drawn brows, he continued, "It is an uncommon talent, but a harmless one, to travel in one's sleep."

"Like sleepwalking, but you leave your body behind," Bertie added.

"We had best tread carefully, as humans put it. The Jorann has signaled her interest, and she favors her Grandchildren."

That statement made sense on a familial level and none at all on any other. *So much to learn*, Kim thought. "So this Jorann has grand-children among the outcastes?"

The Monral lit with amusement. Bertie choked on his tea and spent seventeen seconds coughing.

"No," he said, when he could speak again. "Well, yes, but not that way. It's a mutation."

"Not a mutation," said the Monral. "A recessive trait."

"It's vanishingly rare, whatever it is." Bertie took a careful sip of his tea. "Generations can pass without one popping up. Then *pop! pop!* We get two of them. The Sural and, well. I shouldn't say. We may be mistaken about the second."

"If not, then we may have three, if one is an outcaste Grandchild."

"What a concept!" Bertie said, sparking with something that might be alarm.

"Better to speak of more useful topics," the Monral warned, glancing around the refectory, and then launched into a commentary on the wandering laborers now harvesting his orchards and fields. Kim listened, wishing he could learn more about the Jorann and her Grandchildren, but there would be time for that. *Three hundred years!*

He buried his frustration in a mental mud pool, which was the image he'd chosen when Jeryneth tutored him on barriers and emotional regulation. It did seem to help. Jeryneth had considered his phlegmatic nature an asset, saying that she thought neither skill would present much challenge to him. Then she set him loose with exercises he could use to continue his training on his own, seemingly convinced he would naturally go on to find a suitable mentor.

The Monral nattered on with practiced ease. Kim listened intently, as any information about Tolar was sure to be useful, even if it wasn't what he specifically wanted to know right now. The first harvest of Monralar's long autumn was coming in, and workers were building a new bridge between Monralar and Parania that would make travel easier for those same wandering laborers, who walked from one province to another, harvesting or planting as they went, according to the season. Clearly, border arrangements were made by mutual decision among the provincial leaders affected, with a hint of economic horse-trading to balance things out. The Monral went on to note that skirmishes along the border with Nalevia were cooling down, mostly because Nalevia had lost too many guards to them and Monralar hadn't lost any. He boasted of the skill his guard caste showed in that achievement, although Bertie commented that violence could only incite more violence.

So. Tolari practiced warfare, although the Monral didn't make it clear how or on what scale. And how did they sue for peace? Did Tolari provinces absorb each other, conquer each other, destroy each other? He was fairly sure the number of provinces was stable, at least according to the Kekrax, but human history alone suggested a dozen ways provinces could change drastically as a result of conflict without losing their identity entirely.

"Well," Kim said during a lull in the conversation, "It looks like I have tasks to accomplish that can't be done over breakfast. The usual procedure at the beginning of a project is to check in with the relevant authorities and establish a positive working relationship with them. That means Suralia."

"Be sure to get out your warmest clothes," Bertie said, with a sigh. "It's cold up there."

* * *

KIM MUTTERED TO HIMSELF, looking over the contents of his duffle. He didn't *have* any warm clothes. What few he possessed were in storage on Tau Ceti Station, since he'd had no need for them on Kekrax Main. Bertie had offered him an expensive-looking greatcoat that was far too long, and the Monral offered him winter robes of Monralar lavender in lieu of scholar blue—while Bertie griped that the local scholar caste leader *should* have offered them but didn't, the blasted bigot.

That a high-ranking scholar could possess such bias left Kim wondering just how much of it he would face as a human researcher on Tolar. Setting aside the Terosha, of course, he was accustomed to an ideal of scholarly even-handedness, even among aliens, but that was clearly, and surprisingly, not the case here. Meanwhile, Bertie pointed out that the lavender robes the Monral offered would greatly increase the length of Kim's journey, because the direct route to Suralia passed through provinces at enmity with Monralar. Wearing lavender there would invite attack. So Kim respectfully declined both the greatcoat and the lavender, and instead pulled out the single vest he'd brought, a tan-colored thing with a solely decorative purpose, and fastened it over his shirt, hoping for a better option when he arrived in Suralia. Perhaps the scholar caste there would be more welcoming. Working with Tolar's scholars would be difficult, to put it mildly, if anti-human bias was widespread.

At least it was warm in the transport pod, as they called the vehicle in English. In Monrali it was a single syllable, and upon being asked Bertie had said the word was common across Tolar and its etymology quite ancient. The vehicle was a wonder all by itself. It was a *creature*, alive the way their spacefaring tradeships were alive. This one looked like a giant, somewhat elongated crystalline egg, large enough for two persons to sit comfortably, with storage space behind, where his duffle and a sack of provisions lay. With his new senses he could faintly hear the pod humming happily to itself as it carried them at breakneck speed through the tunnels beneath Tolar's surface. The pods were much more biddable than the living tradeships, Bertie said, and anyone could guide a pod if they knew where they were going. Kim didn't, of course, so the same Monrali servant who'd startled him that first morning accompanied him now, to tell the pod which tunnels to take.

Tell was relative. Bertie had said it was all done with empathic nudges and opined it wasn't much different from riding a horse. Then he had launched into an extended reminiscence of the wonderful horses in his family's stables on Britannia, while Kim nodded along, pretending he wasn't utterly terrified of huge beasts with long teeth and metal shoes. The reality of a Tolari transport pod was comforting by comparison. You couldn't fall *off* something when you were inside of it.

Suralia lay on the opposite side of the planet—the journey would flip day and night for him and consume half a full day, with the result that he would arrive at approximately the same local time as he'd departed. Since the pod absorbed much of the servant's attention, Kim pulled out his tablet, intent on catching up on his professional journals, the ones he had been *about* to read when Nine-Three summoned him to the meeting that had started all this. He fell asleep reading, of course. The pod's cheerful empathic hum and the near solitude of the deep tunnels, combined with a warm and form-fitting passenger seat, did him in. He woke just over six hours later—and how he knew that, he still couldn't say. He wasn't yet accustomed to the keen sense of time the blessing had given him. That wasn't what bothered him now, though. Something else was different. Something...

"What *is* that?" he said aloud. The tunnel didn't look any different. It was long and dark and spotted with patches of light at regular intervals, just like every other transport tunnel he'd seen so far. The pod still hummed to itself as it hurtled along. Something *had* changed though, but what?

"Do you have a concern, scholar?" the servant asked.

"I—" Kim couldn't think of a way to express it. He settled for, "Something changed since we left. The *world* changed."

"We approach Vedelar's city," the servant said, his brows furling as if around a puzzle.

"No, something *changed*. I feel something. Or sense something. It's like confidence. With yearning? Is the pod doing that?"

The servant's expression cleared, and he smiled. "Of course," he said. "You are sensitive enough to hear Vedelar's Song."

"Song. Right. Wait, what?" He looked around as if seeking audio outputs in the pod.

Now the man laughed with evident delight. "Every province resonates with a Song, the hearts of the entire people joined with their ruler. Each is naturally unique. Most of us are not sensitive enough to hear it, although we usually have a feel of it in those we meet. It is difficult to like someone from an enemy province, but simple to love an ally."

"Oh, I see." That made sense of a sort, but each new experience impressed on Kim how much more he had to learn. He was in over his head, dropped by this heightened gift into the deep end of a world of emotion he'd never suspected could exist. It was exhilarating. It was irritating. Sometimes, it was a little painful.

The city they approached now, hundreds of thousands of souls clustered together, was a collective glow bright enough to sting. It must not have been enough to sting him awake from a sound sleep, because he had slept through whatever such cities they had already passed through. Awake, however, it was growing increasingly uncomfortable.

Barriers, he told himself, and closed his eyes, calling up what Jeryneth taught him. *Use whatever is* familiar, she had said, *whatever works*. He pictured the mud of the settling bath in his rooms at the hostel for aliens on Kekrax Main, and himself in it. Mud. Pervasive, dulling mud. Coating his skin, getting in his ears, baked solid to form walls, shutting out everything.

Almost everything. He knew it the moment they reached the city's transport hub, and he sensed a mix of surprise, delight, and idle curiosity around him as the pod wove its way through presences milling about among the pods of all sizes. Some presences wandered about, acutely focused. Those might have been guards, but he didn't want to open his eyes to confirm it. Kim supposed he'd eventually learn to distinguish the castes empathically, but for now, opening his eyes would weaken his concentration and let in the stinging discomfort.

The pod's inertial dampeners didn't entirely disguise the drop when they had crossed the hub and reached the entrance of the next deep tunnel. Shortly, very shortly once the pod accelerated, the stinging brightness fell behind them. Kim breathed a sigh and opened his eyes. The servant was once more engrossed in guiding the living pod in which they sat, insulated from what must be a roaring wind. High-speed underground transit, planet-wide! Kim shook his head. Most alien races used flight, but not the Tolari. The Monral had commented that flight could be dangerous on a planet undergoing a major climate shift, as Tolar was, and no ruler would countenance any loss of life among his people.

Well, that was relative, Bertie had countered. No ruler would countenance the loss of a *noncombatant* provincial, but they were apparently willing to spend the lives of their guards like water when they deemed it necessary, while those who were unwilling to live in a province and serve it were dismissed from their consideration altogether, even by scholars, who should, Bertie emphasized, know better. Then Bertie had regaled Kim with tales of the Monral's exiled father,

Farryn, whose hair-raising adventures in human space probably just confirmed any existing bias in the provincials who heard of them. The man had engaged in espionage and murder for hire, for chrissake, but to be fair, he *wasn't* a typical outcaste. His ruling caste origins combined with an empathic gift that didn't work on other Tolari, but did work outstandingly well on humans, had set him apart. Neither Bertie nor the Monral had been willing to talk about what that gift actually *was*, or whether it was heritable, but now that Kim thought about it, he wondered just what the Monral had done that raised Kim's hackles at the breakfast table.

He fell asleep again on those thoughts and dreamed of the tall outcaste woman again. Halla, the Monral had called her. This time, she stood on a cliff during a storm, though not near enough to the edge that he feared for her life. She wept openly, gazing down at the sea, one hand held out. Without thinking, Kim took the hand. Their eyes met, recognition flashed between them, and Kim woke abruptly to find himself in a city hub of dark stone. Empathically, it was as if curtains had suddenly opened on the glaring sunlight of noon. Kim shut his eyes tight and retreated into his imaginary mud bath. Through the barriers, the empathic glare wasn't *terribly* painful, not really. It was more like sandpaper on his senses, lightly applied. But he didn't like it, not at all.

He tried squinting his eyes open a little. The transport pod slid across a stone floor amid workers in dark green, with a few pale blue robes scattered here and there, watching. Suralian guards wore pale blue, Bertie had said, which Kim remembered from the Kekrax information recorded on his tablet. So. They had arrived in Suralia's city hub. Then the pod dropped down a shaft, which almost immediately curved up. A short ride later, they emerged in a transit room resembling the one in Monralar's stronghold but carved of dark stone, and the pod slid sideways over flagstone flooring patterned in subtly shaded but intricate geometric designs. No guards were visible to his eyes, although he could see their glowing presences, intent and watchful, many more than in the city below, and in much greater numbers than those in Monralar's stronghold. Off to one side waited a Tolari youth and a light-skinned woman with golden brown hair, both in the pale blue robes of Suralia and the elaborate plaits of the ruling caste.

Hold on. The Tolari wasn't a youth, but a child, if a very tall one.

Kim touched the side of the pod. He knew now to do that much, and the pod responded by opening an exit next to him. His servant companion went out the other side, bowed to the woman, and left, while Kim got his feet under him and straightened his rumpled clothing as best he could, goose bumps pebbling his skin. The air, even here inside the stronghold, was winter-crisp and cold.

"Welcome to Suralia," the woman said in a mild Plains accent. Her robe sported bright white ruling caste embroidery at collar and cuffs, and her eyes were a startling white-flecked blue. "I'm Marianne Woolsey." She put a hand on the child's shoulder. "And this is my daughter, Rose."

CHAPTER 14

"*I*'m Kim," he said, and assayed a bow.

The girl started vibrating on her heels as he straightened, patting her mother's arm as if her hands were fluttering bird wings. "Mom-mom-mom," she said. "Can I? Can I? You know only Terrans do it and with the embargo and all it'll be so *long*!"

Marianne gave her daughter a quizzical look. "Do what?"

Rose stuck out a hand toward Kim. "I'm very pleased to meet you!" she exclaimed.

Perhaps he remembered too vividly what he had picked up from Bertie, or perhaps he had taken Jeryneth's warnings about sensitives and physical contact too much to heart. Without thinking, Kim shied back, then cursed himself as Rose's face went blank and she broadcast hurt. *Damn.* The last thing he ever wanted to do was distress a child. But now what? He wasn't sure how to smooth things over with her, and her feelings were so *present.*

He tried a friendly smile and a cordial, "And I'm very pleased to meet you too, Rose," along with another bow.

Rose's blank look turned solemn, and she dropped her hand. *Damn, damn, damn.* He just wasn't very good with children, but Marianne came to his rescue by taking her daughter's hand in her own. She folded her other hand over it.

"You know how Storaas is very sensitive?" she asked.

That elicited a profoundly unenthusiastic grunt of, "Uh-huh." The girl didn't take her now-baleful mahogany eyes off Kim.

"That's how Kim is."

"Oh," she said. Then a moment later, she blinked. "Oh!" Like quicksilver, Rose's mood shifted back into cheerful. "I'm sorry. I didn't know. I don't get the daily briefings yet, because I'm not *really* a member of the ruling caste until after I take the trials. Fafee might let me take them." That had all been on one breath. She inhaled. "But Mom won't, so that'll be at least another year, and then I'll be the legal heir to *Terelia*. That used to be Detralar, of course, until the Detral dishonored himself and his whole province by trying to assassinate Mom even though she has the Jorann's protection. He hit Fafee with a poisoned arrow instead, which was kind of a good thing because Mom couldn't have survived it but Fafee could but even he almost died." Another inhale. "*Anyway*, almost no one thinks I'm ready for the trials, but I am. I wish they would believe me. But I'm still very pleased to meet you!" She bent into a shallow bow, her arms placed carefully at her sides.

Marianne's glow shimmered with several kinds of uncomfortable feelings that Kim couldn't name, and her face was pink. "Rose, please go ahead of us and let Fafee know we're coming. He's in his open study."

"Okay!"

Rose ran out the door of the transit room. Marianne gestured in that direction, still pink, but the shimmer in her glow was settling.

"This way," she said, and led the way in the same direction at a more dignified pace.

Kim fell in at her side. "Is she always this enthusiastic?" he asked as they turned into a long, hall lined with banners, where Rose was already out of sight. It was only slightly warmer here than in the transit room. Another wave of goose bumps rose on his skin.

"Oh no. Usually she's more so."

He bit off a laugh. "The Monral's daughter is very like that. Not so much verbally as physically, but she's only five years old, or eleven seasons, I suppose I should say. Five and a half standard. Bertie calls her the Tornado."

"Rose is eight standard, and she was a living verbal hurricane from her first word." Marianne smiled fondly, while Kim blinked at the fact of Rose's age. He'd taken her for a few years older, perhaps eleven or twelve and getting early growth.

"It will serve her well when she rules, I think," Marianne continued. "Ambassadors from other provinces won't be able to get a word in edgewise. Although I shudder to think what will happen if she comes head to head with Farryneth after *she* becomes Monralar's ambassador. Two unstoppable forces. The stronghold might collapse around them."

Kim laughed again, more because it seemed expected than because he understood Tolari politics well enough to fully catch her meaning. He glanced at the banners lining the walls of the hall, which represented the provinces allied with Suralia, if they served the same purpose as those in Monralar's stronghold. They moved slightly with the air circulating down the hall. He shivered.

"You're cold," Marianne said. It wasn't a question.

"I'm freezing," he replied. "I'm sure you can tell from my accent I'm a stationer. My only experience living downworld was at the equator on Kekrax Main and an internship year in Brazil."

"*Ei, como tá indo?* No one here knows Portuguese, so far, and I'd love to practice mine some time." She pulled a tablet from an almost unnoticeable pocket of her robe and poked at it. "We'll get you something warm to wear. I'm honestly surprised Monralar didn't—he's famous for his hospitality. Whatever was he thinking, letting you go with just that thin little vest?"

"The leader of his scholar caste declined to provide a blue robe, and the Monral himself could only give me lavender. This, apparently, would have added a great deal of time to the trip if I'd worn it, so I declined. Bertie also tried to give me one of his old greatcoats, but the thing probably cost a year's pay and dragged on the floor."

Marianne tittered. "Yes, it would. He's not anything like as tall as the Sural, but he's a good one-ninety centimeters. And no one would have thought of putting you in any other color." She gave him an assessing look. "You must be… Hm. Are you a station rat?"

"Sayyar," he corrected. "I might be. I don't know. Even if I am, I'm lost to my people. I was raised in the Tau Ceti crèche, and I accepted citizenship when I turned eighteen."

"I don't know if that's a pity or not." Marianne's face bore a pensive expression. "We don't think too highly of Central Command around here, but at least you got a good education."

"Six of one, half dozen of the other," he agreed. "On the one hand, the galaxy is my oyster, or it was, until Di Fata bought the farm. On the other hand, I don't have a family to keep me in one place."

"I'll bet that made the decision to work for us easier."

Kim shot Marianne a look. He had only himself to consider, that was true enough.

"Probably."

"I'm sure that had something to do with why I was chosen by Central Command to come here. I was an only child, the child of only children, and orphaned as a teen," she said. "My one remaining grandparent passed away when I was in college. All I had left when they sent me here were a few distant cousins in the Republic of Montana. I had friends, of course, and I miss them, but I'm sure it would have been harder if I'd had family to leave behind. Not that Central Command gave me any choice in the matter."

"No, they wouldn't, would they? Like the gangsters in old hollywoods." He put on a Boston accent. *"Nice friends you got here. Be a pity if somethin' happened to 'em."*

Marianne huffed. "Precisely, as Bertie would say."

"Speaking of Bertie, since you're my other boss—"

"That's almost exactly what I'm not, at the moment," she cut in.

His feet stopped moving. "I don't understand. Bertie said the two of you were in charge of this project, and you more than he."

She turned to face him. "We were, until the Sural stuck his oar in. I declare, that man—" She closed her eyes, and Kim sensed an internal struggle to remain calm. "He's decided he's in charge, because, of course, he's the Sural, so he's in charge. Of everything. I'm *slowly* talking him out of it. This project is pretty far outside his wheelhouse and he knows it, and besides, he's already busier than the Chairman's food taster. But the longer you're on Tolar, the more you'll hear about how arrogant he is. It's all true."

She heaved a sigh, but a tiny smile had crept onto her lips.

"Well. I also need to apologize for giving you no time to rest after your journey," she said. "This was the only time the Sural could fit you in for several days."

"Not a problem. I slept through at least half of it."

She grinned and gestured at the nearby entrance into a large open room with a dais at one end. "I'm glad to hear it. After you."

Once in the room, Marianne angled toward an open doorway along one wall. That led into a spacious study that was even colder than the transit room. Windows made up one entire wall, overlooking a snowy garden dotted with small wooden gazebos. Rose was nowhere in sight, visibly or invisibly, but at one end of the study sat an oversized desk with an oversized man seated behind it in an oversized chair. Bright white embroidery covered every visible part of the man's pale blue robe, and even seated, his size was intimidating. Bertie had warned Kim that the Sural was something of a giant. Kim's imagination hadn't quite been adequate to the description.

His empathic sense, however, seemed to have developed a bit finer resolution since Monralar. Invisible, person-shaped glows stood along the walls of this room, as they did in the halls they'd walked. Guards, obviously, but these were even more alert than the others. He didn't try to touch them empathically—Jeryneth had called that *probing* and said it was rude. More importantly, most Tolari reflexively pushed back at a probe, especially guards and sensitives. The more sensitive they were, the stronger their response. He contented himself with absorbing the feel of these and hoping to remember it in future encounters. Another glow with a less intent air stood to one side of the desk, and as they approached, it dropped out of camouflage and proved to be a servant, with a length of dark blue cloth draped over one arm.

Marianne halted, eyebrows raised. "A scholar's robe?" she asked. Her gaze went to the Sural.

"On my authority," said a man of perhaps thirty who stood at the Sural's left shoulder. He wore a robe of the same dark blue, and— Kim sucked in a breath. This was a sensitive, a strong one. How Kim knew, he couldn't say, but he just *knew*.

"Among his own kind, Dr. Storm-Gale is a scholar," the man continued. "The color is appropriate."

Marianne shrugged and took the robe from the servant, who camouflaged and left the room. She held it for Kim while he put it on like a coat over his blousy shirt and fitted vest, leaving it open in the front. It was lined with some sort of quilted material of the same color and began to warm him immediately. He refocused on the man at the Sural's shoulder, who was, despite his youthful appearance, very, *very* old. The weight of centuries fairly dripped from him, like water wearing away at stone. As he gazed back, Kim saw the moment the man realized that he knew all of this. One corner of his mouth twitched.

An urge to test himself against this man came out of nowhere, and images of roosters posturing at each other danced in Kim's head. He burst into laughter. The scholar's twitching lips bloomed into a friendly smile.

"Two sensitives in one room is two too many," Marianne said sardonically. "Are you quite done playing, Storaas?"

The man—Storaas—chuckled. "Forgive me, high one," he said. Then, to Kim, "I am Proctor Storaas."

"I'm Kim."

The very tall man seated at the desk—the Sural, for certain— stirred, and Kim met his gaze. He hadn't yet uttered a word, although he was the highest-ranking individual in the room. Tolari manners dictated he should have spoken first. Both Kim and Storaas had broken protocol.

"Whoops," Kim muttered, and then winced as he realized he'd said it aloud. Storaas didn't look at all repentant.

The Sural laughed. In a man that size, Kim expected a basso rumble, but instead his voice was a pleasant baritone.

"I am the Sural," he said, as Marianne went to stand to his right and put a hand on his shoulder. He laid his fingers over hers. "And you have met my beloved, Marianne Woolsey, also called the Marann. Be welcome in my stronghold."

Kim performed a deep bow. He couldn't remember the proper phrase to go with it, so he said, "I'm honored to meet you, high one."

That must have been close enough, because the Sural smiled and gestured to a chair before his desk. "Come. Sit."

Kim sat, trying to sort through all the sensations coming at him. The Monral and Bertie had referred to the Sural and Marianne as bond-partners, making it clear that's not what they themselves were. Kim could see the difference now. Bertie and the Monral were deeply in love, and so were the Sural and Marianne, but the latter pair appeared to...complete one another. Kim wondered who to ask about that, or even if he *could* ask about it. What was the etiquette of such questions on this planet?

He'd been at this point in a project any number of times now, mulling the first questions in a new society and searching for the right informants. He'd figure it out eventually, here on Tolar, but things were moving awfully fast. The Sural chuckled, snapping Kim out of his reverie. He'd been staring at the Suralian ruler, silent, for nineteen seconds.

"You have a distinct talent for what our human friends call *the Tolari stare*," the Sural said, with a bemused smile. "Now, tell me of your experiences since leaving Kekrax Main and your understanding of the task ahead, in your own words."

CHAPTER 15

$\mathcal{H}$alla looked up the steep stair winding into blackness and drew a breath. Standing here, with one ped on the bottom step, she could feel a faint upward movement of the air. The dark above the lamplight was absolute, and knowing how far the stairs reached made the climb a daunting prospect. She was, after all, not as strong as she had been in her travelling days, although that strength would return now, thanks to the Mother of All. She swallowed the lump of gratitude that rose in her throat at the thought.

"Free," she murmured to Tarasheth as she began the ascent. "We are free of the pain. Now we can start again."

For a moment, she smiled into the darkness.

Up. Slow and steady, measuring her effort, taking even breaths, her gaze on the next step. As she approached the edge of each bubble of light, the next flared to life. She stopped after a time and sat, drank some water and ate the food Tyrana packed into her bag before she departed. That lightened her shoulder bag appreciably. She continued up.

The Jorann had said the Sural needed to earn her approval if he wanted an interpreter. *Earn* her approval. The burden was not on Halla to convince him of her worth, but on him to convince her that his task deserved her time. She smiled again at that, briefly, then returned to regulating her breathing. Step. Step. Step. Regular. Even. Steady. Time did not quite revolve around her here as it had in the Jorann's cavern, but she could still sense the sun in the sky above, moving up from the dawn horizon.

It was halfway to the day meridian when she reached the top of the stairs and stepped into the Sural's stronghold, breath coming hard and legs trembling. The Marann waited for her there, standing to one side to give her space to recover from the climb.

"Be welcome in my home," she said, with a friendly smile, once Halla's breathing eased. "We have a proposal to set before you, if you will hear it. If not, I can inform Finnic that you have returned, and you may go on your way whenever you wish."

Carefully worded, Halla thought. The Marann's manner was almost deferential. That was extraordinary, coming from a member of the ruling caste to a person in grey. The part of her that had once been part of Tarasheth stirred, murmuring distrust. Halla closed her barriers completely.

"What happened?" she asked, not bothering to keep the suspicion out of her voice.

The Marann met her gaze with a frank one of her own. "The Jorann made her displeasure known at the ways in which you have been mistreated. We cannot speak to anything that happened to you in the sanctuaries, but we can guarantee that no provincial will mislead you, use you, withhold information, or treat you as—" she took a breath "—a contagion of dishonor."

Her own words. Halla could not suppress a snort. "Finnic talks too much."

The Marann grinned. "Finnic is tasked with ensuring that you are never mistreated again in the sanctuaries."

Halla gaped. "*All* of them?"

"He is a little overwhelmed at present, despite assurances of the Jorann's support."

She laughed, and once she started, she found she could not stop laughing at the idea of the sanctuaries behaving in one accord about anything, much less at the behest of the newly adult Finnic, bearing the Jorann's word or not. The Marann waited once more, as the laughter spun itself out, chuckling now and again herself, until finally Halla's laughs subsided and she wiped the tears from her eyes.

"Oh, unfortunate Finnic," Halla said. "He will hate me."

"No, he appears to relish the idea and look forward to the adventure. Should you choose it, that is. Will you hear our proposal?"

Halla was already half-inclined to their project, but she did not intend to tell the Marann that.

"It can do no harm to hear what you have to say," she replied.

* * *

THE MARANN LED her to the stronghold's main hall, and through the audience room, and into the Sural's closed study, where he sat at a desk clearly built for him. When she reached the space in front of the desk, the Sural stood and offered her a nod.

That left her a little faint. What could the Jorann have said to the leader of the ruling caste that he *acknowledged* an outcaste?

When no one spoke, Halla decided to break the silence. He was the supplicant, after all, not her.

"I greet you," she said, in the language of Venak.

"Well met," said the Sural, in the same language. "Forgive, Halla, I speak little of Venak tongue. Suralian?"

He used the Venaki word for *Suralian*. At least he was making an effort, and she could be gracious, could she not?

"Agreed," she said, in Suralian.

His face relaxed, very slightly. Surprising, in a man with such exquisite control, whose barriers were as tightly shut as were her own. She could only guess at what it meant. Relief, perhaps, that he would not have to express himself in a language he spoke so badly. Or else, perhaps, a sense that the first round had been, at worst, a draw.

"Will you sit?" he said, motioning toward a chair before his desk. A *large* chair. It must have been one of his own. She came forward to claim it, defiantly letting her relief show for the chance to rest her legs after the long climb, a wordless comment on the Sural's rigid control. He took his own seat behind the desk after she settled. The Marann went to stand beside him as a servant came in with tea. By the fragrance, it was Suralian tea flower, which only rarely made its way into the sanctuaries.

Halla sipped at the treat appreciatively. "The Marann indicated you have a proposal for me," she said.

"We do," said the Sural. "But an obstacle lies before us which must be cleared first. The Jorann is aware of the deception worked on you by the leader of Aanesh and the shipmaster, and she is quite angry that one of her Grandchildren was treated in such a manner. She has tasked me to ensure it does not happen again."

"Can you?" Halla asked. "It is well enough to give Finnic authority to ensure my people do not starve me, but can you influence Varina? Or Farryn? Or any sanctuary leader?"

"No."

The word pulsed in the air.

"Then of what use are you?" she asked. It was something Tarasheth might have said.

The Marann snorted. Something was passing back and forth between the two of them, but anger was clearly not part of it.

Bond-partners. Halla was glad that she would have a part of Tarasheth with her always, but she had no desire for what these two had. They were scarcely more than one person.

The lack of anger between them decided her. She pressed the point. "The sanctuaries govern themselves. You have no authority over us. No province will trade with us for what little we have. We eat or go hungry at your whim. What proposal can you possibly make which *anyone* will honor?"

"You are a Grandchild," the Sural said. "With that comes a certain responsibility."

Halla frowned at the departure from her question, but replied anyway. "*Responsibility?* No. In the sanctuaries, I am a curiosity and a burden for the food required to sustain me. I am two people walking on one pair of legs, three if I am allowed to eat my fill after a hard day, but I have only two hands to give to the work. I can count on my fingers the number of days this season I have gone to my mat without hunger. And in every sanctuary you will find those who can truthfully say the same."

The Sural's brows rose and the Marann went wide-eyed, radiating surprise. Almost, Halla sensed something from the Sural. *His barriers nearly cracked.*

"Why are you surprised?" she asked. "The sanctuaries exist on land rejected by the provinces as insufficient to their needs. Only Sacaea and Dhashrin can sustain themselves, and we have them only because they are so far out to sea that the provinces found them impractical to fight over. You know this, and yet you limit the food you send us. At any time there are always sanctuaries turning away travelers because they lack enough to share."

Silence met her words.

After a moment, the Marann said grimly, "That explains much."

"Indeed," the Sural replied.

Halla gaped at them. "You did not know? How can you not know?"

"You do not tell us."

"Provincials will not speak to us for fear of contracting dishonor! *You* did not speak to us, though the leader of the ruling caste is excepted from those laws. You only speak with me now *because you want something*, not because you wish to aid us."

The Marann tapped pink lips with a pale finger. "And on the station, where provincials and outcastes do interact, Bertie kept the peace, but a human with his upper caste upbringing might not notice if they scarcely mixed," she said, almost to herself. "Aafreen probably still has her hands too full to address it as an issue, in the aftermath of repairing the hull breach."

"A serious issue, and one to discuss with my allies," the Sural said. He focused again on Halla. "Our project will benefit all Tolari, outcaste as well as provincial—"

"Will it?" Halla demanded. Anger seethed through her veins. Provincials would take advantage of anything they learned for their own use, and outcastes would continue as they always had, with barely enough for survival. *"Will it?"*

The Sural drew a breath to speak, but said nothing.

Good, Halla thought, staring the provincial leader in the eye. She had not felt such anger in years. She had not felt so *alive* in years—not since Tarasheth died. It felt like victory, if only a small one, and the piece of Tarasheth's heart sitting within hers exulted in it.

"No," said the Marann. "No. Beloved, that question is valid. She is right to doubt."

He glanced at his bond-partner, then nodded slowly. "Indeed," he said. "Indeed. We cannot proceed before these issues are resolved."

"Kim is already here, getting his implant—"

"Nevertheless."

Halla smacked the back of one hand against the palm of the other. "Nevertheless, I will do it."

The Sural's barriers did crack then, with a brief pulse of astonishment before he re-shut them so tightly that only her eyes told her he was still present. His face was expressionless.

"Explain," he said, his manner abruptly suffused with ruling caste arrogance.

"No," Halla replied.

His eyes widened briefly, but he said nothing. *Earn my approval*, Halla thought. He needed it, but he had also never needed it to gain her cooperation. She wanted to go on this journey for the sake of the sanctuaries themselves, to tell them about the bond rupture that would have killed her, to find others who might be in need of the Jorann's healing before others like her went needlessly into the dark. If the Sural's expert from the Outside recorded what he found, well, she would try to address that too and do what she could to prevent the ruling caste abusing the sanctuaries. Still, she could see no reason not to take advantage of the Jorann's demand on the Sural as a means to get more out of him.

"I have conditions," she said.

He lifted a hand, palm up. "Name them."

"I do not serve you or the ruling caste. I serve *Tolar*. I am outcaste. I cut my own hair. I act upon my own integrity."

He nodded. "Understood and agreed. Is there else?"

"Word of this will spread quickly, and no one will share freely if they dread our coming. Every sanctuary will receive a *large* supplementary shipment of food, medicines, and supplies as I arrive and at the beginning of every season that I remain. I do not care which province sends it. Argue that among yourselves, but make it be there. Ensure our presence is something each sanctuary anticipates, make it an unqualified benefit, or they will consider your human and myself just one more burden the provincials place upon them."

"Done," said the Marann promptly.

The Sural lifted an eyebrow at his bond-partner. She quirked a grin. Halla again felt *something* between the two, but again, there was no anger or disapproval in it.

"Is there anything else?" the Marann asked.

"No." Halla gave a slight—very slight—nod of acknowledgment.

"Then we will inform Kim, our human scholar, that we have an interpreter." She smiled. "Speaking of Kim, we have one more related suggestion. You are not required in any way to accept it, but we would like to offer you an English language implant. Kim is receiving Suralian today. I strongly believe it can only improve communication on this project if you each speak a language the other understands fluently."

CHAPTER 16

$\mathcal{W}$aking from a language implant was worse than a Kekrax wine hangover, but it didn't torment him with hammers. It hurled asteroids from orbit.

"My head," Kim groaned.

"Can you sit up?" asked a woman's voice. It came from the glow standing next to his bed.

He cracked open an eye. A Tolari in yellow, the apothecary he'd met—what was her name? Oh, right, *Cena*. She stood over his bed holding a shotglass-sized cup. It smelled like medicine.

He groaned again and said, "I think so."

He got his elbows underneath him and pushed upright, only to slump over his thighs. A wave of dizziness washed over him, and the asteroids turned into molten spears. His stomach heaved. The apothecary put the cup to his lips.

"Drink," she said. "Now."

He took a mouthful and almost spat it out. Somehow, he managed to swallow it.

"That was vile," he gasped, but his nausea was already subsiding from the little he got down.

"Drink the rest," she ordered.

He took the cup and glared at it. It was still half-full. "Must I?"

She lit with amusement that didn't show on her face. "Yes."

He glowered, but upended the cup into his mouth and swallowed the contents as fast as he could.

"Do you realize yet that you are speaking Suralian?" she asked, handing him a mug of steaming liquid.

He sucked down several mouthfuls of the hot tea to clear the wretched aftertaste before he replied.

"I—" he stopped, savoring the word. It wasn't English. "I do now."

She smiled, that professional physician's smile he'd encountered at every annual physical exam his entire life. It was apparently universal. "Good. Now speak English."

She'd said it in Suralian. He reached for a response and found only the squeaks and hisses of Kekrax First. That wouldn't do. He closed his eyes. It did seem as if the foul-tasting medicine had worked on more than just the nausea. His thoughts were clearing and molten asteroid spears had stopped falling on his head. Suddenly, like the turn of a kaleidoscope, English was there.

"*I wandered lonely as a cloud,*" he said. He opened his eyes. "A line from one of my favorite poems."

"Good," she said again, still in Suralian. "Your vocabulary and grammar will improve as the implant settles. The most significant improvement will come after your first full night's rest. After that, it will be best for you to speak as much Suralian as you can."

He waved vaguely at the surroundings. "Not difficult in these circumstances."

It was English. He tried again and found most of the Suralian words he needed. As he spoke them, Cena took a thumb-sized scanner out and stared intently at her tablet while she ran it slowly over his head.

"I will probe you now," she said.

"You trust my control?"

As he spoke, she touched him with an empathic probe that he

barely managed to stop himself from slapping away. After some few seconds, she nodded to herself and met his gaze.

"I trust your control," she said in Suralian, pocketing the objects. "How do you feel?"

He took a breath. He felt fine.

"Well enough," he said, and it was easier to find the words this time, replying Suralian to Suralian. "No headache now."

"I will release you from my infirmary, then. Go to the refectory and take a meal, first. Then you may resume most normal activities, but do not engage in vigorous exercise or lift heavy objects for at least ten days. If you experience any dizziness or excessive fatigue, call for assistance at once."

Not that he *wanted* to go for a run or lift weights, but he could see how that might be a dodgy thing to do after letting medicos play around in his brain. "Ce—" He began to address her by name, but the implant actually intruded, coughing up her title. "Apothecary. I understand."

The professional smile reappeared, as did a person-shaped glow near the door, which resolved into a man in yellow.

"Go with my aide," Cena said. "He will take you to the refectory."

* * *

LUNCH, or rather the midday meal, was in full swing when Kim arrived, and every table was well populated. The aide directed him to the high table, the longest table in the room, where the Sural sat at the head in a wooden throne just as large and ornate as the Monral's. Kim had decided after his first meal on Tolar to keep his thoughts about those chairs to himself. He was a professional, after all. He was trained to avoid personal value judgments and psychological assessments of Tolari based on human cultural norms.

But that chair was ridiculous.

Marianne sat in a much more ordinary chair to her bond-partner's left, and across from her in the heir's place was a young woman who must be Kyza, the Sural's legal heir. She looked to be mid-teens in standard years and had none of her father's height. Next to Kyza sat the woman from his dream.

He stared, hand stilled in the act of pulling out his chair. She was even more magnificent in person than as a ghost in Monralar, and she was unreadable in the same way as the Sural. She was also staring back at him.

Another outcaste sat next to her, a young man with an amused smirk on his lips, and *he* was a sensitive. Storaas sat next to him. Kim, feeling outmatched, hastily closed his mouth and sat.

A servant brought a tray of rolls, dried fruits, nuts, and roots, and another servant placed a mug of tea in front of him, since he hadn't gotten his own before taking a seat. He sighed a little, grateful they were making allowances for the fact that he had just awakened from a medical procedure.

"Kim," Marianne said in Suralian, "this is Halla, your interpreter, and Finnic, who will also be accompanying you."

Both outcastes raised their eyebrows at the introduction. Kim thought about it and realized that so far, Tolari manners had dictated he introduce himself.

He nodded carefully, to avoid a return of the asteroids, and spoke the first words that came to mind. "You honor me."

Halla dropped her roll. Finnic's eyes danced and his smirk widened into a grin. No one at the table spoke for what felt like a very long seven seconds.

"Did I say something wrong?" Kim could recognize a cultural artifact when he saw one. Value judgments again, this time from the other side. If he was going to be an objective observer, it would only make sense to treat every Tolari he encountered with the same degree of respect. It would be tricky, and clearly there was a social boundary he was crossing with these two outcastes, but he couldn't pretend to any kind of objectivity if he too treated them as inferior to provincial Tolari.

He turned his gaze on the Sural, who smiled and bit into a vegetable. Marianne cleared her throat, but Kim could sense the way she was holding down a desperate desire to laugh.

This felt like the first week of grad school all over again.

Kim turned back to the tray, grabbing a roll and a handful of thumb-sized dried fruit, each a deep reddish brown. He wasn't hungry, but he tore the roll in half, stuffed two of the dried fruits into it, and took a bite. The combination tasted a lot like Britannic fruit bread.

"So," Marianne said. "Finnic is going along with you as a kind of goodwill ambassador."

Kim looked at her. That wasn't a lie, but it didn't have the ring of truth, either. Marianne rolled her eyes.

"All right, it is more than that, but I cannot explain it here, and everyone needs to eat."

That was truth. He nodded, glancing across the table at the outcastes. Finnic smiled when their eyes met. Halla didn't. She was still unreadable, but he had the notion that she was mildly impressed. Maybe he'd said something right. He'd certainly said something unexpected.

In dutiful obedience to the apothecary, Kim applied himself to the bread, fruit, roots, and nuts, while Marianne started up a conversation about the weather. Halla didn't seem inclined to talk, and simply ate steadily. Finnic, however, was positively voluble about how little weather there was at the bottom of the sea. Kyza, with more skill than he would have expected from a teenager, drew him out on that point, and the outcaste sensitive went into some detail about the benefits of experiencing the tranquility of the deeps, something to which Storaas had introduced him. At the mention of Storaas and the sea in the same breath, the Sural stirred and frowned, Storaas grew completely still, and Marianne changed the subject to a discourse on this year's expected tea flower crop.

It was decidedly odd.

When they had all finished, the apothecary Cena approached the table and stopped beside Halla.

"Will you come with me, Halla?" Cena said.

"You may scan only," Halla replied in fluent Suralian as she rose, finally giving Kim an opportunity to hear her voice. It was a rich, resonant contralto that went straight to his core. "You will take no tissue samples. I am not a subject for research."

"I understand." Cena extended an arm toward the exit. "This way."

Halla rose and followed the apothecary, moving as if she owned the stones on which she walked. She was glorious. Kim ran her words through his mind as he watched the two disappear into the hall.

"Suspicious," he murmured.

"She has been mistreated," Finnic said from across the table, "and none of us trust provincials. I intend no offense, high ones," he added hastily. "It is simply the truth."

"For good reason," Marianne said, softly, in English.

An enormous weight of meaning lay behind those three words. *So much to learn*, he thought. Every society had its trade-offs. Perhaps the provincial Tolari were just beginning to realize that they needed to re-examine some of theirs.

"What do apothecaries want?" he asked in Suralian. "Is she ill?"

"We offered her an English language implant, to facilitate communication between you," said the Sural. "She accepted it. My apothecary merely wishes to perform the required scans."

Kim blinked a few times. That *would* make things easier. "Good idea."

"My idea," Marianne said, with a smug grin.

* * *

AFTER THE MEAL, Finnic announced an intention to go to the beach, as far from the stronghold as he could reasonably get, while Marianne commandeered Kim.

"The Sural wasn't particularly willing to back down," she said in English, as she led him into the family wing. "But he's so overloaded with work and responsibilities that he's willing to delegate the project to me. I intend to delegate most of it to Bertie, because I'm busy with tutoring our daughters most days and with station business the rest. That's probably the best I can do, for now."

Kim frowned.

She glanced at him sidelong. "I know, you probably want to know exactly who your boss is, but things can get a little complicated when the Sural takes an interest in them. In *practice*, you'll report to Bertie, and you'll have a fair amount of latitude when you actually get into the sanctuaries. Will that satisfy any concerns you might have?"

Kim nodded. It was one way to run a project. "I can agree to that."

"Good. Hopefully that will stay settled. Here we are—the family wing library. We'll talk here."

She made a gesture as she approached a door, and a camouflaged guard opened it to reveal a large room that looked very much like any private library he'd ever seen. Books lined three walls, while windows ran floor to ceiling along the last, providing a view of the stronghold gardens in new spring growth. Tables and chairs dotted the room. Kim inhaled. It smelled much like a library too, although with a subtle alien tang.

"I noticed that Finnic couldn't get away fast enough after lunch," Kim said, taking a seat near a window.

"He does that every time he comes for mentoring with Storaas, weather permitting," Marianne said, taking a seat on the other side of a low table. "Most outcastes are uncomfortable in the provinces, in a stronghold even more so, and sensitives most of all. It's not just the unfairness with which they have been treated through much of Tolari history. Something about *us* bothers them. It's why we needed you in the first place."

"Bertie said I won't affect them that way if I'm unpledged. So what is it about that?"

"No one knows for certain. They describe it as an irritation, like a sting or a prick. It might be the connection to our rulers itself. It's very important that you don't pledge your allegiance to a province, or you'll lose the chance to earn their trust."

"I see. I think. What about Aafreen? Is she connected?"

"Pledged. No. Unmodified humans can't pledge. Well, they can make the oath and hold themselves to it, which Bertie did before he took the blessing, but it has no empathic effect. Even if Aafreen were willing to come downworld, she's a station—" She covered the slip with a cough. "Sayyar aren't entirely unmodified. That's mainly what I brought you to the library to talk about—that *you* weren't entirely unmodified when you took the blessing. That's why we were so wrong about your chances to become a sensitive."

Kim stared at her. "What?"

"Bertie's agents did some digging after he found some slight discrepancies in your records from the crèche. The public records say you were three months old when you arrived in 2523. That's not true. You arrived in 2527, when you were four *years* old."

Something akin to panic rose in Kim's chest. "That's not possible! I would remember!"

"Not likely, not that young, and traumatized in the bargain. But we found more than that. When Cena examined your head scans from Monralar, she noticed some discrepancies in the shape of your palate. Your first language is *not* English. She was able to reconstruct your natal consonant inventory, and just as a barely uneducated guess—I speak Arabic but it's not the same—I'd say it's the archaic Persian spoken by Sayyar. More importantly, you have genes, and a lot of them, that aren't Earth Normal. If we were on Tau Ceti, we could find out exactly which mod they come from, but we don't have that kind of data here. I'd bet on it that they're from the Sayyar gen mod. It's probably the reason you ended up a sensitive, because they're known for their intuition."

"No," he said. "No. That can't be true."

"Here." Marianne offered him her tablet.

He stared, then forced himself to put out a hand and take it. It displayed the report from Bertie with all its attachments, all in English, and all less than a day old. He paged through them, one by one, while Marianne waited. Records from the crèche, with the discrepancies highlighted, and more documents proving the alterations. Copies of a genetic analysis—of *him*. Another record proving that Mirza Kumar Storm and James Wu Gale did exist and that they did die in the same shuttle accident, but that they never had a child. Every record contained the proper seals. And none was a birth certificate. He lowered the tablet.

If he really was Sayyar, the birth certificate from the crèche was fake.

"What you're saying is you don't know who I am," he said.

Marianne retrieved her tablet with gentle fingers. "You're Kim. You're a cultural xenologist. You belong to Tolar now. That's solid."

Almost he believed her.

"But Kim can't be my real name. Not if I'm Sayyar."

He looked up at her. Marianne was sitting at the edge of her chair, elbows on her knees, her striking eyes full of compassion.

"We don't know anything for certain yet, but it's obviously not a Persian name, no. Bertie's people are still digging. He thinks they can find out what station you were really born on, and if they do, they can probably find your name and your family. They're looking at 2527."

"The year I was four." Kim laughed, unable to keep the bitterness out of it. "I don't remember anything before the crèche. I was the only one who looked like me, and children...well. Children are children. I was bullied because I was different. I had to hold on to who I was. Who I thought I was. *Which wasn't real.* I was defending my very self *with a lie.*"

"Kim—"

"If I'm Sayyar, my family will shun me for walking on worlds. If I'm not, I still don't have a family, because no one came to claim me after my parents died. And the *name* they gave me! Storm-Gale. *Christ.* It was bad enough when I thought it was real."

He paused for breath, and the final realization hit him. "And you have no idea who did this, or why."

"We know who. We don't know why."

"Then why are you even telling me any of it? Why did you think I need to know *now?*"

Marianne swallowed.

Kim jolted to his feet and wandered aimlessly about the room, breathing hard, a sensation in the pit of his stomach as if the world was falling out from under him. He stopped in front of a window and leaned his forehead gently against the glass. He closed his eyes. Maybe he wasn't being fair. Most people would want to know the truth about themselves. He couldn't blame her for assuming he'd be one of them. Hell, maybe he did want to know—just not like this.

"I'm sorry," Marianne whispered.

He straightened and turned to meet her pained gaze.

"This is a lot to take in," he said. "I need time to think."

CHAPTER 17

*a*fter the apothecaries finished scanning her head, and only her head, Halla went down to the beach at the far end of the Bay of Suralia and found both Finnic and the human there, sitting in the sand, gazing out to sea. Rafts of sea flutters floated just beyond the swells, occasionally calling to each other, diving for sea grasses. It was a grey day, with almost no breeze, threatening a cold rain or perhaps even a freezing one. Halla was grateful for the thermal robe Tyrana provided, which could keep her warm anywhere if it could keep her warm in the Jorann's cavern. It was an open question whether it would keep her dry.

The human still wore his odd clothing, the white half-robe barely visible under a scholar's robe tucked around his torso. His trousers were rolled to just below his knees despite the cold, showing a light froth of black hair on his lower legs, and he was packing sand around his peds...no, *feet*, which were already buried to the ankle. Away from the stronghold, it was easier to sense that he did *not* irritate her senses. Human, but not provincial, and a sensitive. *A sensitive*, she thought sourly. She dropped onto the sand on the other side of Finnic. Traveling the world in the company of not one but *two* of them, she might well run mad and jump in the sea.

"Sensitives," she muttered. "Why must there be sensitives?"

Finnic laughed heartily. The human—*Kim*, she reminded herself—projected a brief burst of perplexity, then returned to piling sand around his ankles and staring at the waves. She closed her barriers as tightly as she could and looked past his, hoping Finnic would not notice. Kim was preoccupied with something, and it pained him.

She turned her senses away and focused on the horizon, where dark clouds gathered. She had not expected to find the human— No, he had a name and she should use it. She had not expected to find *Kim* in distress, after he had seemed so at ease and even rather confident in the refectory, despite that he was a newcomer to Tolar. She glanced at him sidelong. The disquiet showed on his face, briefly, at intervals.

"What troubles you?" she asked, after one such interval.

"It is obvious?" he replied.

"Yes," said Finnic, deliberately wide-eyed.

Kim smacked the sand round his ankles until he exposed his feet, bare of any slipper or covering, toes wiggling. Disturbingly, each moved separately, and in different directions at once.

"To do work...properly...I need to hold myself back," he muttered. "I need more control of thoughts and feelings."

Halla was unsure what he meant to say, but Finnic's upper lip curled as if he understood.

"Among us, that is a provincial belief," the young man said.

If Kim meant he needed to regulate himself, she could agree with Finnic to an extent, but she had experienced far too much of that attitude in the sanctuaries to believe it existed only in the provinces.

"Not entirely," Halla mumbled, her gaze still riveted on Kim's wriggling toes.

Kim followed her gaze and buried his feet in the sand once more.

Finnic looked up at her and said, "Of course you feel that way. You lost your *life-partner* and Aanesh expected you to moderate your grief for her. Sacaea is not like that. You should have come to us after—" He interrupted himself. "We would have welcomed you."

"It mattered little where I went. I was dying." A pulse of alarm came from Kim as much as Finnic, and she hastened to add, "We had a bond, my lover Tarasheth and I, a very old kind of bond, and it ruptured when she died. My heart was torn. The Jorann told me that if I were not a Grandchild, I would not have survived as long as I did."

"*Daakh*," Finnic cursed. "That must be why some individuals cannot survive losing their life-partner, even though they are not pair-bonded. I heard my grandmother speak of it, but only once. No one cares to speak of it aloud."

Halla nodded. "The sanctuaries need to know that the Jorann can heal such a wound. They *deserve* to know."

"So that is why you agree to come," Kim said, softly, nodding slowly to himself.

"Yes."

"Your decision makes sense now," said Finnic. "I could not understand why you would agree when you were clearly so angry."

"What happened?" Kim asked.

Halla said nothing, instead making a small gesture to Finnic.

"Storaas told me a little, by way of a briefing. Halla was tricked into agreeing to go to the station, using her interest in languages to snare her rather than simply asking for her help. It is the same old tale. Provincials." Finnic spat the word, as if it were an insult.

It *was* an insult, after all.

"Not provincials this time," Halla corrected, and told them of how Varina and Farryn deceived her. By the time she finished relating the tale, both men were appalled.

"I not meet Farryn," Kim said, then frowned and said, slowly, "I have not met Farryn. I do not wish to meet him."

"Excellent!" Finnic exclaimed. "Your Suralian is already improving."

"It is," Halla agreed. "And you already have the measure of the shipmaster."

Kim smiled and ducked his head. Halla risked a look past his barriers again. He was still...haunted.

"You never told us what troubles you," she said.

Kim's smile disappeared. He turned his gaze back to the ocean.

"I have a difficult...a difficulty," he said, in a voice barely audible over the surf.

"Are the provincials pressuring you?" Finnic asked.

Kim shook his head. "No. They gave me informations that I—perhaps I was not ready to hear. It can be hard to be in a new place with a new people. This, I have done before. But here, the Tolari empathy comes. I have a new way to see things. And I find out I am not who I think I am, and it is...harder. Much harder."

Halla's lips parted. She shut them.

"I am young and only newly adult," Finnic said. "But I found myself different once I could do as I please. Is it like that, after taking the blessing?"

"No, but you should stay that way," Kim said. "A good way to be."

Finnic laughed. "We all grow old." He grew solemn. "I think we are more alike than different, you and I."

Kim's face twisted. Halla had a sense of something breaking, and a sudden burst of agony crashed into her.

"*Who am I?*" he shouted to the sky. He dropped his face onto his knees and sobbed. "I not want to know this. Not!" His awkward Suralian had deteriorated significantly.

Finnic reached to touch Kim's shoulder and jerked his hand away as if burned. He looked up at Halla, anguish written across his own face.

"Too much," Finnic said, in a strangled whisper, clearly struggling against a desire to flee.

Halla moved. She knew what it was to suffer alone, and she was better than those who had left her to her pain. She *would* be better than Varina. She shuffled on her knees around Finnic, checked her barriers were tight, and wrapped her arms around Kim—

—and learned why Finnic had been unable to touch him, sensitive that he was. Kim was a storm of chaos. It almost froze her in place, but she pulled him in until he put his arms around her and sobbed into her robe.

Underneath it all, she could hear his heartsong, devastated and sere and so, so beautiful.

"*Nuu*," she found herself murmuring, as a parent would to a distraught child. "*Nuu*."

"Who am I?" he cried, amid the sobs. "What the *hell* am I? Why am I here?"

"You simply are. We all simply are."

She rocked him as he wept, murmuring. What could he have learned to shake him so?

"You are who you are now," she said. "You have work to do and tasks requiring skills that no one else on our world possesses."

That had an effect. His sobs hitched and began to calm. *Mother of All* but his heart ached, and her heart ached for him, for the isolation and loneliness he felt. Surely, he would not remain so desolate, not with that spirit, so centered, so even, with a heartsong that beautiful. Surely, someone would appreciate it, once he began his journey through the sanctuaries. He would find someone eager to share his life, as she had found...Tarasheth.

When his sobs faded away, she continued to hold him, listening to the waves crashing against the beach, feeling his warmth in her arms. Finnic sat in silence, gradually relaxing as the storm inside Kim eased. She could sit like this for— She cut the thought short. It had been long since anyone wanted her touch. Of course she would take it in the way parched soil drank the rain. She loosened her hold a little.

"What happened, there with the provincials?" she asked.

"How we say—it is a long story," he replied, his voice muffled by her robe.

"We have time," Finnic said. "And we wish to help."

He pulled a cloth from a pocket and used it to tap Kim's wrist. Kim pulled away from Halla, full of chagrin, and proceeded to wipe his face and clear his nose with the cloth.

That seemed a good sign. She sat back.

Kim took a breath and began to tell them of the place where he worked, which sounded like a provincial scholars' tower, and of his decision to take a year away—a human year, which was only two seasons—to study the Kekrax. They were highly intelligent, he said, and deeply kind-hearted. When he spoke a few phrases for her in their hissing, clicking language, part of her perked up, and she made him explain the meaning of each sound.

Then he spoke of the humans who tried to abduct him, although that part made hardly any sense, and of the Kekrax who helped him escape, and of his arrival at the trade station. An odd sensation crept up her spine when he spoke of the Monral's human and his offer of help with human laws.

"I thought my parents died when I was an infant," he said. He straightened his scholar robe. "I grew up in a place with other children of no parents. Bertie discovered, and Marianne told me, that the place lied to me. I am not the son of the people they say was my parents. She showed me *proof*. That when I become...upset. I—I...I do not know who I am."

Halla sucked in a breath.

"A child with no parent, no trauma-bond, nothing," Finnic murmured.

"How did you survive?" Halla asked.

Kim blinked rapidly a few times, brows drawn. "How did I *survive*?" he repeated slowly. "They take—they took care of me. Fed me, clothed me, educated me."

"Oh!" Finnic said, and his voice rang with realization. "Halla. A human child has no parental bond to follow into the dark! But Kim, how do you—how do children know they are loved?"

"They...do not, exactly, except what they experience."

Halla stared. Finnic's astonishment beat against her. "*Mother of All*," she whispered.

"I cannot understand your surprise."

"Do you know about our bonds?" Finnic asked.

"A little. Tolari have a pair-bond, like the Sural and Marianne. I can sense that. And Marianne talks about pledges and a province bond. I am not sure if I sense that, but it irritates you."

Finnic nodded. "But first we all have the bond between parent and child. Through it a child always knows a parent's love. Without that bond, we die."

Kim froze. "You *die*?"

"Yes," Halla said. "Always."

"But…" He took a breath and expelled it in a huff. "Well. That makes my problem look small."

"No," said Finnic and Halla at once. Finnic's lips twitched, and he lifted a hand toward her.

"Who you are is what you have to give," she continued. "It is at the heart of everything that makes you a person. Why would the Marann shake that when you have already lost so much?"

"What?" Kim's brows quirked in different directions, one up, one down.

"Did you *need* to know you were lied to as a child, in order to do your work here?" she clarified, with a spark of anger coming to life in her. "Why was it necessary to tell you *now*? It could have waited."

Finnic nodded.

Kim frowned, and an answering anger sparked in him. "I asked her the same." He took a deep breath and blew it out. The spark dimmed and faded away.

"Can you still do your work with us?" she asked.

Kim took a sharp breath, but before he could reply, Finnic interrupted. "What *do* you do, exactly?"

Kim looked back and forth between them, then said, "I watch how people live, how they think, how they treat another like them, another different from them, I listen, I ask questions, I study, I compare what I learn to what I know. Other things, but the words are hard to find."

"And you learned these skills from your human scholars, yes? Did you have a favorite mentor?"

He nodded. "His name was Kuan. He came from Earth, and he was the best of all our scholars who study alien cultures. It was an honor to study with him." Kim paused frequently now, listening to his own words, but his Suralian was much better. He wiped at his nose with the cloth. "His English had an accent so thick that even students from the same place as him could not understand him, and they asked me to translate." A weak chuckle escaped him. "Truthfully," he added, "I had difficulty too."

"Your entire being lit with the telling of that," Finnic said. "He was like a father to you?"

"More like a grandfather." Kim took a deep breath. He paused and seemed to think. "He was very old, very gentle. Everyone respected him. I wish I could tell him what I learned about the Kekrax. But he is gone now."

A single tear rolled down one cheek. Kim swiped it away.

"Forgive me," he said. "I am not like this."

Finnic snorted. "If you were not like this, you would be *much* less interesting."

CHAPTER 18

Kim kicked off his shoes and lay down fully clothed on the sleeping mat in his guest quarters. *Damn* he was tired. The talk on the beach, the unexpected comradery—it helped. He could hang on to the growing fellowship of his new team and to the task at hand.

He took a deep breath, expelled it, and tried not to cringe at the memory of sobbing in Halla's arms. He didn't want to remember how good her arms felt, even while his identity spun away from him. While he sobbed like a child. He did cringe at that thought, and then Finnic's words came back to him. There was at least one Tolari who thought a human in an emotional mess was interesting.

He snorted. He'd lived among Kekrax, among V'kri, among A'aan', without breaking down. Every student of xenology learned about PCD—profound cultural disorientation—but until now he'd thought he was largely immune. Perhaps it was the empathy knocking him off-balance, or the novelty of working in a culture so close to human and yet subtly alien in ways he'd never seen. Certainly not knowing where he really came from affected him more deeply than he could have predicted. He wished Dr. Kuan were alive to discuss it.

Who am I?

An outcaste of sorts, just as he'd always been. At least Tolari outcastes had more of a sense of privacy than the provincials he'd met. There was so little real solitude in this stronghold. Hell, there was an invisible guard in the sitting room on the other side of the sleeping room door. And he more than half suspected that Storaas or another sensitive beholden to the Sural had been listening nearby when Marianne gave him that report.

Before they separated, Halla and Finnic had told tales of ruling caste surveillance that he could scarcely credit, but he'd agreed to their plan to use the beach for privacy from now on. Kim could explore the city, too, but that wasn't a good option for Finnic or Halla, whom the city denizens would at best treat with suspicion if not outright hostility. And the grey-robed pair clearly feared worse than that.

He closed his eyes and began methodically to relax his muscles, starting with his feet and working his way up. When he reached his shoulders, he realized he was clenching his toes again, thinking of the moment he'd noticed Halla gazing at them with a look of fascination. She was so—so much. So much her, so much *of* her, with a quick mind, and it had been *so long* since he'd experienced anything more than a handshake. Her arms had felt good. So good.

He pulled himself up short. *No, Kim, you can't indulge your taste for tall lovers. Not now, not with her.* The very last thing he should do at the start of a project was lay siege to the widow who would be interpreting for him, just because *he* was lonely. They could probably be friends, though. She wasn't suspicious of him the way she was of the Suralians. Reserved, yes. Suspicious? Not that he could detect with his new empathy.

He'd met her only today. How did he know so deeply they could—

No. He opened his eyes and sat up. The exact number of minutes and seconds he'd lain there floated into his awareness. This was absurd. He refused to violate the University's Code of Ethics by seducing his interpreter, for chrissake. Why was he even thinking about this?

Because she'd touched him, that's why, and he'd been alone since

CHRISTIE MEIERZ

Min-Jae broke up with him, a year and a half ago. He told himself, firmly, that Halla had held him the way a mother holds a child, even crooned to him as she would an infant. It didn't mean anything, and certainly not what the physical need driving him wanted it to mean. With a guard on the other side of the door, the only reasonable solution was to take a nap on his stomach and hope the problem took care of itself in his sleep.

He expelled a sigh. He needed to keep working on his barriers to have any chance of not making a fool of himself. The evening meal was a couple of hours off; he could spend at least some of that time firming up the walls Jeryneth had shown him how to form. He sat up and crossed his legs, hands loose on his knees, his gaze on the majestic, snow-capped mountain peaks outside the sleeping room windows. There was so much to learn here and so many mistakes to make while he was learning, such as convincing a bereaved woman he was inappropriately interested in her. Storaas could probably teach him how to sublimate that kind of interest, but he was no longer sure he wanted to ask. There was too little privacy here to invite a strong sensitive into what was left. Could he keep Storaas out if he had to? Maybe. He didn't want to have to, and it would only excite suspicion. Besides, he liked the man.

He'd liked Marianne too, until today. Even Halla was angry about the way Marianne had thrown his identity into doubt while he was adjusting to an entirely unfamiliar culture. Still, he had to find a way to cool his anger. Treating Marianne as if she had deliberately pulled the metaphorical rug out from under him for no good reason—that wasn't fair. She probably thought she was being helpful to him. But her timing was wretched as far as Kim was concerned, since all she'd accomplished was to knock him off his pins. The personal cost to Kim had been high, perhaps high enough to scuttle this mission entirely. Dr. Kuan's watchwords had been *Know yourself thoroughly, then forget yourself entirely*. That was impossible now.

He grunted. Marianne was educated, obviously, since she was a professional tutor. But she wasn't an anthropologist, much less a xenologist, and neither was anyone else, according to Bertie. Marianne therefore couldn't have known the risk she was taking. Still, he didn't want to deal with her just yet. The beach, as much as it had served as something of a team building experience, had left him feeling too raw. And he *could* use some time to practice his empathic barriers. Supper could wait.

* * *

WHEN IT BECAME clear that Kim was not coming to the evening meal, Halla walked up to the head of the high table to stand between the Sural and the Marann. The Sural very deliberately put down his food, folded his hands on the table, and looked up at her.

"You have *laws*," she said, putting all her contempt into the last word, and opening her barriers enough for him to *feel* it. "*We* have principles."

She slammed her barriers shut hard enough for everyone in range to sense it and stalked toward the exit. When she passed Finnic, he rose and followed her. Her pace forced him to half-jog to keep pace, as she swept down the main hall, into the guest wing, and up to Kim's door.

To her astonishment, the camouflaged guard opened it for her.

Kim was on the balcony outside the sitting room, leaning on the railing, staring into the evening darkness. He turned as they approached.

"When I have English, I will wish you to speak it," she spat. "Suralian burns in my mouth."

"What happen...happened?" Kim asked, eyebrows raised.

His barriers were up and firmer than they had been previously, but he did not have her gift and could not close himself off completely. She looked past his defenses despite Finnic's presence and refused to feel guilt for the intrusion, but Kim had calmed a great deal. Good. She could speak her mind.

"They have yet to do anything at all," she replied. "I spoke to the Marann, briefly. It will be tens of days before the ruling caste chooses a route for us. Perhaps more."

159

"Ah," he said.

"We could begin our journey now," Finnic said. "Halla can learn your English as we travel, and I ought to learn it too."

"I am happy to teach, but you cannot be serious." Kim leaned back against the railing and crossed his arms, frowning. "You are serious?"

"We cannot speak of this here," Halla warned. "Suralia pledges the largest guard caste in the world. What little privacy might exist in any other stronghold is impossible to achieve here."

She turned back into the sitting room. The two men followed her, and they all took seats inside, where it was warmer, though not as warm as Halla would like. A camouflaged guard stood on each side of the door to the hall. *Mother of All*, Suralia even put a guard in a guest suite. It was irrational.

"If we speak of leaving, someone will come to discuss it with us," said Finnic. "The Sural or the Marann or both. Perhaps Storaas. Or all three."

"Provincials," Halla said. Her upper lip wanted to curl. She let it. "No respect."

"I agreed to work for them," Kim said. "I cannot simply go. But I think we *should* discuss the project and where we go first."

Halla stared at him. Did he want the high ones to come? Perhaps he did.

"I suggest Sacaea," Finnic said, with a bright grin. "Afterwards, east or west makes little difference to me."

"I will agree to Sacaea," said Halla. "We should begin our journey there. Finnic knows it, and Sandbird and his life-partner were kind to me."

"The extra shipment will be welcome. We can grow enough food, but supplies are short. We are so far from anywhere."

"You come from Sacaea?" Kim asked.

"Aye."

"Marianne and Bertie leave to me to run the project, but I do not know Tolar at all. Will you know a place where we can stay in Sacaea? A place to work, to sleep, to meet those who live there?"

Finnic's grin grew several magnitudes brighter. "Of course! The sanctuary leader is my grandfather. He and my grandmother will take good care of you."

"Oh!" Halla exclaimed.

Finnic laughed. "Did they not tell you?"

"No. I thought— Sandbird went to 'those who exercise' to ask about a pod, and returned with you."

That drew a hearty laugh from him. "My father is one of those, yes. And I enjoy exercising with him, but I do not spar." That last word was new, but the implant helpfully identified it as a verb limited to guards and the ruling cast, and clearly a euphemism, as Finnic employed it.

Kim pulled a small tablet from an inside pocket of the Tolari scholar's robe he still wore over his human clothing and made a quick note, tapping at it for a few heartbeats before tucking it away again. Then the door opened, and both the high ones and their sensitive Storaas came in. Halla refused to stand or acknowledge any of them. Finnic and Kim looked at Halla, looked at each other, and then imitated her rudeness, even amplifying it by each settling back in his chair to make himself more comfortable.

The Marann cleared her throat. "I seem to have sparked a rebellion," she said.

Halla turned on her. "What did you expect? You gave me your word no provincial would mistreat *me*. Did you think I would accept it if you mistreated one of my companions?"

The Marann drew a breath to reply and stilled, lips parted, for several heartbeats. She closed her mouth and frowned.

With Storaas present, Halla could not risk a look past the Marann's barriers, but she thought she saw a flicker of emotion on the woman's face, quickly suppressed.

"Was it necessary to your project to tell a man who has nothing that he is not who he thought he was? Did you consider the impact of such words?"

The Marann's eyes widened.

"No. You are human, but you are ruling caste and bonded to its leader. Every person is only a tool to your hand. Still." She paused until the atmosphere in the room began to shift toward resignation. "If you honor your agreements, I will serve Tolar, as long as you remember that I do not serve the ruling caste. No outcaste does. No outcaste will."

The Sural laid a hand on his bond-partner's shoulder.

"I understand," he said. "We will honor the promise regarding shipments to each sanctuary you visit. Do you truly intend to leave ahead of schedule? It is yet some days until your English implant will be ready."

Halla grimaced. English was unrelated to any language she already knew, and it would take time and effort to learn without an implant.

"We will remain long enough if I also receive one," said Finnic.

The Marann twitched a grin. "You *are* a bold one."

Finnic flashed his teeth, and Halla was grateful that it lightened the mood in the room. Finnic was audacious to the point of foolishness, perhaps, but then, all the Sural could do if he was offended was to expel the young wretch from the province.

"In truth, I learn languages but slowly," Finnic said, more seriously. "An implant would be of use to me. And from what Kim told us of his work, English would serve us well as a common language."

The human high one looked up at her bond-partner. "Beloved?"

The Sural nodded. "Agreed."

"I will see to it," said Storaas. He beckoned to Finnic, who was grinning widely, and the pair of sensitives left. Halla breathed a sigh of relief before she could catch herself.

"Yes, I feel the same way sometimes," said the Marann, with a tight smile. She took a deep breath. "Well. It looks as if I have some apologies to make."

At a gesture from the Sural, the door-guards broke camouflage and brought two chairs, one for the Sural and one for Marianne, then left the room.

CHAPTER 19

The moon was waxing. It was definitely brighter than it had been a few nights ago. Yes, waxing. Wait. The mountains were north of the stronghold. Was it setting in the east?

Yes, it was. That way was east.

Kim sighed and lowered his forehead—gently!—onto the blanket over his knees. That had taken up far too little of his attention. The apologies and the planning had gone late. The tiring and tiresome planning. Some people just loved it. Marianne certainly seemed to relish it. Kim, on the other hand, couldn't get them out of his quarters fast enough, only to find afterward that he couldn't sleep. It was well past the night meridian, what they called midnight on this planet. Dawn would come in a few hours, he reckoned.

His identity, his real identity, remained a question mark.

He tried lying down again. The ceiling wasn't any more interesting now than it had been the last several hundred times he'd stared at it, but who knew, maybe something would change.

Nothing had. He grabbed a stylus and began sketching an interview methodology, using his implant to build a cultural inventory to start from. It was clear he needed more experience with the Tolari than he could generate from first principles.

He laid back and yawned. Closed his eyes. Yawned again. Opened his eyes.

Light shone on the ceiling and his eyes were gritty. He'd slept after all, for three hours, four minutes, and twenty-two seconds.

Well, and that was better than nothing. He groaned and rubbed his face, yawning, and hauled himself onto his feet and into the bathing area. The water wasn't as hot as he wanted, because Tolari were adapted to cooler climes in general, but it got him clean. Then he dressed. Smalls. Shirt. Trousers. Vest. His warmest socks. His only shoes, which fit better than his boots. A scholar robe over it all. The wardrobe in his sleeping room contained several such robes alongside his shirts, and a number of the loose trousers Tolari wore under them neatly folded next to his own. Maybe it was a ploy to get him to adopt a provincial mode of dress. Perhaps it was just all they had; everything he'd heard in the refectory suggested the Tolari were frugal by nature. He'd use the robes as coats, but he wanted to wear his own clothes and keep his own identity. Whatever that was. Did he even *have* his own identity?

The servants had left his shoulder bag on a shelf in the wardrobe with his clothing. Something sparkled redly just inside an open pocket. The data crystal from Two-Five. He'd somehow forgotten about it.

He fingered the crystal and found a smile on his face. At least an hour remained before breakfast, time that could be put to good use. He pulled out his tablet and set it to holo, then slipped the crystal into a port, casting about for a good place to settle in and watch. The low table in the sitting room caught his eye. Excellent. He took a seat on the nearest divan before activating the crystal.

A high-quality rendering of the food room in Two-Five's house appeared. The table was loaded on one side with Kekrax foods squirming in bowls and plates or wriggling on sticks. On the other side was a Boston holiday feast of turkey and mashed potatoes, stuffing and string beans, pumpkin pie and chocolate cake. *Chocolate cake?* He didn't remember the cake. In sum it was more food than any ten people could eat, much less one unaccompanied Kim.

And there was wine. Several bottles of Kekrax wine. *That* he remembered.

Two-Five and Four-Three sat protectively to each side of Two-Three on their side of the table. Kim sat across from them. They all spoke in the Kekrax languages and English by turns, and Kim watched himself interview Two-Three and draw him out with as much skill as he had ever learned, while at the same time becoming flown on the wine. He had been, he thought, masterful. Dr. Kuan would be proud. His stylus flew as he annotated the screen; the first analysis of new data was generally the most innovative. He could theorize later.

Most of an hour into the recording, the door to the hall opened, and Halla and Finnic came in, chattering and animated. They fell silent as they took seats beside him on the divan. Neither could understand the English, much less the Kekrax, but Kim was riveted on the holo, and they didn't try to pull his attention away.

Toward the end, it was quite clear to Kim that not only was a third Kekrax language involved, one used to teach the norms of Kekrax culture to the broodlings, but that the broodmale was key to the conservation of that culture. It explained why broodlings were so carefully closeted with the parental trio's broodmale at first. More questions crowded Kim's mind. He almost wished he could return to Kekrax Main for the answers, but perhaps he would see Two-Five again.

In the final segment, he gasped to see Two-Three expose his pouch and allow the baby broodmale to emerge and eat with them. *No one* had ever captured visuals of a Third this young. He was tiny, perhaps half the size of his fellow broodlings. Two-Three allowed Kim to feed worms to the baby, one by one, until he was sated and sleepy in the crook of Kim's elbow. Kim cradled the precious creature there, an incredulous smile on his face—and finally succumbed to the wine, falling sound asleep, still faintly smiling.

Two-Five turned to the recording device and said, in English, "He forgives them, the First, the Second, and Two-Three of Three. The venerated Kim male forgives them. They gave orders, the judges. They will take him so he does not die in a mine, the venerated Kim male.

They need a cultural xenologist, the Tolari high ones. They hope he embraces their purpose, the venerated Kim male. They hope to see him again, their friend."

The recording ended. A lump had formed in Kim's throat. He swallowed around it.

"These are the Kekrax who rescued me," he said, turning to Halla and Finnic. His voice was rough, but the Suralian came more easily this morning. "They must have known they would bring me here before they offered me that meal." He gazed at the now-blank tablet and murmured, "They must have known before I encountered them on the avenue. Did Nine-Three send them? Did the Kekrax judges conspire with Marianne and Bertie? Two-Five was so proud of himself when we arrived at the station."

Halla was nodding slowly. "Before you arrived, Varina spoke of the provincials bringing a human from Outside."

"After I arrived, Bertie told me my dilemma came at a perfect moment for them."

Halla squinted, leveling an assessing look at him, one Kim had seen on her face a number of times, but always before, she aimed it at a Suralian. Outcastes didn't trust provincials, he reflected, and even Marianne, fully pledged and a member of the ruling caste, admitted it was for good reason. But *he* wasn't a provincial, and he found he wanted Finnic and Halla to trust him.

"What will you do now?" she asked.

"My work," he said, with a wink and a slight movement of his chin toward the camouflaged guard at the door.

She frowned.

Finnic, quiet until now, barked a laugh. "I have an idea," he said. "Let us eat the morning meal and then take a walk on the beach. There are too many people in this stronghold. I need to rest my senses."

* * *

ONCE ON THE BEACH, strolling just out of reach of the waves on the firm, damp sand, Halla felt Finnic and Kim both begin to relax. In truth, a stronghold was a difficult place for anyone to spend time, but it could only be worse for sensitives. She could not imagine how Storaas lived there. He was stronger than Kim, and Kim was *strong*.

She breathed in the sea air, savoring the tang, wondering about human one-eyed blinks, and whether the one Kim performed back in his sleeping room had a meaning. The part of her that had once been Tarasheth fastened on the possibility.

"What did it mean when you closed one eye, then opened it again?" she asked.

Kim smiled. "That I intended a listener who could not see my face to hear something entirely different from what I meant."

"Storaas thinks that humans put more meaning into physical gestures than we do because their culture is based on sense-blindness," Finnic said. "He said you even have a word for blinking with one eye. But how are we meant to understand all the possible meanings?"

Kim shrugged his odd, two-shouldered human shrug. "It might take a lifetime of practice. I should have realized you would not understand its meaning. Where I come from, everyone does it."

"Is it like a language?" Halla asked.

"Not exactly. Or maybe." Kim stopped and rubbed his face. "I slept badly. Finnic, is this far enough for you? I would like to sit."

Finnic grimaced.

Halla waved a hand at him. "Continue your walk. I will stay with Kim."

Kim plopped onto the sand. Finnic half sprinted for a few steps and then settled into a loose-limbed stride that soon took him out of her range. Her range—but likely not his, the unfortunate man. Kim gazed out to sea, exhaustion written in his face and in the sag of his shoulders as he sat with arms draped loosely about his knees. The sky was clear and yesterday's dark clouds gone from the horizon. Sea flutters called and waves crashed, and the wind was a light breeze, steady and chill. Kim heaved a deep sigh.

Halla let herself down beside him. "You could not say what you wanted, so you blinked?"

"Yes," Kim said. "I have discretion to decide the importance of anything I learn in the sanctuaries. Some things, general things, will do no harm for Suralia to learn, but if they believe I will share anything you hold secret, well, they can believe that if they like."

She stared. Did he mean to become outcaste? She smiled down at him, half in wonder. He glowed a little under it. A pulse of attraction, *his* attraction, flowed between them, and her own body's response to it caught her breath. Even the part of her that was Tarasheth, who had never felt the slightest interest in men, felt drawn to this one.

"You—" he said. He frowned, the moment gone, the desire flown.

She closed her barriers tightly on the disappointment. "What troubles you?" she asked.

"Sometimes you are...different. And still yourself, at the same time. As if you have another heart. Or part of one—" He stopped, mouth open. "Oh."

"Tarasheth," she said. "You sense Tarasheth."

"But how?" he murmured, almost to himself.

"The Jorann healed the wound in my heart and spirit, and she sealed in the piece of Tarasheth's heart left behind. She will always be with me."

"Always," he murmured. "That must be a comfort."

She swallowed hard. He understood. Somehow, he understood. She eased her barriers a little.

"Yes," she said, simply. She leaned back on her elbows, stretching her long legs in front of her, regretting that the glowing moment had slipped past. She should have taken his hand when she could have done. Now? She sighed.

"Has it been long?" he asked softly.

She nodded. "Three years, yes."

"Three years on Tolar," he breathed. "Six where I come from. I had thought you newly bereft."

"For most of it I was, because I could not heal. I am still newly healed and recovering, but I can feel interest again."

Another pulse went through him, but he turned his face away.

She would not miss this opportunity. She laid a hand on his. The song of his heart came clear in her senses, not as devastated as it was before. She was glad of that.

"Look at me," she said.

He expelled a breath, shaking his head. "I cannot seduce my interpreter, Halla."

"Look at me."

"I have been alone for a long time. Do you understand? I do not even know if it is *you* that I want or only the—" He let out his breath, and his voice dropped almost to a whisper. "I should not have let you hold me yesterday. Only I...I could not bear to push you away."

He finally looked at her then, his gaze locking on hers. Then he shook his head slightly and lowered his face back into his knees, throat rippling from a hard swallow.

"Foolishness," he said through the muffling fabric. "We met only yesterday. I know nothing about you. But something in me thinks I know enough to be convinced that you are—" He shrugged and shook his head and lifted his chin to rest on his knees. "No. You would laugh."

She pressed her fingertips between Kim's fingers, lacing them together. "You are very different from my Tarasheth," she said.

He sputtered a kind of sobbing laugh and buried his face in his knees again, but he did not let go her hand. "I would think so."

"You are one of us now, with a sensitive's gift, but you cannot know our history yet, or everything we can do that humans cannot. No?"

He shook his head against his knees.

"Sometimes we can hear the song of another heart. It depends on how sensitive we are, and how well we would fit together. I am not a sensitive, but I heard yours when I touched you yesterday. I hear it now." She squeezed his fingers lightly. "You are a strong sensitive. You can surely hear mine."

Kim lifted his head, turned it to look at her. "Is that what that is? Your heart?"

"Yes."

"Beautiful." He put his chin on his knees again, staring out at the ocean, and blew out a breath. "This is so hard."

Her heart squeezed. *He said my song is beautiful.*

But still he held back.

"Do you not want me?" she asked.

He sputtered a laugh. "Oh yes. Very much."

There was bitterness in his voice, where there should have been joy. Human misunderstanding? The more recent ruling caste gossip said that the Monral and his human lover had misunderstood their desire for one another for years. Perhaps Kim was misinterpreting hers. She took a deep breath. If he needed the words, he needed the words. She would say it, as hard as that was.

"I want you," she said. "Share my blanket. Find joy with me."

He let out a sob and buried his face.

"Was that wrong? Did I break a human custom?"

"I cannot!" he cried, and this time he did let go her hand to wrap his arms tightly around his knees and repeat, in a whisper, "I cannot."

It made no sense at all.

"Why not?"

"You are my *interpreter*." His voice sounded as if his throat had been scraped raw. "We must work together. What you offer is inappropriate for me to accept. A crime in some circumstances. Not allowed in any."

Halla sat up and hugged her own knees. It made no *sense*. "But we are both adult. No one has a right to interfere if we freely choose to share our bodies with one another."

"I am bound by the ethics agreement of...of..." he uttered some English words. "I cannot find a Suralian word for it. The place of scholars where I work. We all sign the agreement before we can work there. We stamp it with our genetic code. Those who break it are dismissed. Shunned."

She nodded. An agreement. Human scholars had principles, the way outcastes did, but they wrote them down, like provincials. A hybrid culture. A split path. One that split the two of them apart.

"Is it a law, then?" she asked.

"Not exactly. More of a code of conduct, but the ethics agreement protects students and—" he paused "—those who serve the scholars."

"Such as interpreters."

"Yes." He blew out a breath. "Halla, humans are *sense-blind*. They can hide the ugly side of their nature from one another. They can lie. They can take advantage of their authority. Even when we bind ourselves in oaths and agreements, some of us break them, but as we say, it is better than nothing. We have to watch out for each other."

Halla frowned. "I think I do not like your people."

He stood, uttering a short, bitter laugh. "That might be wise."

He turned and walked toward the city.

CHAPTER 20

The sun was down before Kim woke from his nap. He was munching on food a servant brought and reading the most recent issue of *Cultural Xenology & Education Quarterly*—apparently pushed onto his tablet during Two-Five's brief layover at the trade station that orbited Kekrax Main—when the hall door opened and Marianne strolled in, her usually lively presence a little subdued.

He waved at the chairs opposite his divan.

"At least you're sorry for making my life hell," he said. "What ken I do ya for?"

Marianne snorted as she took a seat. "Educated Iowans stop speaking Plains as soon as they leave home."

"You have the accent."

"Stationers are the ones with the accent."

"Because Iowa is the standard-bearer of all things?"

"No, that's Boston." Her lips twitched. She took a breath. "Pax?"

He held her gaze. She didn't flinch from it. Well, Marianne was certainly no coward.

"I'm not angry anymore," he said. "But I need a little time."

"Fair enough." She squared her shoulders. "I have a little news from Bertie. You were declared truant before the Kekrax courts yesterday, a week late. We don't know the precise reason for the delay, but it can only mean the debt owners knew you were still among the living when they arrived at Kekrax Main. Finding out that you're *here* is only a matter of time, since Bertie's agents got to Tau Ceti University with our offer before they could fire you, and word of that *will* get out."

"Word of a research project on a planet no one has ever studied? Hell yes. That kind of plum assignment might remain secret at the high table in Oxford Hall for all of three seconds, if that."

"Bertie did say it might have been easier to clear your debt if they'd fired you first."

"And then I'd never be able to publish again. No respectable journal would touch me."

"Egad, Kim. You really are a thoroughgoing academic, aren't you?"

"Absolutely."

"All right. Well. I'll make a note of that." She took out a tablet and tapped at it. Put it away. "Our outcaste friends will get their English implants the day after tomorrow. They'll need a day or two while those settle. Bertie should have a contract for you to sign not too long after that, and then you can head off into the sanctuaries."

A thought occurred to Kim. "Tell me you're not the template for their implants."

She shrugged.

"God, will I have to listen to Plains English for the next 300 years?"

"Is that how long you plan to stay with her?"

He froze as he realized what she'd said.

"Got you," Marianne chirped.

He scowled. "I hate you."

"Liar."

"I don't like you."

"Yeah," she said on a sigh. "But you'll get over it."

He growled and bit into a piece of fruit. "Are you done?" he said, with his mouth full.

"No," she replied, suddenly all business. "We have to talk about this. You're going into the sanctuaries with a woman you're in love with and feel ethically constrained from touching. That's not a good combination, and it will affect your ability to work."

"I'm *not*—"

"Yes, you are. Halla told Finnic about it."

"It's none of your damned business!" he shouted.

The guard at the door dropped his camouflage. It was a warning, he supposed. He jumped to his feet and headed for the balcony window, veering before he reached it. He turned again. And again. He couldn't be in love. It had been one day. An eventful day, sure, but *one day*. That wasn't love; it was lust. Infatuation, at best. Turn. He liked Halla. He *wanted* to meet her people. Turn. He wanted the best for her, of course he wanted the best for her, just as he wanted the best for her people. For everyone. Not just her. All the outcastes.

Turn. At some point, the guard had re-camouflaged. Marianne sat with crossed arms, regarding him with an insulting amount of sympathy on her face.

"What do *you* know about it anyway?" he snarled.

Turn.

"The Sural is my boss."

He halted in his tracks, stilled inside and out, and pivoted to face her.

"What?"

She uncrossed her arms and clasped her hands around one knee. "You heard me."

"How is he your boss? He's your bond-partner. I can see it with these new senses your damned gen mod gave me. The pair of you are practically the same person."

"Engaging my services to tutor his daughter is what brought me here in the first place. I'm still tutoring her. According to Bertie, who seems to have spies—excuse me, *agents*—all over the place now that his father has acknowledged him again, I'm still drawing a paycheck back on Earth, courtesy of Central Command. It's all very official. I'm sleeping with my boss."

Kim walked back to the divan and sat on the edge of it. "Go on."

"In the beginning, I was *just* like you about the whole thing," she continued. "I'm a tutor, he's my employer, I have to be professional, so forth, so on, et cetera. I didn't even realize how I felt about him, not really. Everyone else knew, because empaths are nosy."

He sputtered a laugh despite himself. "Aren't they just? So how long did that last?"

"Eight years, standard."

Kim whistled.

"The thing is, Tolari empathy makes everything very different here, that and the fact that they have never truly faced scarcity—"

"The outcastes do."

"Yes." Marianne cleared her throat. "We're looking into that. May I continue?"

"Go on."

She lifted an eyebrow at him. "Thank you," she said sardonically, and continued, "In the provinces at least, individuals have everything they need, so if they give their service to someone who abuses it, they simply leave. It doesn't affect how they're going to eat or where they're going to live."

"Infatuation and love always change the power dynamic."

"Not on Tolar. The noncombatant castes don't have much of a power dynamic here, since those who serve are free to go elsewhere without penalty. If they get emotionally involved, it's done freely. If it's not, everyone around them knows it, and trust me when I say the pressure of general disapproval is enough to stop most Tolari from misbehaving. There's almost no crime on Tolar."

"Almost?"

"You do pick up on the little words, don't you?"

"It's my job."

"Yes, well. What crime there is happens *almost* entirely in the ruling caste. Farryn, for the most recent example, the shipmaster of our trade fleet who used to rule Monralar? He murdered a provincial heir. That brought about the death of her toddler son, because below a certain age, Tolari children can't survive the death of their bonded parent unless there is a very determined adult nearby to catch their bond. Farryn made sure in this child's case that there wasn't."

"Halla and Finnic told me Tolari children can't survive without a parent."

Marianne nodded. "It's absolutely true."

"So how did Farryn get away with murder? I thought you said social pressure is enough to stop Tolari from misbehaving."

"I said *most* Tolari. Rulers are always scheming, so the councilors and advisors who work with them get used to it, and Farryn, well. Everyone in Monralar's stronghold knew Farryn was up to something, but no one suspected it was murder." She stopped, eyes flicking for some seconds, then grinned. "Egad, you're good. *My point* is that the rules are different here because the conditions are different. Everyone knows you're not taking advantage of Halla and that she's pretty keen on you."

"*Pretty keen?* I thought you said you gave up Plains."

"It's perfectly good English."

"You're trying to wiggle off my hook."

"Oh look, a robin!"

Kim leaned back. "So. The rules are different, therefore I can be as unethical as I like?"

"That's not what I'm saying and you know it."

"Do I?"

Marianne crossed her arms again.

"I'm serious," he said. "Just exactly how are you not saying that it's okay for me to commit a crime?"

"It's not a crime."

"A rose by any other name."

"It's not a rose, either. Look. There is no crime because the antecedents don't exist. There is no interpreter at your mercy. She's not a student. She's fully adult. She's probably twice your actual age, in fact. She could walk away if she wanted to, and I'm pretty sure nothing could stop *that* woman from doing whatever she decides to do. You're not forcing her to put up with unwanted attentions. You're not pressuring her into something she doesn't want. If anything, you're trying to convince her you *don't* want her and that she *shouldn't* want you."

Kim grumbled. He couldn't deny that.

"Plus," Marianne added, "and this is the most important part: you're on Tolar. Everyone around you is an empath. That changes everything. If all you do is hold hands, each of you will know exactly what the other truly feels. The ethics rules that make sense at Tau Ceti University aren't necessary here."

He took a breath, then expelled it.

"I need to think about this," he said, finally.

"Do that," Marianne replied. "But don't take too long. Halla is feeling rejected and humiliated, and speaking as a woman I can tell you that whatever you say to her, 'I didn't mean it' will probably backfire. If she even gives you another chance."

"For chrissake, Marianne, why did you even come here if she won't hear me? Do you make a habit of telling people things they don't need to know?"

Marianne set her jaw. "We want—need—both of you for this to work, and there's no chance if you don't try. Just be honest with her. Nothing is certain when it comes to the heart, but that's the only thing that will work, if anything can."

* * *

KIM PACED HIS SITTING ROOM. Then he paced the balcony outside his sitting room. Eventually his ears started to ache, because spring nights in Suralia were frigid. He went back inside and paced there again.

He didn't know what to do. He'd made a mess out of his team and alienated the woman he— *No.* He couldn't possibly love her. Just because he craved her presence. And the sound of her voice. And her touch. He stopped pacing and made a wordless noise of frustration.

The guard at the door popped into view.

"Oh go away!" he snapped.

He'd said it in English, but the guard disappeared again. Maybe the man spoke English. Or maybe Kim's intent was obvious enough. Not that he was really gone or that Kim couldn't see his glow standing there, senses outstretched, making sure enemies didn't come crawling out of the woodwork, but at least the guard couldn't see when he was camouflaged.

If I can't see you, you can't see me. Or so they'd told him. It had something to do with the laws of physics.

To distract himself, he stared at the woodwork that Suralia's enemies currently weren't crawling out of. It was, he had to admit, beautiful, richly dark and elaborately carved with unfamiliar motifs. The entire suite was every bit as luxurious as its counterpart in Monralar, with elegant furniture and ornate carpets and exquisite works of art, but where the Monral's stronghold was light, the Sural's was dark, with bright lighting to compensate. He supposed there was interprovincial rivalry going on even here. The Monral had lodged Kim in his best guest suite? The Sural could do no less.

He sighed and rubbed the back of his neck. He should talk to Halla, if she'd let him. But what if he made another cock-up of it? If he upset her enough, he'd need a new interpreter. Marianne would have told him—probably—if Halla had abandoned the project. That gave him some hope that things between them weren't beyond repair. At least she hadn't left. Yet.

So he should try.

He took a breath, breathed out hard, and headed for the door. The guard opened it for him, and he let resolve fuel his pace down the hall to Halla's door.

The guard didn't open it for him.

His heart sank. He shouldn't be surprised. He *wasn't* surprised, in fact. Halla was in there; he could sense her in her sitting room with Finnic. His range wasn't huge, but he could sense that far. They'd told the guard not to open the door, and they knew he was here. She was more hurt than anything else, but anger simmered in that hurt, and an unwillingness to let him worsen things between them.

"Fair enough," he said on a sigh, and turned back toward his own rooms at a much slower pace.

* * *

HALLA WAITED until Kim was well out of hearing range before she sobbed into a cloth.

"You should speak with him," Finnic said.

She shook her head. "And let him hurt me again?" she asked through her sobs.

"I do not believe he will."

"He believes that touching me is a crime!"

"He is *human*. They have strange beliefs. It is not as if one of *us* said such a thing."

She leaned over and sobbed into her knees.

"Halla," he said softly. "The Marann visited him before he came to your door."

The words jolted through her and interrupted her sobs. She sniffled and looked up. "To save her project?"

"Probably," Finnic replied. "She is a provincial. But she is not heartless. I saw compassion in her. I think her intentions are good."

"You are young." She sniffled again. "You think everyone is good."

"Perhaps," he said. "I am young, that much is true, but I am not *stupid*."

She sighed and buried her face in her knees. "Forgive me."

"The sanctuaries have much to lose if you abandon this."

Halla looked up again. Finnic gazed at her steadily.

"And your sanctuary, first of all," she said.

"Yes. We *need* those shipments. Do not deny them to us because you are too proud to forgive a man whose heart is clearly yours."

"And if he crushes *my* heart under those obscene feet of his?"

Finnic's lips twitched, but he shook his head. "You know my range. I saw a shift in him as the Marann spoke. I believe he came to apologize."

Halla swallowed. If Kim would be open with her, it could be so different.

"Not tonight," she whispered, and gave herself up to the tears.

* * *

HALLA'S TEARS were dry by the morning meal, where a young woman in dark mauve joined the Sural's table. She took the place next to the Sural's heir Kyza, pushing Halla and Finnic down a seat. Across the table, Kim sat next to the Marann, his barriers as tight as she had ever seen, but his shoulders drooped slightly and he picked at his food. Storaas was seated next to him, followed by the Sural's head apothecary. Those two were clearly entwined, sitting close, sharing private smiles and murmuring to each other in the moments when Finnic did not strive to dominate Storaas's attention.

The young woman cleared her throat and caught Halla's eye.

"I am Thela," she said, addressing her introduction to Kim and Finnic as well. "Bond-daughter to Suralia. I have just returned from music studies in Parania. I would like to play for you later, if you wish, after I have had some rest. It was a long journey."

It was a fair introduction, and a good start. "I am Halla."

"Kim." A monosyllable only.

"And I, of course, am Finnic." Finnic's eyes sparkled. "Were you in Parania long?"

"A season. I went to study with their laerta master. And I visited with my friend Laura, the beloved of Parania." Kim looked up at that, with a measured gaze.

"How is Laura?" the Marann asked.

"Very well," Thela replied, with a bright smile. "She is rapt in a new art, learning to create images on brushed metal. She is *so* talented."

"As are you, daughter," said the Sural, with an affectionate smile.

Thela radiated pride. "I thank you, Father. Oh! And I had time to play for the Monral and Lord Bertie."

The Marann clicked her tongue. "He hates it when you call him that."

"I know." Thela giggled. "But he always smiles and calls me a *teenager* when I do."

"You *are* a teenager, in Terran standard years," Kyza said. "We both are."

Thela nodded and bumped shoulders with the other girl, and they giggled together. Halla marveled at it. She had never thought to see provincials, constrained to only one heir, acting like sisters. All knew, however, that the Sural had three parental bonds—with his heir Kyza, with his bond-daughter Thela, and strangely enough with the Marann's heir, whom Halla had never seen.

That was odd, as she thought about it. She had been days in the Sural's stronghold. Why had she never seen the Marann's daughter? But it scarcely mattered. Halla would be gone from Suralia soon, and the Marann's heir was, after all, only a child, and a provincial one. It would likely be years before she took the trials and became a scourge to ordinary Tolari.

Halla ate steadily, as was her usual habit, listening to the conversations and occasionally feeling Kim's gaze on her. If she looked up, he was already glancing elsewhere, sensitive-quick. She stopped trying to catch him, and simply let him gaze at her while she kept her eyes on her food. Perhaps it would change his mind about her or about them. Finnic had said he saw Kim shift under the Marann's suasion, but Finnic was young. He could be mistaken.

Kim stood, slowly and with none of his usual vibrance. "I need to rest my senses," he said. "I will be on the beach."

Halla groaned inwardly. She had intended to take a walk on the beach herself. It seemed likely he would head south, toward the place they had been meeting. Well, she would go the other way.

After she ate enough to feel comfortably full, she left the stronghold, heading toward the northern tip of the bay. It was considerably warmer this morning, enjoyably so. The sea flutters gathered in large, delirious flocks that flew in undulating clouds above the waves, calling loudly. She breathed deep and stretched her legs into the arm-swinging, ground-eating pace she adopted when alone. A cliff of dark Suralian bedrock rose at her left. The waves crashed to her right. Ahead, the tip of the bay came into view.

What would she do now? Could she work with Kim, mired as he was in strange human beliefs? *A crime. Not allowed.* Despite the attraction that swirled between them. He regretted his words—that was obvious. He had seemed almost dejected at the Sural's table.

Was that movement up ahead, on the rocks? She stopped and squinted, but it did not repeat. She resumed her pace.

She stopped again. There *was* movement. Someone was climbing up the end of the cliff at the top of the bay, naked but for a bit of fabric wrapped around the hips.

It was Kim.

She cursed. He was the *last* person she wanted to see right now.

Then her heart nearly stopped. He had reached the top of the cliff and knelt at the edge, looking down, perhaps measuring the drop. She started to run. Even at this distance, the determination in his posture was clear.

"No!" she shouted, though she was probably out of earshot. "*No!*"

He stood and raised his arms.

She ran faster. *No! No, no, NO NOT HIM TOO!*

Kim lowered his arms and swung them up again as he jumped out and away from the cliff. He was so far up. He could not possibly survive the fall.

Every nerve in her body lit on fire, and she ran faster. She had to be there. She had to catch him.

Kim twisted in the air as he fell, the poetry of his motion a stark contrast to what she knew was coming. He would hit water; she could see that now. Maybe he had a chance to survive. Halla reached the edge of the pool at the base of the cliff and flung herself beneath him.

CHAPTER 21

Kim sat on a divan in the apothecaries' common room, leaning over his uninjured leg. His eyes swam, but not because his broken leg and foot ached. Those weren't broken anymore. An apothecary, with no hint of the reproach he deserved, had repaired his damaged limbs with Tolari technology while others worked on Halla. The ache persisted. He deserved it.

Halla's back was broken, crushed when she broke his fall. She had almost died. Her glow was so dim when help arrived that he thought she *was* dead. It was brighter now, on the other side of that wall where the head apothecary was working on her, but it was still not as bright as the moment he dove right onto her. It happened so fast. He didn't even see her until he straightened to enter the water, and suddenly she was there beneath his feet, moving with frankly impossible speed, arms reaching to catch him.

The hell of it was that she probably thought she was saving him. He could see how cliff diving might resemble suicide to a people who shunned the sea, if she had caught sight of him just as he tried the top of the cliff rather than when he was warming up with dives from lower down. As she so obviously had. It had been stupid, no matter his training in the sport. *Never dive alone.* It was doubly, trebly, *almost fatally* stupid.

So what? he'd thought to himself at the top, too angry over how he'd hurt Halla to care about his own safety. Besides, it was a perfect diving location. He was confident after testing his new, genmod-enhanced reflexes on the lower ledges, and certain that his muscles remembered the moves. And they had, but look at what happened anyway. It was a hell of a way to learn a lesson, and Halla was paying the price for it.

She had a lot to forgive him for, and maybe he didn't merit it. He stared at the toes he was destined to lose, listening to the murmurs of apothecaries, nurses, and aides, smelling medicines and astringents.

Marianne came in from the hall and angled straight for him, taking the next seat on the divan.

"She's going to live," she said.

He continued to stare at his feet. "I know," he whispered hoarsely.

"How are you holding up?"

He shook his head. Teardrops wobbled off his chin.

"Kim," she said. "I'm so sorry."

He looked up at her, vision swimming, and narrowed his eyes, which squeezed more tears out of them. "Are you?"

"Of course!"

"Bertie said the blessing heals serious injury. Give it to her."

"Kim, we *can't.*"

"You mean you *won't.*"

"She's outcaste!"

"So?"

"Kim—"

"Outcastes are good enough to work for you or to *serve* you, but they're not good enough for the level of medical care you give your-selves." His upper lip curled. "Hypocrite."

She recoiled. "It's not like that."

"It's exactly like that." He returned to staring at his feet. "I wonder what your Jorann will say when she learns you're keeping the blessing from Halla. She's special to the Jorann, isn't she? And the Sural is the

Jorann's gatekeeper. I'll eat my hat if he doesn't have a direct line of communication. Have any of you ever asked *her* if you can give outcastes the blessing? Or are you afraid of the answer?"

Marianne swallowed audibly. After exactly eight seconds, she left him alone again.

* * *

KIM STILL SAT THERE hours later when the apothecaries finally emerged from the treatment room where Halla lay. He glowered at Cena as she approached.

"I have sent for Finnic," she said, as she took a chair across from him. "You both need to hear all the options."

"Only because you reserve the best for yourselves," Kim growled.

Cena lifted an eyebrow. "I serve Suralia."

"You are a healer refusing to heal," he shot back, and watched the words hit home. The flare of anger only raised an eyebrow on the outside, but her presence seethed with outrage and calculation that he could see through imperfectly closed barriers. The anger flared brighter when she realized Kim was looking *past* those, but he didn't care. He didn't care if she got him thrown off the planet, if that's what it took to get Halla the treatment she needed. Cena took a breath, but Finnic walked in at that moment. Instead of answering Kim's rudeness, she motioned the young man toward a chair.

Such exquisite control, Kim thought. *I don't want to be like that.*

"We have repaired the damaged bone in Halla's spine and ribcage," Cena began. "The more difficult task concerns healing the damage to the large cord of nerve tissue protected within the spine, but full healing of this, too, is possible. Monralar possesses therapies and equipment based in human medical science—"

A sensation like thunder about to break came over Kim, and then the Sural was in the middle of the room, dominating everything. Cena rose and bowed deeply.

Kim crossed his arms and remained seated. "What took you so long?"

Cena gasped.

"The Jorann required me," he replied, voice calm, face serene.

"Really? And what did *she* have to say?"

The Sural drew a small object from a pocket. "She tasked me to give you this. You are directed to do with it as you please."

He placed it in Kim's outstretched hand. It looked very like the small crystal box given him by the apothecary in Monralar, and it held an identical milky white cube.

The blessing.

Kim jolted to his feet, stifling a groan of pain from his stiffening injuries, and limped as quickly as he could into Halla's treatment room. Finnic followed on his heels. Behind them, a murmur of conversation started up between the Sural and Cena. Kim shut the door on it.

A nurse bent over Halla, who was covered with a sheet, holding a shot glass sized cup to her lips. From the look on Halla's face, the contents tasted as wretched as the medicine he'd been given. He could smell the acrid scent of it from the door.

"Kim," she said when the nurse eased her down and moved a polite distance away. Halla's voice was hoarse, and she sounded sleepy. "The apothecary said you were not badly injured."

"No. A few broken bones, already mended."

"Halla, my friend, I heard you were a hero," said Finnic. "You saved Kim!"

Halla managed a smile at that. Her gaze went back to Kim and dropped to his hand. He held up the box.

"Are you ready to begin healing?" he asked.

"I cannot feel my legs," she said.

"I will take that as a yes." He slid onto the edge of the bed beside her and opened the lid, while Finnic took a nearby chair.

Halla peered groggily at the tiny milky cube. "Stay with me? Both of you?"

"Of course," Kim said.

Finnic nodded firmly.

She picked the cube out of the box, paused a long moment, and placed it on her tongue. Nothing seemed to happen, until Halla relaxed a little and settled back, eyes half-lidded.

Kim caught the nurse's eye. "When I took the blessing, I fell unconscious, and stayed that way."

"When you were human?" he asked.

"Yes."

"That was normal. This is the way of it for us. It takes time to heal a serious injury, however, and she should rest."

That sounded like an invitation to leave.

"Stay," said Halla, quietly.

Kim remained where he was, as did Finnic. The nurse sighed, then bowed slightly and left, closing the door behind him. Kim blew out a loud breath.

"Provincials," Finnic muttered darkly. He brightened. "Halla, my friend, you should have heard Kim. *I* wish I had heard Kim. The talk among the servants is that he argued with the high ones on your behalf and prevailed. That *never* happens."

"They exaggerated," Kim said. "I rather think it was an order from the Jorann."

"Who would tell her? The Sural?" He scoffed. "I must tell you, Kim, that you have gained a reputation for being a pleasant fellow until someone makes you angry."

Kim barked a laugh. "I can live with that."

The door opened again.

"As can I," the Sural said as he stepped into the room.

Kim glared at him. "Leave Halla alone."

The Sural spread his hands in front of him.

"Let him talk," Halla said.

She locked eyes with the Sural and nodded. Exhaustion and determination glowed in her in equal measure.

God she was magnificent.

"My thanks." The Sural pulled the remaining unoccupied chair to the side of the bed and sat on it, looking like an adult on children's furniture. "Halla, I think you will understand that we must postpone your language implant until you are recovered."

She bobbed her chin a fraction. "Yes."

"An apothecary's aide could have been sent in to tell us that," Finnic said, a note of challenge in his voice.

"Indeed," the Sural replied, barely flicking his gaze away from Halla. "But I am uniquely qualified to explain what you can expect as a triggered Grandchild. Would you prefer to hear it from my head apothecary? She can certainly explain everything you need to know."

"No, I will hear you," Halla said. She still sounded groggy, but determination outmatched the exhaustion now. "But triggered? As you are?"

"Yes. There can be no mistaking the changes. They were not present during your last scan, and we assume the events on the beach are responsible. Kim could account only for the last moments before your impact, which prompted us to look for the signs. I can attempt to identify the trigger itself if you feel equal to telling me what you remember."

Halla took a breath and stared at the ceiling for several seconds.

"I will try," she said.

"Unless you are too tired," Kim said.

She shook her head. "I can do this much." She took a breath and continued, "I saw Kim on the cliff. I thought," she swallowed. "His mood had been so low. I thought he sought to end his life. I ran to stop him, but he jumped before I could reach him, and...I remembered my Tarasheth drowning in a riptide and not being able to save her—and everything inside me caught fire. Suddenly I was fast enough, and I was there to catch him." She smiled faintly. "I did not think about what would happen when I *did* catch him."

"You see?" said Finnic, grinning brightly. "You are a hero."

Halla shook her head again, the smile turning rueful.

The Sural was nodding. "Everything inside you caught fire. An apt description."

"That was it?"

"Yes. A strong emotional crisis and what you believed to be a life-death situation. It pushed your body past the threshold." He turned his mahogany eyes on Kim. "Your will to live does not appear diminished. I must ask, however, if you were indeed seeking to end your life."

"No, I was—" Kim frowned. He couldn't find the words in Suralian. "Cliff diving," he continued in English. "A sport I took up when I was a teenager, although I mainly dove on the station. Tau Ceti has an Olympic diving pool, ten meters deep. I could never compete past the amateur level, but I placed in a few school competitions."

The Sural stared. Then he said, "A *sport?*"

"A sport. It's fairly popular on Britannia. On Earth, too, but Britannia is a water world with a great many more excellent locations for it."

"A sport." The Sural shook his head and switched back to Suralian. "He jumps into the sea from the top of a cliff to prove superior skill and to provide entertainment to enthusiasts of the practice."

Halla and Finnic looked at each other. Halla's eyes were as wide as Kim had ever seen them, and her lips slightly parted. Finnic was squinting, and his upper lip drawn up to show his teeth.

"Humans are mad," the young man said.

"I cannot say you are entirely wrong," Kim replied.

CHAPTER 22

The tingling woke Halla. Her legs were tingling. *Abominably.*

She pushed herself up against the head of the bed in the room to which she had been moved, thankful that she still retained a fair amount of arm and shoulder strength. She rubbed at what itching she could reach without bending more than the slight amount the aides and nurses allowed. That was only partway to her knees, but it was something. She could feel her hands on her thighs, more by the diminished tingling under them than anything else, but rubbing had no lasting effect. After a few fruitless attempts at each leg, she gave up and gritted her teeth.

Finnic was still with her, sound asleep in his chair, a comforting presence, if a sleeping one. Kim was gone, and so was the nurse. Well. She was glad of that. She had much to ponder, as the Sural had been surprisingly forthcoming and detailed about what a triggered Grandchild could do, and about the more personal effects of using those abilities.

She could expect to find reserves of strength and speed well beyond normal limitations. *That* she had already experienced. The Sural also recommended against using more than a minimum of her new strength except under the most dire of circumstances. She could easily damage her own muscle and bone.

Beyond that, the personal effects were discouraging, to her as an outcaste. She would need to consume more food in general. It made sense, she supposed, but it would make her even more of a burden than she already was. In addition, using her abilities would require a great deal more food in order to replenish herself. That too made sense, but then the Sural added that when her stomach was satisfied, she would experience an intense desire for sex. Finnic laughed uproariously at that and offered himself should she ever need relief. Kim's reaction was entirely and oddly different. Blood had pooled in his face, and his presence shimmered. It was a compelling sight, and Finnic had not attempted to hide his enjoyment of it. Even the Sural had offered a brief smile.

The Sural then pointed out, at the end, that in the absence of a willing sexual partner, heavy physical exercise would work to ease the need.

That was good to know. Kim was not willing, and she *would* not ask Finnic.

Presences caught her attention, moving about in the common room. Kim was out there now, and the head apothecary, Cena. They both approached.

Finnic woke as they opened the door and he stretched, uttering a sleepy, yawn-distorted "Fair morning."

Kim was no longer limping, but his stride hitched as his gaze fell on her. He blinked, swallowed hard, and offered a falsely bright smile as he stopped beside her bed, one hand extended. A crystal box rested on his palm.

"More?" she asked, as she plucked the box from his hand.

"I was told to take the box," he replied as he took a chair beside the bed. He shrugged his strange, two-shouldered human shrug. "I was not told what to do with it. And you clearly need it more than I do."

She opened the lid.

"Delay a moment," the apothecary said. "I wish to scan you."

191

Halla replaced the lid while the woman ran a scanner over her legs and up to her waist, slowly, gazing intently at her tablet. She nodded.

"You are experiencing some sensation in your legs?"

"Tingling," Halla said. "*Strong* tingling."

"Good." She pocketed her tablet and scanner. Then she smoothed the sheeting over Halla and drew it up to her shoulders from where it had pooled at her waist.

Kim relaxed a little. Halla bit one side of her lower lip hard. He had scant skill at concealing his attraction—and then she remembered that despite it, he was not hers, nor she his. He had made that clear. Her amusement died away.

"The tingling should subside by the end of the day, possibly sooner, if you partake of what the scholar here has brought you," the apothecary was saying. "You may also begin to regain some use of your leg muscles soon." She pointed her chin at the crystal box in Halla's hand. "You may consume that now."

Halla reopened the box and placed the blessing on her tongue. It tingled a little as it dissolved, and a feeling of refreshment spread through her. She took a deep breath. She had a sense of unreality about all of this. She might be the first outcaste in two thousands of years to take the blessing—twice!—but she was certain the provincials had not intended to give it to her. After all, they had spent thousands of years refusing to share with the sanctuaries, claiming the blessing only gave outcastes more time to live in dishonor. As if the provinces were the arbiters of who deserved to live.

Did the Mother of All know what provincials did in her name?

"Finnic," the apothecary said. "Your language implant is ready."

She headed out the door.

Finnic straightened and grinned. Then he frowned, looking back and forth between her and Kim.

"Oh go on," Kim said. "You can practice your English on me afterwards. It will give us something to do while Halla sleeps."

Finnic shot Kim an innocent grin. "I can think of many things we can do."

"Finnic." Kim rolled his eyes.

"I am coming!" the younger man called, and hurried after the apothecary.

Kim muttered something in English as the door closed.

"What did you say?" Halla asked.

He stared over her head, thinking. Then he said, "There is no direct translation, but the base meaning is that I am sure he was. *Coming*, that is. Which is one way we humans refer to the height of intimacy."

She thought about that, caught a flash of embarrassment in his emotional presence, and laughed a little when she realized his meaning. "Yes. But Finnic has a good heart. He is young and newly free of restrictions, and many of us become a little focused on the physical for a time at that age."

Kim chuckled ruefully and fell silent.

Halla fingered the sheet under her hand. It was the first time they had been alone together since he rejected her on the beach. Her heart stuttered at the thought. She needed to do *something* to resolve it between them.

"Halla," Kim said softly.

She glanced up. He was leaning forward in his chair, hands resting on his knees, dark eyes intense.

"No." She shook her head, eyes on her fingers again. "No."

"I need you to know—"

Her breath came short. "No! Anyone would have done that for you. No." Her eyes stung and filled with tears.

"Halla—"

"No! I understand. I *have* to understand. I am not yours. I cannot ever be yours. You explained why and I understand." She took a shuddering breath. "I cannot work like this. We should part for a time, to allow our hearts to calm. To adjust to...reality."

A stunned silence met her words. She refused to look up. If she looked up, she would lose her resolve. If she lost her resolve, she would do or say something that forced Kim to reject her again.

"Is that what you want?" he asked, voice hoarse.

No.

"Yes."

Another silence. *He knows I am lying, but what else can I say?*

"All right."

Kim stood and walked to the door. Stopped. Hesitated. For a moment, she thought he would turn. *No! No! If he turns, if he comes back, I am lost!* She wished him away, though her barriers were closed, and finally he opened the door and went through, closing it behind him.

Halla pulled the sheeting over her face and sobbed. Then, moments later, the nurse returned. Halla groaned and struggled to control herself, trapped on the bed and unable to hide. The nurse sat on the edge, scanned her, even probed her. Then he sat back and regarded her with brows furled.

"Is there a way I can help?" he asked.

She was about to shake her head when an idea occurred to her.

"Monralar has therapies for my injury that Suralia lacks," she said, her voice thick with tears and, yes, even a touch of frustration. "I wish to go there. Now."

* * *

KIM STARED out at the ocean. The day was just as warm as yesterday, but more cloudy than clear and easier on the eyes. That, and distance from intrusive presences, had brought him to the beach, because he had to think. *Had to.* The project was on hold while Halla recovered, obviously, but her last words to him cast doubt on its future as well. Could they work together now? Could *he?*

They were adults. They could work it out. They had to.

Finnic approached and flopped onto the sand beside him, wincing from a whole-body impact that even Kim could feel. Finnic held his head in his hands.

"That hurt," he said in English, his accent thick but comprehensible.

"Then don't do that," Kim replied. "How do you feel?"

He straightened. "Angry."

Kim peered at him sidelong. He knew where this was going. "Kim and Halla are Kim and Halla's business."

Finnic took a deep breath, then spoke slowly in heavily accented but near-perfect English. "No. We are a team. And you, my friend, are a fool. No, you are two fools. She is gone."

"*What?*"

Finnic regarded him with a flat expression. This wasn't the carefree new adult he put on as a mask to hide how much he cared about people. This was the man underneath. Kim felt a little honored and a great deal concerned.

"She left for Monralar this morning."

"*What?*"

Kim ran a hand through his hair. *Gone.* She was *gone*. He really had made a thorough cock-up of this project. If he'd just kissed her when she wanted him to, when they *both* wanted to, everything would still be on track. There would be no accident, no broken back, and no brokenhearted woman running all the way to the other side of the planet to get away from *him*.

No project dead in the water.

But no. He wouldn't have kissed her, not then. He couldn't have done that and retained any self-respect. He knew better now, but the resulting miscommunication had driven away the woman he— He sighed, admitting defeat. The woman he loved.

"The head apothecary said Monralar has therapies for her," Kim sighed. "And I'm sure Bertie will find some way to get her as much of the blessing as she needs to heal. Or maybe two was enough. I don't know."

"You are *three* fools in one head." So much for near-perfect English, but his meaning was clear.

"Probably."

"The sanctuaries need Halla. The project needs you."

"Actually, that's an idea. It doesn't have to be me. There are plenty of qualified xenologists who are more respected than I am."

"You speak nonsense. The Sural sent me to tell you he wants us follow her."

195

"What? Why? I'm the last person she wants to see."

"You are the only person she wants to see, but she needs to learn that. You need to learn it too." He stood and brushed the sand off his hands and robe. "Come with me. We will go to Monralar. Or by every rock in my mother's garden, I will *carry* you there."

CHAPTER 23

$\mathcal{H}$alla gazed at the treatment room around her while the Monral's head apothecary, face carefully neutral, scanned her and performed a thorough physical examination. How much of the information the apothecary gathered was necessary to her treatment? Better to have too much information than not enough, where it concerned recovering the ability to walk again, but she had placed herself in the hands of provincials.

Monrali provincials, whose ruler's lover had a reputation for advocating in favor of the sanctuaries. That *did* weigh in their favor, and so far, she had been treated with nothing but careful respect. Halla tried to quell her suspicions by concentrating on the treatment room. It was large and airy, and built of white stone, like the stronghold as she had seen it in her dream. A vibrantly colorful painting of dancers in motion hung on the wall near the door. But it shared the smell of the treatment rooms in Suralia: the bitter tang of medicines mixed into the astringent odor of cleansers.

At length, the apothecary pocketed her tablet and scanner.

"How do you feel?" she asked, in Suralian.

"The tingling stopped during the journey," Halla replied. "If I press on my skin I can feel it. And I can move my legs now, but it is like swinging a piece of wood. No control."

"Excellent," the apothecary said. "As the aides have already measured you for the mesh, we can begin your nerve therapy when it is ready."

Halla pressed her lips together. "Do I need it? I was given the Jorann's blessing. Twice."

"Aye, you need the therapies. I reviewed the record of your injury and treatment." One corner of her mouth lifted. "The blessing will considerably speed your healing, but you must still relearn how to walk. That will require time and effort."

Halla nodded, and the apothecary smiled. She was friendlier than the one in Suralia. It was a relief.

A light-skinned man with light gold hair and blue eyes, the one she had seen talking with the Monral in a dream, stuck his head through the treatment room door.

"May I come in?" he asked. He spoke Suralian with a distinctly different accent than did Kim or the Marann.

The apothecary gestured him in. He was fairly tall and dressed in a Monrali guard's robe, as he had been in the dream. He prickled as much as any guard, but he also had a feel of the station to him, somehow.

"I am Bertie," he said, with a friendly smile and some kind of provincial bow. "You may have heard of me?"

She nodded, wanting to be suspicious of him, but he reminded her too much of Finnic to feel anything but a reluctant amusement. That was clearly the effect he wanted, because his smile broadened.

"I am Halla," she said.

"Very good to meet you, Halla. Well! I have some news, but whether it is good news or bad depends upon how you feel about it."

The hairs went up on the back of Halla's neck. "Kim and Finnic followed me."

Bertie, who had already taken a breath to continue, stilled. "Yes," he said, brows quirking. "We have news that they left Suralia, most likely to come here. We do not, however, know when they will arrive."

She frowned. "What? How can you not know?"

"We have no idea precisely where they are. They simply took a pod and departed while the Sural was still negotiating permissions for them to use the interprovincial tunnels."

"But Finnic cannot know the tunnels well enough to guide a pod through them. None of us do."

"Which is apparently why they left by sea."

Halla gawped. "By...sea...?" She shook her head. "Finnic. That was Finnic's idea. He loves the sea. And Kim has no fear of it. He jumps into it from cliffs. Neither man has any *sense*."

"They should be fine."

"Fine? How can they be fine? They are traveling halfway around the world in a *pod*. On the ocean! There are storms. There are waves. Anything could happen!"

"Well..." Bertie rubbed the back of his neck. "I will ask about the weather if that would help. Perhaps they will have smooth seas. But how did you know they were coming?"

"I know Finnic."

Bertie's lips twitched, but he said, "Marianne claimed responsibility for this. She told me she asked the Sural to send them after you to save the project."

There was more to the matter than *that*. It seemed unlikely that the Marann had told Bertie where her real fault lay. "*Send* them? Stubborn as those two are, the Sural can only send either of them somewhere they already wish to go. But Finnic would follow me simply to tell me I was wrong to leave."

Bertie snorted. "Then did Kim follow without thinking, or did Finnic bully him into it?"

"Finnic bullied him into it." *That* made sense.

"And the Sural was negotiating with his allies to let an outcaste use their tunnels when they simply left. I wonder what concessions he may have already made that he must now honor?" The human lit with amusement at his own words. "Well! Leaving aside the matter of a pair of flutter-brained diggerwits on a voyage by sea—I have to admit that I want to save the project too, but not at the cost of anyone's peace of mind. How do *you* feel about continuing? No one will tell me."

"No one knows."

"Not even you?"

Halla sucked in a breath. This man, this *human*, was far too perceptive. Guard training, she thought. Guards, ruling caste, and sensitives, they all saw too much.

"No," she said, softly.

The apothecary pulled out her tablet and poked at it for several heartbeats. "The Suralian nurse recorded that she slept a great deal during the journey," she said to Bertie. "I will allow you to stay and converse as long as you refrain from upsetting her any further. Emotional stress will adversely affect her recovery."

There was a warning in her voice.

"Yes, apothecary," he said meekly, as she headed out the door.

Bertie pulled up a chair, face serious. "Halla, I truly believe they will be all right."

She sucked half of her lower lip between her teeth. He was trying. She took a breath and tried to smile, but she could not have convinced Bertie, because she failed to convince *herself*.

"In other matters," he said, gently, "Suralia sent the template for your English implant, although no apothecary will give it to you until you are recovered, or as recovered as you need to be for the actual procedure. That gives you a new option. The Suralians used Marianne Woolsey for their template. There is more than enough time to build another using me. My vocabulary is less Earthbound and more interplanetary, and of course there is my superior Britannic accent."

Bertie grinned toothily—just like Finnic.

"Oh?" Halla's eyebrows rose despite herself, but given the choice, she would rather not remind herself of that woman every time she heard herself speak English.

"Do you prefer a Britannic template?" he asked more seriously, pulling a tablet from a pocket.

"Yes," she said.

He lifted an eyebrow at her quick answer, but tapped at his tablet before tucking it away again.

"We have your scans from Suralia, but our apothecaries want to scan your head again. Something about being triggered, along with regenerative changes from the blessing. I am not fluent in medical terminology in any language, but those seemed to be the main reasons."

She drew a breath, but said nothing. As injured as she was, she was helpless to stop the Monrali apothecaries from doing anything they liked. For all their fractiousness, the ruling caste could unite when they deemed it beneficial—and Monralar was allied with Suralia. Would Monralar's apothecaries honor the Sural's promise?

"Halla," he said. His smile was gone, replaced with a sober expression. "I understand your fears. For this one thing, the apothecaries need fresh scans. Nothing else, only scans. On my honor as a guard of Monralar, you can rely on our hospitality. All right?"

She let out a breath and nodded. "All right. But will you tell me if you hear any news about Kim and Finnic?"

"You will be the first to know."

* * *

FOR THE MIDDAY MEAL, Halla managed, with the help of a muscular aide named Jeddin, to sit upright in a chair at the apothecaries' refectory table. Servants put a large amount of food in front of her. Warm, herby breads, fresh fruit, vegetable soup, bowls of nuts, it was as good as—no *better* than the food in Suralia. She ate every scrap and then simply enjoyed sitting upright and sipping the excellent tea. It was not Suralian tea flower, which was the only provincial tea she could easily identify. What she drank now was rich, smoky, and completely unfamiliar.

"Do you enjoy the tea?" said a light, male voice, and the Monral, looking just as he had in her dream, appeared in the doorway, and Bertie just behind him.

Halla did not move. Neither did she lower her mug as the Monral took a seat across the table from her, and Bertie took the chair beside him, with a cordial nod in her direction.

"It is excellent," she said.

"This kind grows in a single valley in the southernmost region of my province," the Monral said. "Nowhere else."

"Nothing like this comes to the sanctuaries."

"No, I regret. The supply is small and it is popular among my people. We have only a small surplus, which we trade with Parania because the Paran's beloved favors it."

"Of course."

His eyebrows lifted slightly. Then his gaze fell on his own hands. She followed it. He was toying with a small crystal box, rotating it in his fingers.

"Am I wrong to suppose that your tea is not the only offering available to me but denied to the rest of my people?"

"An astute question," Bertie murmured. "Particularly relevant today."

"Indeed," said the Monral. He met Halla's gaze with unusually pale eyes of a clear amber color. "It is my duty to act on the Jorann's wishes with regard to you. I can offer the blessing to no other outcaste unless the ruling caste meets and decides otherwise."

"Ah. And the nerve therapies?"

"I have authority to offer those to any who serve Tolar."

He held out the box.

"No," she said. "No more. I will take nothing not freely shared with any other outcaste in need."

The Monral paused, then pocketed the box. "I understand."

"But you will begin the nerve therapy?" Bertie asked, his brows pinched into an earnest expression.

"Yes," she said. "I can accept that."

Bertie's face relaxed into a smile. "Good. We do wish to see you restored to full health and strength, Halla. Believe that."

"I will try. But no more of the blessing."

"I—" Bertie sighed. "Is there anything else we can do for you? Anything at all?"

She expelled a hard breath. "I do have a request."

The Monral lifted an eyebrow, curiosity coloring his presence.

"I need to make a gift to Aran, the deputy stationmaster. A life-gift."

"A life-gift?" the Monral murmured. "In what manner did he serve you?"

"I was—" She hesitated for a long moment.

Bertie put a hand on the Monral's arm, and they exchanged a look.

"Do you wish to speak with my guard alone?" the Monral asked, gently.

"I—" She gusted out a breath. It was strangely difficult to speak the words. "No. It is a simple tale. I was dying when I went to the station, my life draining from a wound no one could see or even know I had taken. Aran told me the Jorann could heal me and offered to make the arrangements. If not for that, I would be nearer the dark than not."

The Monral nodded. "Then a life-gift is indeed appropriate."

Bertie straightened suddenly, his expression bright. "You have come to the right man. I know of something Aran will appreciate. Consider it done."

* * *

KIM SPENT the first hour of the undersea voyage enduring a silence that Finnic somehow managed to style into a criticism of Kim's very existence. Well. That was not an insurmountable problem. Kim escaped by taking a nap.

When he awoke, the critical atmosphere had vanished, and Kim was filled with peace, and wonder, and even awe.

"What is *that*?" he said, sitting up straight and straining to see, but the darkness was complete. "Where are we?"

"The hevalra," Finnic replied in Suralian, with no hint of his previous censure. "Can you reach far enough to sense them? They know we are here."

"What is a *hevalra*?" Kim asked. "And you should speak English."

"Shut up and listen," Finnic retorted in that language, because apparently he was still irritated with Kim even in *this*...whatever it was. Well of tranquility? Sea of peace?

Kim *reached* and felt nothing other than the sparks of tiny deep-sea creatures floating in the current around them.

"Down?" he asked.

"Down."

Kim reached again, downward, and this time his senses encountered something huge and incandescent, glowing in his empathic vision. His angular resolution was improving; the creature was strikingly similar in shape to the sculpture he'd seen in his guest rooms in Monralar, but on a much grander scale. "Is that a hevalra?"

"A *hevalrin*. Yes. There are two hevalra today."

"I only sense one."

"The other is deeper. Sometimes there are many, but there is always at least one. I think they maintain this place."

"Why?" A rustle of fabric, and Kim sensed Finnic's shrug. He scrubbed at his face with a hand and yawned. "We can't have gone far."

"That depends on your definition of *far*. We are about half the way between Suralia and Sacaea." Finnic nudged the pod gently, and a sense of motion resumed. "Kim. We need to talk."

"About what? If you want to tell me again how thoroughly I've offended you and Halla, you can save your breath. I'm already aware. If you want my apology, you have it. I wish I knew how to make things right with her, but I really have no idea. And this is all so impossible. Days. I've only known her a few days. It shouldn't be like this."

"Go to her."

"I *can't*."

Finnic made a noise between a grunt and a growl.

Kim rolled his eyes at the darkness. "She told me she cannot work like this. If she can—calm her heart—while she recovers from her injuries, enough to work with me afterward—"

"She will."

"How are you so certain?"

His glow shrugged a silent shoulder. "She listens to me. Sometimes. I will do what I can. This project is important, and my sanctuary needs it. Every sanctuary needs it."

"So you keep saying."

Finnic snorted derisively. "Did they not tell you the terms Halla demanded for her service, and to which the Sural agreed? Every time we arrive at a sanctuary, a generous shipment of food, medicine, and equipment will come with us. Another will arrive every season we remain. My sanctuary, her sanctuary, *every* sanctuary needs this. Once the ruling caste has done this once, they will see what has changed, and all that *could* change, and how blind they have been. Others will follow us, provincials and outcastes alike, and we can begin to make a better life for everyone in the sanctuaries."

Finnic fell silent, and Kim sensed him let his attention be absorbed by the transport pod. Kim settled into his seat, marveling at the magnitude of his misstep with Halla until the darkness around them grew into gloom, and then became daylit waters. At last the pod broke the surface to slide onto the sands of a crescent-shaped island so small it consisted of barely more than its beach. Another island curved off to each side like a tiny archipelago. Finnic let the pod rest while they both stretched their legs and unpacked some of the abundant supply of food and drink they had taken from the kitchens before leaving. Finnic spoke not a word.

Then they were off again, skimming the surface when it was calm, diving beneath when the seas became rough. Kim lost track of the stops they made; twice they stopped to sleep on small islands. The third night, Finnic drove the pod onward as darkness fell. As they passed a peninsula, clear under the waxing moon and bright stars, he said, "Sanctuary Aanesh. The next city is Monralar."

Kim breathed a sigh of relief when Finnic finally brought the pod out of the water on a white sand beach. Neither he nor Finnic was entirely surprised to find Bertie approaching, followed by a pair of servants and a woman in dark green.

"Welcome back," Bertie said as he stopped in front of them, eyes glittering and presence sparking. "Finnic, is it? Charmed. I've heard a great deal about you." Then his voice hardened. "Do the pair of you have any idea how many people you left in the dark while you risked your lives haring off over the ocean in a *transport pod*?"

Finnic swallowed hard.

"Oh," Kim said. "Uh. There was no reason to worry. We were safe. We took breaks."

"You're very fortunate you didn't encounter a typhoon."

Kim felt the blood run out of his face. "Typhoon? I had no— I guess we didn't think. So... Um. How is she?"

"Asleep, at the moment. It's the middle of the night, as I'm sure you can see."

Kim nodded, wincing at the ache in his legs as the circulation returned. He grabbed his bags from the back of the pod, and Finnic collected his, only to have the servants immediately divest them of their luggage and walk off with it.

When the woman in green approached the pod and laid a hand on it, Finnic said in Suralian, "Be gentle with her. She is very old and it was a long journey."

"Of course."

The pod went willingly with the woman, who murmured softly to it as she led it back the way she came. Now that Kim could focus his attention on something other than struggling to stay awake, he sensed the creature's weariness and hunger.

"Oh," he said. He felt like he had inadvertently kicked a puppy.

"Indeed." Finnic took a harsh breath and continued in English. "I should have borrowed another, but I could not leave her there alone. She knew no one in Suralia."

"She?" Bertie asked. "I didn't know anyone could tell."

Finnic straightened abruptly. "I can," he said defiantly.

Bertie lifted his hands. "I believe you, my friend. You and your pod are welcome in Monralar, and *she* will receive the best of care." He swept an arm toward the city. "If you will come with me to the stronghold, guest quarters await."

And Halla, thought Kim. *Damn. Damn Finnic, damn the University, and damn me.*

CHAPTER 24

The sun was well up in the sky when Kim woke. The first thing he noticed was that he wasn't cold. He luxuriated for several long seconds in the warmth of equatorial Monralar's autumn breeze, redolent with the fragrance of flowers and the scent of the sea.

The second thing he noticed was that the glass door to the balcony was open to admit that breeze.

The third thing he noticed was that he wasn't alone.

"Finnic." He weighted his voice with all the disapproval he could summon.

A shadow fell across him.

"Good morning," Finnic said, from the balcony door.

Kim expelled a long, loud sigh and sat up.

"Why are you in my sleeping room?"

"Why are you?"

"I'm *sleeping*."

"Not anymore."

"Finnic!"

Finnic walked in and squatted next to the sleeping mat. It was the man beneath the mask again, serious and concerned. "Halla knows we are here."

"Of course she does. Someone probably told her we were coming as soon as we left Suralia. How is she?" Kim blinked. Bertie hadn't answered that question last night, had he? And Kim had been too tired to notice. "Do you know how she's doing? Did they tell you? Does she want to see us?"

Finnic shook his head and said, in much improved English, "I think if she were ready to see us, Bertie would have answered you last night."

"You noticed that too." Disappointment began to pool in Kim's stomach. "I hope it doesn't mean she's abandoning the project. Do you think she'll talk to you?"

Finnic stared off, thinking about that. Then he took a breath and expelled it, clearly trying to work himself up to saying something he didn't want to say. Kim waited.

"Kim," he said, finally. "Did you really tell her it was a crime for you to touch her?"

"*What?* No! I—" He froze. With dawning horror, parts of the conversation on the beach came back to him. *To share a blanket is inappropriate. A crime in some circumstances.*

"Oh damn. *Hellfire* and damnation. I did say something she could take that way."

"She took it that way."

"*Damn.*" He scrubbed his face with his hands. "How many different kinds of an idiot can one man be?"

"I do not know, my friend, but I suggest you cease trying to discover the answer." He clapped a hand on Kim's shoulder and stood. "Bathe and dress. You missed the morning meal, and Bertie said he has news for you."

Kim got to his feet. "If you see him, tell him I'll be out as soon as I'm dressed," he said as he headed into the bathing area.

When he emerged, Finnic was gone. The young man's presence had left Kim's guest rooms while he was turning up the water temperature, and the solitude had been delicious. Kim shook his head and ran his fingers through damp curls as he contemplated his wardrobe. Smalls, the usual shirt, the usual trousers. No vest or robe—he wouldn't need those in *warm, sunny* Monralar. The memory of Bertie's good-natured pushing brought a slight smile as he reached for his sandals. Yes, definitely sandals.

The air felt good on his feet, but the spaces between his toes itched. He clenched them together. It didn't help.

It was cooler in the hall outside his suite, a few doors from the one he'd occupied before. He got himself turned around trying to find the refectory and finally hit upon the idea of following the brightest of the glowing empathic trails on the floor. It took him straight to the main hall, and from there he knew his way.

The refectory was nearly empty, but there was still some food on the tables near the kitchens. He grabbed what he could, filled a mug from a steaming carafe of tea, and took a seat at a small table by himself. Less than a minute later, Bertie appeared in the doorway, heading straight for him. He detoured past the food tables to pour himself some tea before taking the other seat at the table.

"Good morning!" Bertie said cheerily.

"I'm so surprised to see you," Kim replied, deadpan.

Bertie chuckled. He took a sip of his tea, then said, "We've made a bit of progress on the contract negotiations with Tau Ceti, if you're interested."

"The only thing I'm interested in finding out is how Halla is doing. You didn't answer me last night."

Bertie set down his mug and studied Kim for a few seconds. "It's like that, is it?"

"Yes, it's like that. Do you plan to help or get in the way?"

"I plan to do whatever benefits our project most. Do you still care about that?"

"I tell you what. I'll tell you how I feel about the project if you tell me how Halla's doing."

Bertie took several sips of tea while he considered that.

"All right," he said, finally.

"You go first. I've learned not to trust provincials, and human or not, you're a provincial."

"Ouch. I really must have another talk with Marianne. She's turning into a person-sized version of the Sural."

Kim snorted. "Something like that. And *Halla?*"

"Yes. Well." Bertie cleared his throat. "About Halla. She's doing quite remarkably well, as I understand things. We've some human medical technology that our shipmaster Farryn turned up with his salvage corp, and we're making good use of it with Halla. She's on her feet today—or peds, rather—but not walking yet. For now, the apothecaries have her standing while gripping supports, in addition to doing various exercises while sitting or lying down. They do expect to start her walking soon."

He fell silent.

"And?" Kim prompted.

Bertie blinked. "And what?"

"Her spirits? Her mood? What's your *impression?*"

"She's heartbroken." Bertie stared him straight in the eye, face neutral.

Kim sucked in a harsh breath.

Bertie's expression softened. "What happened in Suralia?"

"You don't know?"

"I'm just a guard. No one tells me more than I need to know to do my job."

Kim let out a long sigh.

"Oh dear. That bad?"

"You mentioned that you're an attorney. They have ethics rules about fraternizing with interns and clerks and the like, don't they?"

Bertie's eyes widened. "We don't need those here. Tolari culture is resistant to the exploitation they're designed to prevent."

"No one told *me* that until I'd made a hash of things by trying to keep to the University's Code of Ethics. The one I signed. The one I *gene-stamped.*"

Bertie buried his face in his palm for a moment. "I am very sorry. I wish I had thought to mention sexual and romantic mores. I'll add them to the list."

"Yes, do that. Too bad you didn't before I explained the ethics of our professional relationship to Halla." *After she told me that she wanted to share a blanket with me.* He wasn't about to tell Bertie *that* part of it.

Bertie winced. "She can't have taken that well. No Tolari would do, I shouldn't think."

"She didn't."

"Well that's—" Bertie interrupted himself. "The project is obviously on hold while Halla recovers, but you've not said if you still want to continue at all."

"I'm currently leaning toward *not without Halla*, but if that's as impossible as it currently looks, I might reconsider. Or not. I don't know."

"Your ability to say yes, no, and maybe in one go is inspiring." He leaned back with his mug cupped in long-fingered hands. "Are you up for hearing what I came here to say?"

"Sure. Why not."

He lifted an eyebrow. "Such enthusiasm. Well. The very *first* thing we did was send a demand letter to Milosrdenstva Konglomerat, the corporate entity that purchased your alleged debt for pence to the pound, on behalf of you and just over five hundred other unfortunates conscripted by Di Fata at about the same time—it was a large sweep, but I've heard of larger. They've not answered us yet, but they will do."

"Who is this 'us'?"

"The Rembrandt Pharmaceuticals legal department." Bertie bared his teeth. "Nearly all the victims were employed by Di Fata properties that are going bankrupt, but a few worked for Rembrandt or one of its subsidiaries in the past. That gave us the political cover we needed to add them all to the case. Once Milosrdenstva realizes that Rembrandt is serious, they'll release the debts and sue Di Fata to recover their losses, which should be substantial."

Bertie drained the rest of his tea and set down the mug.

"In the final accounting, when the Kekrax took you aboard, they saved 507 other individuals unfortunate enough to be employed by a corporate predator. I'd call that a good day's work."

"Kekrax really don't get enough respect," Kim said.

"No, they don't." Bertie looked earnestly at Kim. "And it's obvious that you are coming to identify with the outcastes."

"Is it?" Kim returned the gaze, carefully blank-faced.

"Have you noticed yet that you shift uneasily around provincials, especially the fully pledged?" He paused. "Such as myself?"

"You know, I'm not even sure what *pledged* means. Marianne said it's some kind of oath."

"More of a vow of fealty. Adults normally pledge to their caste leadership. It's more than loyalty and extends to the province and its ruler. For guards, it's *much* more. We pledge everything, body, life, and spirit, directly to province *and* ruler. That's why guards—why *I* irritate you more than a servant or an apothecary does. I don't entirely understand how the irritation comes about, but the Monral doesn't find it surprising that it's begun to affect you. We can feel it, you know, your reaction." He leaned forward. "You can do a lot of good for the outcastes if you stay with the project."

Kim took a deep breath and expelled it. "I know, but any competent xenologist or anthropologist can do my part of the job. No one else can bring what Halla negotiated for the sanctuaries, and without her, you'll go through interpreters like ice on a hot day. I know you're still negotiating with the University on my behalf, but you'd have to negotiate anyway for a project of this magnitude and length. Advertise the position. Even if it requires a gen mod, you'll still get dozens of qualified applicants, and I have a couple of months left on my sabbatical. I can help you sift the candidates. If Halla won't work with me, surely she'll work with one of them."

"I wouldn't be so sure." Bertie gazed at him thoughtfully. "And it would be a very bad idea for you to leave Tolar before we have a treaty with Central Command."

"*Damn it!*" Kim slapped the table with the flat of his hand, but it produced more pain than noise. He winced.

"Quite." Bertie said. "If I'm honest, I'd rather the negotiators not shift position at this remove if they can avoid doing so. Talk to Halla. See if you can patch things up."

Kim stared. "No."

"Trust me."

"She told me to stay away."

"What can I do to convince you to reconsider?"

"Nothing."

Bertie held his gaze for nine seconds, then leaned back again with a heavy sigh.

"All right. But do let me know if you change your—"

"I *won't,*" Kim said savagely. He stabbed the table with his index finger. "Until and unless she *asks* to see me, I will do as she bid and stay away."

"That begs the question of why you've come to Monralar in the first place."

Kim snorted. "Because Finnic threatened to carry me if I didn't."

* * *

KIM TOOK a pod from the stronghold to the city, guiding one solo for the first time. It was time he learned, after all, and the pod handler in the stronghold opined that even a child couldn't get lost in such a short, dedicated tunnel. Once in the city hub, it was a short walk to the beach, which was his real destination.

He strolled along the edge of the waves barefoot, carrying his sandals, trousers rolled up to his knees. The breeze was warm, and it felt good to get away from all the *people.* Monrali were friendly enough, but something about most of them grated against his nerves. Bertie was right: he identified with the outcastes now, enough that pledged provincials made him uncomfortable. He might as well start trying to puzzle that out, even if only to leave some notes for whoever would do the real research here.

He'd walked at least a kilometer down the beach when he spotted Finnic ahead, cavorting naked in a large tide pool. He stopped. He should probably turn back and leave Finnic to his solitude, but with his range, he'd already know Kim was there. He sighed to himself and resumed walking. He would issue a polite good morning and continue on his way.

"Join me," Finnic said when Kim came near. He stood in a large pool confined by a rocky outcropping at the edge of the waves. "The water is warm. But stay away from those." He pointed at several brownish-green, crab-like creatures the size of Kim's foot, scuttling about here and there. Then he held up his hand to show Kim a crescent-shaped red mark on outside the edge of a palm. "They bite."

Kim snorted. "Don't harass the wildlife and they won't bite you."

"I was not *harassing* them. I was investigating them."

"Right. Well. I'm not half finished walking. Enjoy your dip."

He'd skirted the pool, hopped over a rock on the wave side, and started to mince his way across a patch of unreasonably sharp gravel when the man spoke again.

"She wants to see you."

Kim froze, wincing at a pebble digging into the bottom of one foot. He hopped onto a flat rock.

"Did she *say* that?" he asked.

"Not...exactly."

"Have a nice day." He contemplated the gravel. It looked a little smoother to the right. Then he held up the hand holding his sandals and snorted at himself.

"Kim, stop."

"Why is everyone trying to convince me to ignore what Halla said?" he shouted at the sky. He swung around to face Finnic. "I know she was lying when she told me she wanted me to go. But it's what she *said*, Finnic. I have to respect it."

Finnic uttered a wordless noise of frustration. "Humans!" he spat.

"Well what do you expect me to do?" Kim yelled, anger boiling in his chest.

"Give her time to calm down. Then go back."

"Despite what she said?"

"*Mother of All*, you humans are worse than provincials about words."

"*It's all we've got!*" he shouted, furious now.

A burst of something resembling shock radiated out from Finnic.

The man frowned. "I had not thought of that. I should explain it to her." He began to climb out of the pool.

"You do that," Kim gritted out with clenched teeth. "See if you don't make it worse!"

Finnic straightened. "Then tell her yourself!"

"*No!*" he shouted and, heedless of the gravel stabbing his feet, stalked away.

CHAPTER 25

"*L*ift your knee," the aide named Jeddin said.

Halla gripped the frame and willed her leg to move. It was easier this morning. She had recovered all the sensation in her legs, and the apothecary told her the cord of nerves in her spine was functioning properly. As much as the blessing could do, however, it could not reteach her legs to walk or replace lost muscle strength. That required work on her part. So it was good that she came, the aide had said. Monralar possessed unique therapies to speed that part of her recovery. They were, even now, fabricating the device she needed, a mesh of some kind that would lie against her skin and communicate with her nerves.

"Flex your ankle. Yes, good. Now place your ped in front of the cube. Chin up. Shoulders straight."

She straightened and saw Finnic in the doorway, and her heart stuttered. Her ped thumped on the floor.

Jeddin frowned and turned to follow her gaze. His glower deepened.

"Do you wish me to send him away?" he asked.

She shook her head. She had known they were here, after all. It was only a matter of time before Finnic showed up.

"No," she said. "If you help me to sit, I will hear what he has to say."

With disapproval lighting his presence and darkening his voice, he said, "Very well," and assisted her into her chair. When he had done that, he cleared away the frame, then turned and beckoned to Finnic before striding to a desk at the other end of the room.

Finnic approached warily and pulled a chair closer to hers. Despite herself, she could not be angry with him. She let her expression soften to something not quite unwelcoming.

A tentative, relieved smile touched his lips.

"I can guess why you came," she said. "You need not defend him."

His brows quirked. "I think I do."

"Why?"

"Well." He shifted in his chair. "I have been learning about humans from him and from the other human here, the guard Bertie. Very many of the differences between us are because unmodified humans are sense-blind."

"Yes, of course."

"Think about the way the humans here *speak*, Halla. They have our senses now, but do not trust them; they continue to use words as if they were still sense-blind. If you want to change what you said, you must explicitly say so, or they will assume you still mean it, no matter how much your feelings say otherwise. Kim is very stubborn about that. He needs to *know* what you want. He needs to hear it from you."

"Just like a provincial. Perhaps he should pledge. He might be happier."

"Halla, grow some sense. If he did that no one in the sanctuaries would talk to him."

"A pity."

"Halla!"

Jeddin's glare from the other side of the room was almost audible.

Finnic lowered his voice. "Halla. Stop pretending you do not want to see him."

"I do *not* want to see him."

"Yes, you do."

"No—"

217

"*Yes*, you do. You cannot hide it from a sensitive." He paused. "Or a friend."

She grumbled. "You are a very bad friend, Finnic."

He grinned, with plenty of teeth.

Halla sighed. "All right. Yes, I want to see him. But how would that help? He cannot touch me. It would be agonizing for both of us. *That* is what I do not want."

"Do you intend to leave the project?"

"Not—" She sighed. "Jeddin suggested I should make no decision on the matter until I have recovered."

"You confided in a *provincial*?"

She shrugged a shoulder. "He has been kind to me."

Finnic's inner landscape jolted. He smiled ruefully. "And you have had little enough of that in recent seasons." He nodded. "I understand."

"I need to think. If I must *send* for him to see him—" She sighed "No. If I send for him, it changes nothing."

Finnic pressed his lips flat. "He is *thoroughly* yours. As much as you are thoroughly his. Another thing you cannot hide from a sensitive."

She glowered at him. "I will teach my legs to walk again. And then I will see how I feel."

* * *

KIM'S FURY propelled him a fair distance down the beach before it began to give way. The city had long since disappeared around the bend of the coast, which curved gently south. In retrospect, he should have headed west from the city, not east. He would not have run into Finnic, and no one would care if he trespassed into Parania, if they even considered it trespassing. The two provinces were allies, after all. But eastward lay hostile Nalevia. The provinces were much too large to walk all the way there in any reasonable length of time, but the looming idea of it made him uneasy. As the anger with Finnic faded, his healing leg began to make known its unhappiness with his pace. He slowed, then made his way up the beach to give it a rest.

The sun was hot, and the breeze pleasant. Waves rolled gently along the beach. Eyes closed, flat on his back, the sand's warmth seeping through his clothing on one side and the sun's on the other, he considered his situation. He'd made an unforced, disastrous error. In his own defense, it all seemed down to a collision of cultures, and not only two, but three. Just as provincial culture had begun to make sense, he'd encountered Halla and Finnic, with their outcaste principles and beliefs. The way he as a human moved through the world conflicted with both types of Tolari culture in some significant details. Ethics, in particular.

University ethics. His own ethics. Much of that was unnecessary here, and simply *keeping his word* was different here. Halla told him to stay away. Finnic told him to speak with her anyway. Which was the correct course? And what else could he do other than stay away as she requested?

A distant hum caught his attention. Kim opened his eyes and sat up as a nearby flock of seabirds screamed and flapped away in a panic. Monralar's orbital shuttle, of all things, whizzed over the waves in front of him, doing a barrel roll. He couldn't picture any of the Monrali guard pilots indulging in such antics. Probably. Well, they might, he supposed. But it was far more likely to be Bertie.

"Showoff," he muttered.

The shuttle came around for a landing, not quite far enough to avoid blowing sand onto Kim, and when the hatch opened, yes, a grinning Bertie stuck out head and shoulders.

"Come with me!" he said. "I have a surprise for you."

"I don't like surprises anymore." Kim stood and shook the sand out of his hair. Like a dog. He certainly felt like one, and *not* in a good way.

"Oh." Bertie grinned sheepishly. "Sorry, old man. Hurry up!"

"And where are we going?"

"The station! *Vai-vai!*" That last sounded like Monrali. It wasn't Suralian, according to his implant. Bertie beckoned impatiently.

Kim went a few paces closer. "What the *hell* do I need on the station?"

"That's for me to know and you to find out. Skates on, or we lose this launch window! *Vai-vai!*" He clapped his hands together, twice.

"All right, all right."

"Splendid!" Bertie cried. He disappeared inside.

Kim trudged into the back of the shuttle. For all he knew, the legalities had been settled, and Two-Five had returned to ferry him to Tau Ceti and home. Except for the part that leaving Tolar's space was apparently a bad idea now that he'd taken the Tolari gen mod. Still, Bertie had saved Kim's career by sending negotiators to the University, so what did he have to lose by humoring him and going up to the station? Halla didn't want to see him, after all.

As he made his way to the copilot's seat, Bertie punched the hatch closed and was already spinning up the shuttle's launch engines.

"Here we go!" he said.

Kim barely had time to fasten his safety straps before the shuttle shot upward, with only a mild sense of acceleration. Very good inertial dampeners, Kim thought. Very good. But it was an A'aan' vehicle, after all, and they took pains not to ruffle their strands of jewels. Then he lost himself in the view out the front ports. It wasn't the first time he'd left a world by shuttle, but it was always breathtaking. It felt like a fresh start, every time.

Bertie started chattering about what they were looking at, which province lay below them, and on and on. Kim didn't listen. He smiled, nodded, and murmured when it seemed appropriate and otherwise kept to his own thoughts.

He'd never broken his own heart by breaking someone else's before, but surely he could get over it. Eventually. Given enough time. Fortunately, he had some time while Halla recovered her ability to walk. But then he'd be back to where he started, unable to act on his feelings, even *if* she had any left, which wasn't something he could predict. The simplest but apparently most dangerous solution to the entire dilemma was to return to his position at the University. He had Two-Five's data crystal, a significant compensation for the time he spent on Kekrax Main, one which would contribute to his field and keep this mess from making too dark a blot on his quest for tenure. Unfortunately, Central Security was *very* interested in Tolar's gen mod, along with anyone who might have taken it.

Or he could stay on Tolar, and do this job, and eventually he'd get over Halla. He hoped. What else could he do but abide by his own principles? He would respect her decision. *Damn* that ethics agreement. *Damn* that gene-stamp. *Damn*—

He froze.

Bertie shot him a concerned glance.

"Bertie," Kim said. "How close are you to landing that contract with Tau Ceti University?"

"Fairly close, as I have it from the negotiators. Why?"

"Oh. Nothing. It's nothing." *Damn.* If only Tau Ceti weren't the premier University in human space! He couldn't just leave without seriously damaging his career. Thanks to this dust up, he would already have a lot of fences to mend with the senior faculty.

After a sidelong look, Bertie resumed his chatter, and the shuttle headed toward a bay near the middle of the station's spire. Bertie sat back as the landing field grabbed them.

"Almost there," he said with a smile.

"Almost there for *what?*" Kim demanded. Bertie's antics were wearing a little thin.

A look of concern briefly crossed the man's face, quickly suppressed.

"I'm sorry. I really thought the surprise would make up for it." There was a bump, and all motion ceased. Bertie tapped his controls. The hatch opened. "And it's...complicated. Can you wait just a little longer? Let me take you to C&C, and all will be revealed. Will that suffice?"

Kim glowered. "All right."

C&C was relatively quiet. Kim wondered at that until he remembered that midday in Monralar equated to the middle of the night in Suralia and on the station, which ran on Suralian time. He heard Aafreen's voice coming from the direction of her office, speaking what he thought was probably the antique Persian proper to her people. The papery thin voice of an old, old man answered her, and then the creak of a similarly old woman.

A peculiar feeling crept up Kim's spine.

"What's this about?" he asked.

Feet dragging, he followed Bertie, who sported a grin that could blind unsuspecting passers-by. In the stationmaster's office, Aafreen occupied the seating with two ancient humans, a balding, white-bearded man in a simple tan tunic and loose brown trousers, and a woman whose tunic and layered skirts were bright red and purple and yellow, with a dark green and blue floral scarf covering snow white hair. Both elders were thin as wraiths and their faces were deeply wrinkled. Aafreen helped them to their feet. They had the look of refugees, or perhaps travelers. Either could be true, since they were obviously Sayyar.

"Kim, this is Hassan and Sadira." Bertie stepped to one side to get out of the way. "Your maternal grandparents."

The woman's hands went to her mouth, and her rheumy eyes filled with tears. "Hassan!" she whispered. "Look at him!"

The old man took a step toward Kim.

"Karim," he said, in a quavery voice. "You look just like your mother."

Hassan took Sadira's arm and helped her shuffle forward, then turned back to Kim and wrapped him with thin arms that were still possessed of a little strength. Sadira joined in the hug, sandwiching them all together in a much weaker embrace. Their joy, their hope, and their exultation flooded into him through the touch.

"Karim," the old man whispered, and said something in his own language, which Sadira echoed, and then both elders were openly weeping.

Kim put one arm around Hassan and one around Sadira. Carefully, he said, "Bertie? Is this— I mean, are you *sure* they're my grandparents?"

Bertie sniffed a little, eyes luminous, smile still beaming. "As the

Rock of Barking Fields. The DNA analysis leaves no question. You are their grandson."

Kim's own tears came then.

CHAPTER 26

*a*fter the tears and the long, very *gentle* hugs, Hassan and Sadira—his *grandparents*—sat close together on a divan, neither of them quite able to take their eyes away from Kim, not for very long. Truth to tell, he couldn't get enough of looking at them, either. More hugging would have to wait, as he was feeling a little overwhelmed, but looking would do. For now.

"You were born on Liaoning Station, at New China World," Sadira said, dabbing at her eyes with a cloth. "Our daughter Parisa, your mother, she went there for the work after the riots in 2522. She met your father there. His name was Armon."

"Now there was a man with a good beard," Hassan said, stroking his own.

"Very good beard," Sadira agreed.

And that explained the loads of nanites it had taken to tame his own, Kim thought.

"Armon's family liked our Parisa," his grandmother—his *grand-mother*—continued. "And they married with our blessing too. You were born the following year."

"But we did not know Armon's family was full of radicals," his grandfather interrupted.

"Or that they had attracted the attention of Central Security. When you were four years old, they decided to bring you to Satendra Platform, at Far India, so we could meet you. But the shuttle blew up on the way out to one of our ships."

"How you survived, only Allah knows," Hassan said.

"I can help you there," said Bertie.

Everyone turned to look at him.

"We found a record of the theft of a safe-child seat from station stockpiles just before Armon's and Parisa's flight. Suffice to say that the method of it had all the marks of a station—of a Sayyar, ah, acquisition. It seems they were aware they might be in danger, so they took measures to protect their child. To protect *you*. We haven't found any record of the recovered seat, and we won't, if it was picked up by Central Security, but five days later, backdated records of one Kimberly Storm-Gale appeared at the Tau Ceti crèche."

"Sayyar are banned from Tau Ceti Station," Aafreen said in a dark voice, a fact which Kim knew well already. "They took you to a place where no one might recognize you or speak with you in our own tongue."

"Your mother was our only child," Hassan said. "We were never blessed with another."

"Although we tried," said Sadira, chuckling and patting her husband's hand. "We were young once. We did try. But we started to grow old and the time passed, and then Parisa was gone. *You* were gone. And we were alone on Satendra Platform."

Aafreen sniffled in the quiet that followed. He could sense her anger, too, but she would not let it show, not in front of non-Sayyar.

"How did you get here?" Kim asked, to break the silence.

Hassan pointed at Bertie. "That young man."

"My agents found them," said Bertie. "It's amazing what Rembrandt's resources can accomplish."

"I don't know what to say."

Aafreen coughed. "You say, 'Thank you, Bertie.'"

Kim laughed. Then he nodded, face heating. "Thank you, Bertie. I owe you."

"All in a day's work."

"I already owed you my life—"

"You owe Two-Five and Four-Three your life," Bertie interrupted.

"—and I don't know how to repay you for this, much less with what. But—" He turned back to his grandparents. His *grandparents*, who didn't even know him but who sat, their presences glowing brightly with love, gazing at him expectantly. "I have to tell you, before you get your hopes up, that I can't go back to your colony with you. I have work here. And the government crèche that raised me offered me citizenship. I accepted it. I walk on worlds. I don't speak your language and have only the barest academic knowledge of your ways. Your colony would shun me."

"Young Aafreen here told us all of *that*," Hassan said. "Do you think we care? We would not be here if we cared about that."

"Then—I don't understand. Why did you come?"

"Because you are all we have left, *navam*," said Sadira. "Grandson."

"Your grandmother is right," Hassan said. "We had to come. We had to know you."

"Hassan-joon," Aafreen said. "Do you have anyone at home to take care of you?"

"No, *dochtaram*," Hassan replied.

"A Sayyar stationmaster!" Sadira said to Kim, then lowered her voice to a confidential tone. "And she is so very respectful."

"At home we only have ourselves." His grandfather continued, shrugging. "Inshallah. Perhaps this is where we come to die. I will go to Paradise happy, knowing my grandson's face."

"Not on your life!" Kim said. "We will take care of you here, on the station. *I* will take care of you. I can stay as long as you need me. I..." He swallowed. "I'm resigning from the University."

"What?" Bertie's eyes went wide, but he recovered his composure quickly. "I see. That must be why you asked about the negotiations. Well. It simplifies matters considerably, but could you not have decided the matter just a *bit* sooner?"

Kim uttered a half-laugh. "*You* try giving up your career."

Bertie cleared his throat.

"And three begins a colony," said Aafreen. It sounded like a quote, and her empathic presence began to fill with something Kim thought might be a blend of anticipation and hope.

Sadira extended a knobby hand toward Kim. He took it in both of his, and a warm wave of love washed over him that brought a smile to his face and tears to his eyes once more. *So Tolari empathy works with humans as well*, thought part of his mind. *Deal with it later*, replied the rest.

* * *

KIM GAZED out the door after Aafreen took his grandparents—*his grandparents*—away to a place where they could rest, promising to let him know when they woke.

He wasn't alone anymore. These ancient Sayyar had traveled across the sector just to meet him. Just to *love* him. After spending a lifetime believing he must have some family somewhere, but that none wanted him, the reality staggered him.

He took a shuddering breath and wiped at his face.

"Well that didn't go to plan," Bertie murmured.

"What?" Kim blinked. "What plan?"

"Oh, there was no plan. I'd not thought past *This will cheer him up*, and *This will be fun*. But... Well. I once had to ask myself what I was willing to give up for love and family. I see you've asked yourself the same question and found your own answer. A tenure-track professor, resigning from Tau Ceti University and pulling a coveted project out from under them at the same time? It's just not done, and they'll take it poorly. You're giving up your career at the most prestigious educational institution in human space."

"As soon as they receive my letter of resignation."

"I'll ask Control to give you use of the L-space transmitter to transmit it, as a personal favor to me. The University will cancel negotiations when your notice arrives, of course. Have you chanced to think over what you'll do to salvage your career?"

"I haven't had the time. But the project is key. I can't give up on it.

It might be the only way to make a name for myself in xenology after turning up my nose at Tau Ceti. You've not advertised the position?"

Bertie shook his head. "No. The question remains how to prevent Halla running off when she's able to do. But I imagine you'll want to stay here on the station for now?"

"I didn't think past *I'll take care of my grandparents* and *I can be with Halla now*, but that would seem the logical next step. I can't abandon them and head back down to the planet after they came all this way just to see me. I'm all they've got, at least until more Sayyar arrive."

"Yes, I caught the part about Aafreen declaring the station a colony. She's been alone here a long time, but there's enough commerce now to support a small one."

Kim frowned. "The food isn't safe for them."

"Sayyar are nothing if not resourceful, and they've got one of their own for a stationmaster. They'll be fine." He stood. "Well! I need to go back downworld and inform the Monral of this development. I shouldn't speak for Aafreen, but the station has plenty of room in the living quarters for outcaste staff, far from any provincials, and C&C can set you up with door permissions and a room assignment. Just head out there—" he waved at the doorway "—and tell them you'll be residing up here for a time. Don't forget about the L-space transmitter. I'll have your belongings sent up on the next shuttle."

"Bertie."

"Yes?"

"Thank you. For everything. I'll do what I can to smooth things with Halla. Believe me, I want to help the sanctuaries and get to work as much as you and Marianne want me to. A project like this is a once in a lifetime opportunity. It won't be easy for either of us, but surely we can work together."

"I've no doubt of it. Well. Best be off!" Bertie smiled, offered a half bow, and strode out the door, heading for the shuttle he'd left waiting in the bay levels below.

* * *

AFTER THE EVENING MEAL, Bertie and Finnic came to stand in the doorway of Halla's small room in the apothecaries' quarters. The two men appeared reasonably impassive, but something bothered her, something other than one of them being a fully pledged guard.

"Did something happen?" she asked.

They took that as permission to come in, and each pulled up a chair beside her bed.

"A number of things happened," Bertie said.

"All right." She flexed her legs into a position Jeddin had taught her and held them there.

"You know that I had representatives searching for records of Kim's real identity, yes?"

"Yes." She felt a sudden fear, remembering her first dream of him in the Jorann's cavern.

"We found what we were looking for. We also found two relatives, his mother's parents, still living."

"Oh?" She switched the direction of her flex.

"Yes." Bertie smiled. "They are extremely old, but they expressed such a strong desire to see their grandson that we brought them here. They are on the station now, and Kim is there with them."

She found a smile creeping onto her own lips. She relaxed her legs. "He must be overjoyed."

"He certainly seemed to be." Bertie smoothed his face into a more serious expression. "This is where I need to talk to you about the state of the project. Kim will be living on the station for now, taking care of his grandparents and spending as much time with them as he can while they are still with us. And until you regain your ability to walk without assistance, the project is arguably paused."

Halla nodded.

"Accordingly," Bertie continued, "Marianne and I suggest that the project will be best served if you and Finnic join Kim on the station. Once you have the mesh, Station Medical can continue your treatments and therapies easily enough, as well as give you the English implant when you are cleared for it. At the same time, you and Finnic can tell Kim everything you know about your respective sanctuaries and anything else you can remember about outcaste history and culture. Anything that might help him once he is in the field."

Halla sucked in a breath. She'd seen too much, experienced too much to just go back home. And the sanctuaries needed what she would bring. "If…if he will work with me."

"He will work with you," said Finnic, with no doubt in his voice or his presence.

"Do you have any objections to the current plan, as I have outlined it? Either of you? Or do you have questions?"

Finnic grinned. "How is the food on the station?" Then he swung his gaze to Halla, from top to bottom. "And will there be enough for all of us?"

CHAPTER 27

*J*eddin and another muscular aide helped Halla into a seat in the back of Monralar's shuttle. A metal mesh lay warm against her skin, provided by the apothecaries, fitted to her only two days past. It covered her from the bottom of her peds all the way up to the lower half of her ribcage. It was a human design, they said, that Farryn had salvaged from a human medical ship, and it told her muscles and nerves what to do, as best she could understand their explanation. Or perhaps it was that it helped her nerves tell her muscles what *she* told them to do. Whatever the case, it had taken time to have it made especially for her, but with it, she could walk, slowly, with the assistance of two canes. Jeddin remained at the shuttle after the other aide left, along with Finnic, Bertie, and another prickling guard, all bearing medical devices and apothecary drugs to be packed into the shuttle's storage.

She wanted to help and sat cursing the fact that she could do nothing useful while others worked. Soon enough, however, Finnic and Jeddin and Bertie took their seats, the hatch closed, and Bertie urged the shuttle into the sky.

The view moved her nearly as much as it had the first time, but her belly began to feel as if she had swallowed a flutter when the station came in sight, blinking its lights at the stars. *Kim is there*. Fiercely, she told herself that Tarasheth would love this view. Then it dawned on her that she no longer felt a need to tell her lost life-partner her every experience. How long had it been? Days. A bittersweet twinge panged her heart when she could not recall how many. That was good, she told herself. She was moving on. She focused on the station, and her stomach fluttered again. How wise it was to send her to the station in the first place, she could not decide, but Bertie insisted. If he were not convinced that Kim would work with her, would the Monrali guards be making such an effort to take her to the station? Kim must have agreed to it. He must have.

She would see him again, and soon.

How did he feel about her now? He was a trained scholar of some experience, not a child or an impulsive young adult. He would surely be polite and well mannered. But enjoy his work, when as translator she would be present for every conversation? That would be difficult for both of them.

He might be distant, which would only be natural, given her last words to him. A sigh escaped her. If she had tried to understand his reasoning instead of reflexively thrusting away everything that hurt, they might be friends now, or perhaps even lovers. Her heart stuttered at the thought. She had hurt him, and herself at the same time, but now that they understood each other it need not happen again. He certainly had no reason to give her another opportunity. And now he had his grandparents, for however long or short a time that might be, and that thought brought the next, that she had no idea how long humans lived. But Kim had family, after a life spent alone. That was good. She could be happy for him on that ground.

She shut her eyes on the view. How was it possible to have so many conflicting thoughts at the same time? The mere idea of seeing him set her into disorder.

The shuttle bumped. It had settled into a landing bay while she pondered, unseeing. Yellow robes were visible through the front viewport, moving toward the shuttle now that it had stopped moving. Outcastes crossed the bay, carrying tools and hoses. One kept pace with the medical workers, pulling an empty equipment hauler. One yellow robe pushed a folded litter. They all claimed Halla, wrestled her into the litter with surprising care, and took her off to Medical, where she knew no one but Jeddin.

On the other hand, this was no different from all the times she and Tarasheth had arrived together at a sanctuary where they knew no one at all. They had met people, made friends, worked for the benefit of the sanctuary. She had arrived at the last sanctuary alone, newly bereft, and unbeknownst to her with her life draining away, and *still* she had managed it. She could do better now. She was healing. She knew Aran, the deputy stationmaster. She would call on him, thank him for saving her life, and offer him the gift Bertie had obtained for her in Monralar. She fingered the small embroidered bag containing that gift, safely tucked in a pocket, as the aides guided her litter into the station spire. Bertie had assured her Aran would appreciate it deeply.

In Medical, Jeddin accompanied her into a small treatment room, where an older man with an authoritative air examined her thoroughly, paying particular attention to the mesh around her lower body.

"Fascinating," he murmured, running his scanner over it, eyes fixed on his tablet. "Simply fascinating technology." He looked up at Jeddin. "It is of human design, you say?"

"Yes, apothecary."

"Superb. Now, to look at—" A long, pregnant pause. "I see no remaining damage to her spine or the nerves within. So soon? Was she given the blessing?"

"Yes," Jeddin replied. "Twice."

The apothecary grunted and continued scanning. "Ah, I see the new connections. It was a complete injury? No, you need not answer that, I have all the records. Well." He straightened and looked Halla in the eye. "You need little from me, so I shall leave you in Jeddin's capable hands. Do as he bids and you will make a full recovery. I can see now why our Monral's head apothecary logged no objection to moving you here so soon after such a serious injury, and I see no reason at all for you to remain in Medical." He turned his gaze on Jeddin. "Engage one of the outcaste apprentices to aid her and ask for room assignments in staff housing for each of you. Fair evening!"

He swept out of the room.

Halla blinked. "I wonder if he is always that way."

"He is in charge here, so yes," Jeddin said, lips quirking into a grin. "I have been here before," he added, by way of explanation. "When Bertie was ill after he first coupled with the Monral."

"We heard about that in the sanctuaries."

"*Everyone* heard about that. It offended Bertie extremely to have his encounter with the Monral discussed around the world." Jeddin chuckled. "Come. We have a small cafeteria here in Medical. I want you to eat a meal, and while you do, I will see to the room assignments."

She was, in truth, a little hungry. After collecting a young outcaste apprentice named Ormric and taking the longest walk she had yet attempted, Jeddin settled her in the cafeteria with a large, steaming mug of Suralian tea flower and a tray overflowing with a variety of rich food, much more than she would have taken for herself.

"You are still underweight," he said. "Eat as much as you can. Is there anything else you need?"

She took a breath. "I would like to speak with the deputy station-master," she replied. "If he has some time available."

Jeddin nodded. "I must go to C&C for the room assignments. I will leave a message for him."

"My thanks."

Ormric settled into their own tray of food, and the two of them ate in silence for a time, until she looked up to find Aran coming to their table. He stopped to pour himself a mug of tea before taking a seat, his face lit with a delighted smile.

"Fair day! You appear much improved, apart from those." He tilted his head toward her walking sticks, leaning on the chair next to her. Realization came, suddenly, that the mesh fit so closely that it hardly showed.

"I took a severe injury."

"So we heard, and my heart regrets that you underwent such an ordeal." He nodded to Ormric and returned his attention to her. "It was the first we heard of you after leaving us. I must assume the Jorann aided you as she did my brother?"

"She did." Halla took a breath. "I asked you to join me to give you proper thanks for your assistance. I would give you a gift."

He took a sip of tea, eyebrows rising. "Entirely unnecessary."

"It is a *life*-gift. You earned it." She pulled the small cloth bag from her pocket. It was outcaste grey and stitched with delicate representations of undersea plants.

"I?" The rising eyebrows tried to meet his hairline. "How?"

She proffered the gift with both hands. "I was far gone on what might have been my last journey when you told me of the Jorann's healing. Arranging for me to see the Jorann saved my life."

Aran's eyes went wide. "It was so serious, then?"

"Yes. So said the Jorann herself, and I can only believe her."

He reached a slow hand to take the little bag. Then he loosened the string to let the sparkling pebble within roll onto one palm. He gasped.

"A hevalrin stone! I have always wished for one." He closed his fingers around it and took a deep breath, gusting it out with a burst of joy and an incredulous grin. "I can sense him and—he can sense me! Even here! I must—I ask your pardon, I must find my life-partner." He stood and bowed deeply before almost running across the room.

She found herself smiling.

"Carry it in good health, Aran," she called, as he disappeared out the door.

* * *

As Halla stood at the door to her rooms with her thumb on the lock plate, a tired-looking Kim, wearing an outcaste robe loose over his human clothing, strode around the nearest corner and narrowly missed colliding with Jeddin and Ormric. He halted, wide-eyed.

The problem with letting someone else make the living arrangements rather than doing it oneself, Halla thought, was that things such as *this* could happen.

"Forgive me," Kim said, and disappeared through a door directly across the hall.

Halla's heart thundered in her ears. She thought she would have more time to prepare herself before seeing Kim again. She leaned against the wall beside the door, trying to breathe.

"*Mother of All,*" Jeddin muttered under his breath. "It might be too late to repair this today." Halla had told him only a little of what happened with Kim, but it seemed to be enough for him to understand her feelings. The man had been an apothecary's aide for far too long, and he was as observant as a guard. She sagged.

Ormric shoved her bags inside the open door with one ped, then took her elbow and gently urged her in. Two chairs occupied the space near a window that was really a viewscreen showing the planet below. Jeddin took her other elbow and the two of them helped her into a chair.

"Do you need me to stay with you now?" Ormric asked. The youth's face was full of compassion, as was their presence.

She shook her head, a desperate desire to be alone clenching her throat so tight that she could not trust her voice.

Ormric shared a look with Jeddin. The provincial pressed his lips together, then nodded.

Ormric thrust one hand into a pocket and withdrew a small disk on a cord. They placed it around her left wrist. "Press this to summon me. Use it the moment you need aid with anything. Will you do that? Call me for anything at all. It will be no trouble, and I will not be far."

Halla nodded, sighing.

"You will be well cared for," Jeddin said. "I will attempt to find another room for you today. One less inconveniently placed."

She took a deep breath and tried her voice. It shook only a little as she said, "All right."

She closed her eyes and listened to the door shut behind Jeddin and Ormric. The walk from the lift had exhausted her, short as that was, but she stretched out her senses. She could feel the individuals around her in the nearer suites of rooms.

Kim was across the hall.

This particular section, located in the levels of the spire above the south observation deck, seemed designed for provincials, or humans, or perhaps even aliens, without prejudice. The outcaste need for *space* had not factored into its design, and perhaps it could not have been otherwise, considering the difficulties of wresting living space from hard vacuum. She shut her barriers tightly, hoping it would at least relieve him of the burden of her presence. Her eyes hurt. Her heart ached. She was so tired.

Kim stirred, moved toward and through the door of his quarters, and stood outside her door, waiting.

Her stomach clenched. Well. Ready or unready, best to have it done, she decided. *Do not burden him!* she told herself firmly, and checked her barriers. They were as tight as she could make them.

"Come," she said, in wobbly Suralian. A tear rolled down her cheek, and she quickly wiped it away. Another followed, traitorously.

The door slid open. Kim came in. He perched on the arm of the other chair, never taking his eyes off her face.

"Halla," he said softly. He lowered his voice even more. "You are weeping."

"I am tired," she replied. "I told you to stay away."

"You told the door to open for me." A hint of something hopeful shaded his voice.

She lifted her eyes. His were bright with unshed tears.

"I meant none of this to happen," he said. "The more I tried to fix it, the more I hurt you. I never meant to hurt you."

She swallowed hard. "I hurt you too."

He gave her half a smile. A tear finally overflowed and slid down his cheek.

"Look at us," he said.

"Finnic says there are things I cannot hide from a sensitive."

He almost laughed. "That might be true if I could sense you, but you are almost not there." He sighed. "I do not know how to say what I feel for you in Suralian."

Her breath hitched, and she hesitated, but she wanted to know. *Needed* to know. "My heart is yours?" she offered, as if her voice were not shaking, as if her heart were not stuttering in her breast. She had not relaxed her barriers. *Could* not. Not yet.

"My heart is yours," he repeated, swiping at the tears on his cheek.

No. She stopped breathing, as the cruelty of their situation pierced her like a needle to the heart. Each heart given to the other, and his not free. Desolation drove the words from her in a kind of whispering wail. "Why are you telling me this?"

"Because I did a thing." He took a breath. "I—cannot find a Suralian word for it, for the place I served, the scholars' tower at Tau Ceti. And perhaps it is too late now to change anything between us, but I no longer serve them. I am no longer bound to their ethics agreement. If that makes no difference to you now, I understand. But I want you to know that I can continue the project. I can work with you, for the sake of your sanctuaries. I cannot shut my barriers completely as you can, but I will do my best not to burden you with my feelings."

Burden. The word impaled her. She gasped and nearly sobbed.

Something like despair radiated from Kim. "What wrong did I speak this time?"

She shook her head, trying to breathe. Again and again and again, they spoke past each other. Again and again and again, they hurt each other.

"I should leave." He stood. "Before I make this even worse."

If she did not *tell* him, if she did not let him *see*, they would go on hurting each other, again and again and again.

He was almost to the door.

"No!" she cried.

He stopped. Turned. He had sucked one side of his lower lip between his teeth, and tiny flares of hope sparked in his presence.

She softened her barriers, just a little. For anyone but a strong sensitive, it would not be enough to read her, but Kim gasped and moved—not as fast as she could, that day on the beach, but fast enough. Suddenly, he was on one knee beside her chair, his eyes locked on hers.

"Halla," he whispered, his expression full of— Longing? Hope? Both? "Do you mean— Are you—"

His breathing hitched, and he could not seem to continue. She lowered her gaze to his hands. One rested on the arm of her chair, the other on his own knee. She took them both in hers and drew a breath as she returned her gaze to his face.

Kim had closed his eyes. Through his hands, his heartsong resonated into her. Hers, her song, would be flowing into him. As sensitive as he was, he must, he surely must, know now what was in her heart.

Deep within her, something said, *Be happy, my love*, in Tarasheth's voice.

She swallowed hard and let a smile escape onto her lips as she whispered, "My love."

His eyes flew open, wide and startled. A smile curved his lips, echoing the joy beginning to fill his presence, and he leaned forward until their faces were a breath apart. Then, suddenly, he straightened.

"Halla," he said, a tiny line forming between his brows. "Do Tolari —do your people—do they kiss? Touch their lips together?"

It startled a chuckle from her. "Yes. Why?"

"Not all human cultures do."

That sparked Tarasheth's interest. *No*, she thought. *This is not the time!*

"Does yours?" she asked, her voice suddenly rough.

"Yes."

"Then kiss me."

He leaned forward again, said something in soft English, and slanted his lips over hers.

It was very like Tarasheth's first kiss, but for the salt of their mingled tears—the first gentle brush of lips, the tender press, the questing tongue tip. She pulled her hands free and wrapped her arms around Kim's shoulders with as much of her strength as she dared, reveling in the startled thrill of pleasure she sensed go through him. He thrust his hands into her hair and pressed his mouth hard against hers, and that was *not* like Tarasheth. A smile pushed at her lips. He broke the kiss to return it.

"What?" he asked, throatily.

"I want to discover all the ways you are different from my Tarasheth."

His smile widened. "I will be delighted to show you."

* * *

KIM STRETCHED LANGUOROUSLY AND YAWNED. He curled into Halla's side, breathing a sigh onto her shoulder. They were naked on the floor, both of them glowing with contentment—and then the door opened to reveal Finnic and a provincial in yellow. Kim threw his robe over Halla, torn though it was from their initial enthusiasm, because hers had ended up across the room. As he arranged his robe over her, she lifted an amused eyebrow.

"Well," the yellow robe said. "We need not find alternate room assignments after all."

Finnic grinned. "Who could guess that all we needed to do was put them in neighboring quarters?"

"Finnic," Kim warned.

The young man's grin only grew.

Kim stifled a sigh. "I would guess that your yellow-robed friend is here for Halla. Why are *you* here, Finnic?"

"I bear a message from Bertie. He apologizes for not coming himself to tell you, but—" He gestured vaguely around the room. "Jeddin's presence here is bad enough. Bertie's would provoke an outcry, and that would distress everyone."

Kim allowed a reluctant nod. It was surely difficult for the outcaste staff to be pained by Bertie's presence after working so closely with him for so many years. Kim experienced that discomfort now just from the presence of this provincial in yellow, apparently called Jeddin. He filed the name away.

Kim had loved Monralar, those first days after taking the blessing, and while Suralia had been stifling for its lack of privacy, it *felt* otherwise unremarkable. Then on his return to Monralar, Bertie had noticed and pointed out his discomfort, and now? Now just being around the provincials on the station felt like sandpaper, and he shuddered at the idea of going back to a stronghold full of the even more strongly pledged guards. Without knowing how it worked, he had *become* an outcaste.

Finnic was smirking.

"And the message is?" Kim prompted.

"Debt cancelled. You are a free man."

The air left the room. Kim exhaled hard, suddenly lightheaded. If he'd been standing, he might have gone weak at the knees.

"My thanks," he said, on a shallow breath.

Finnic sobered and bowed. "Bertie told me how much this means to you, Kim."

"What does it mean?" Halla asked.

Kim smiled at her.

"We had best go now," Jeddin announced.

"Must we?" asked Finnic.

"Finnic," Halla growled.

He whirled and quick-stepped to the door, Jeddin on his heels. A soft pair of whooshes, and the door opened and closed with the intruders on the other side.

Kim returned his gaze to Halla. *Halla.* He had not expected the intensity of empathic lovemaking, how he could anticipate where she wanted to be touched, how she could anticipate him in the same way. It had been a breathtaking upward spiral of ecstasy. No wonder the Tolari called it *finding joy.* This, *this*, was meant to be a shadow of what pair-bonded couples experienced?

He found that damned near impossible to believe, but Halla had explained about her ruptured bond with Tarasheth and *apologized* that she couldn't give more. *More?* How could there be more? Making love to Halla was already *more* than he had ever dreamed lovemaking could be. It was everything he wanted and needed. *More* would be too much.

CHRISTIE MEIERZ

He pulled the robe slowly away from her long body, exposing warm brown skin. *Magnificent.* And *his*. And wearing a suggestive smile.

"Again, so soon?" he asked, but his own lips shaped an unbidden smile.

"Do you remember the Sural's words?" she said in reply. "Grand-children of the Jorann possess strong passions. But if you find you cannot keep pace with me, I can call Finnic." An eyebrow twitched.

"Oh, I can keep pace with you," he growled.

For her, he would *make* that be true.

CHAPTER 28

A night of joy magnified her stomach's appetite, Halla thought, as she waited at a table in the staff cafeteria. She had forgotten it during the years of grief and pain, although Tarasheth had often teased her about it during their time together. Suppressing another complaint from her midsection, she watched Kim and Ormric make their way through the serving lines on her behalf as well as their own. Finally the two returned, bearing trays and mugs, and it took all her self-control not to snatch the food they offered and devour it like a starving child. To judge by the amusement sparkling in Kim's presence, she did not entirely succeed in concealing her eagerness to eat.

As the worst of the hunger subsided, Aran walked in, an ancient woman in colorful clothing on one arm and an equally ancient man in much plainer colors on the other. Kim jumped up to take the arm of the woman, who gazed up at him with such love and happiness glowing in her presence that for a moment Halla could scarcely breathe. The two elders could only be Kim's grandparents.

When they reached the table, Kim settled them in the places across from Halla, then took the seat beside her.

"*Babayi, mamani,*" he said, looking at each of his grandparents as he

243

said the words, and those were the only words Halla could decipher. Names, perhaps, or titles? He continued in English, until he indicated her with a hand and said, continuing in Suralian, "Halla. Halla, these are my grandparents, Hassan and Sadira."

Halla pronounced the names carefully. "Hassan. Sadira." She gave each of them a seated bow.

Hassan nodded, smiling gently, and Sadira cupped her hands together in front of her.

Finnic arrived with a tray full of steaming mugs. He placed it on the table and dropped into the chair on the other side of Kim, while Aran and Ormric laid down trays of food before the elders and took seats on each side of them.

"Finnic!" the young man announced, patting his chest and adding some English. Then he said to Halla, "The tea is safe for humans."

Aran said the same of the food, and added some English of his own, while smiling all around the table.

Halla really needed that implant *now*.

The old woman's gaze flicked from Halla to Kim and back again. Then she smiled brilliantly and said something in English to Kim. He answered intensely, and at length, while both elders listened, their white eyebrows rising steadily. After Kim finished, his grandmother put a hand to her heart, met Halla's gaze, and spoke a few words.

Kim froze.

Finnic broke into another grin. "She is very perceptive. I can see where you acquired your sensitivity, Kim."

"What did she say?" Halla asked.

Kim took a breath and smiled up at her. *"Welcome to the family."*

* * *

"YOUR OUTCASTES," Hassan said as he settled into a chair by the viewscreen in Kim's quarters. "They are much like us."

"A pity they walk on their planet," Sadira added.

"There is hope for the ones who live here. They have time to learn better ways."

Kim grinned as he handed them mugs of hot tea, sweet and fragrant, and perched on the arm of his grandmother's chair. He'd need more seating if his grandparents intended to visit often, but he was grateful for the distraction of their company. Halla was in Medical getting her English implant. Apparently Bertie had had a part in that, though Kim wasn't quite sure how. It weighed on his mind that she might wake to the kind of pain he'd experienced from his implant. It was apparently a common side effect, although not universal. He hoped she would escape it.

"None of the men have beards," Hassan grumbled, interrupting his musing.

"Tolari don't grow beards at all," Kim replied. "They can't."

"And where is yours, navam?"

"Eaten by nanites."

"*Ekh!*" Hassan shivered as if disgusted, but beneath it he was unperturbed. "What did they teach you growing up in that government place?"

Kim shrugged. "Government ways."

Sadira patted his hand. "You poor thing," she said. "But tell us about this outcaste lady of yours, Karim. This Halla."

"Hm." Kim couldn't suppress the smile. "You saw her. What do *you* think?"

"She is a lot of woman," said Hassan. "And older than she looks. Older than you, I can tell, but not so old as we are."

"Y-yes," Kim replied, slowly. Not only was Finnic right about his grandmother's perceptiveness, his grandfather shared it. And, Kim could add to that, they were *clever*. "Tolari live longer than we do."

"How much longer?" Sadira asked.

Kim took a breath. "About twice as long."

"Merciful Allah! She will lose you one day, then, most likely."

"No, I—" he blurted, before he could stop himself.

His grandparents shared a look. "And how is she not to lose you, if she can live to twice *our* years?" said Hassan. It was much more of a demand than a question, although his voice remained gentle.

"I..." Kim paused, and closed his eyes. How did Sayyar feel about gen mods? Would they reject him for having taken one? He wracked his memory, kicking himself for his sheer cussedness in passing over articles about the Sayyar in his professional subscriptions, and silently admitted that he couldn't remember what little he *had* read. Steeling himself, he said, "Tolari have a gen mod. It both heals and extends lifespans, and...I took it."

He held his breath.

"Ah," said Sadira, and Kim loosed the breath in a gust when her glowing presence filled with amusement rather than rejection. "That is well then. A long life together is a treasure." She gazed at Hassan, then chuckled like a rusty hinge. "A blessing from Allah, your grandfather will say. And you thought we would shun you for it."

"So little you know," Hassan added.

"How can he know us, or our people's ways?" Sadira chided.

Hassan's laugh sounded like tumbling gravel. "More of us are coming here soon. Are you sure you do not want a proper Sayyar girl?"

The tension drained out of Kim. He smiled. "I'm sure, babayi. I would outlive a Sayyar woman by too much."

Hassan grunted. "Not if she too takes this Tolari gen mod you mention, but no matter. We can see how it is with you and your outcaste lady. That one is enough to keep anyone busy."

Sadira chuckled, then sobered. "Karim. We are keeping you here when you have work to do. That Aran fellow, he told us about your project. You should go to it."

"No! Mamani, no, I..." He swallowed. "I don't have to leave right away. You saw Halla. She was badly injured recently and needs time to heal. So it's not urgent, and I don't want to lose a moment of the time we have together, the three of us."

"Your Tolari outcastes are taking good care of us."

"They give us plenty of food," Hassan added placidly. "And we had the pick of the best places to sleep because we are first."

"Aafreen was first," Sadira said. "The others who came with her moved on, poor child."

"Aafreen is the stationmaster. She has *quarters*. That does not count."

Kim interrupted their gentle bickering. "But there's so much I want to know. About you, about my parents, about our family. Everything! We'll need all the time we can get."

Sadira pondered that. "He makes a good argument, *azizam*. You know my heart is not good."

Kim started. "What?" He slipped off the arm of her chair and onto his knees.

"Did you think that people as old as we are would be in perfect health?" She patted his hand. "We will not fall dead tomorrow, and we are content now that we know you, navam."

"I won't leave you, mamani. Maybe if you were younger and stronger, but not like this. I said I'd take care of you. I keep my word."

"Ah, that would be Armon speaking," said Hassan. "I wondered what your father might have given you, other than his clever mind."

"You should not worry about us," Sadira said, solemnly. "We have our ways."

*   *   *

"Halla will sleep a little longer," the head apothecary said when Kim showed up in Medical a few hours later. "She is well."

"Good," Kim said. "But I came about my grandparents. Just how bad is my grandmother's health?"

"It is a deterioration brought on by age more than by illness." The head apothecary glowered from behind the desk in his office, sparking with irritation that Kim had found someone willing to help him barge into Medical unbidden after Aran took his grandparents off to whatever Sayyar bolt hole they had chosen. "As for why you were not told—there has scarcely been an opportunity. You *are* the son of their heir, however. The results of a quick scan I bullied them into when they arrived showed that your grandmother—" He shook his head. "Her condition is, as I said, deteriorating, though slowly. She refused our offer of treatment, saying that her people use their own medicines. The substance she takes is not without virtue, and it is likely the reason she still lives. However, it will not heal her, and although she is in no immediate danger, I am uncertain how long it can keep her alive."

Kim's stomach sank. "Are you sure?"

"I am. Your grandfather is in better health. He is frail, but absent significant trauma, he may live for years more, assuming losing your grandmother does not shock him into the dark, as can happen with elders who have lived so long a life together." The apothecary took a deep breath and visibly gentled his manner. "Scholar. I cannot predict how much life is left to your grandmother. She may keep herself alive for years by force of will. But I recommend that you spend as much time with her as you can."

CHAPTER 29

T he apothecaries told Halla she would likely wake up with a headache, but with such a headache? She had not expected this.

"How do you feel?"

The voice, and the presence, belonged to the head apothecary. She gazed up at him blearily, and at Ormric standing beside him, and winced. "Surely you already know."

Both of them chuckled.

"Indeed, I do know," the apothecary said.

She frowned. Something was not right. Her eyes went wide on the realization of what it was.

"You speak English," she said. "And I understand it. I speak it!"

She got her elbows underneath her, groaning as her head pounded all the harder. Ormric held out a potion cup, and she grimaced at its bitter scent as she took it from them. The liquid tasted as vile as its smell, but her headache began to dim by the time she choked down the last of it.

The apothecary took out a scanner and tablet. He ran the scanner slowly around her head, then nodded and moved down to her legs.

"Astonishing," he murmured, still speaking English, then straightened. "Your injuries appear tens of days older and more healed than one could normally expect so soon. I simply *must* learn how this technology works." He pocketed his tablet and scanner. "I am obligated to tell you not to engage in strenuous exercise or lift heavy objects for the next ten days, but I believe you are at little risk of such behavior. Take a meal as soon as you may, and speak as much English as possible. You will have numerous opportunities for practice here."

He swept from the room. A moment later, he swept back in.

"Oh, and tell your lover that if he tricks his way into Medical again, I will ask Security to arrest him."

The apothecary turned and was gone.

"Kim what?" she asked Ormric, still speaking English. "Why?"

"He discovered his grandmother is in poor health and convinced an aide to admit him in order to confront the head apothecary about it."

"How bad?"

"Her heart is deteriorating, but she refuses our apothecaries' offers of treatment. She prefers the medicines of her own people, which are not sufficient to sustain her."

"*Daakh.*" Grimacing, she pushed herself up and used her arms to swing her legs over the side of the treatment bed, one at a time. The pain in her head had subsided now, and she had to see Kim. Such news had surely upset him.

"Aishyn expects you to take a meal," Ormric said. "You need to eat."

"I need to see Kim." She stared at Ormric until they frowned.

"Will you agree to come with me and take some food if I send him a message to meet us in the spire cafeteria?"

It was a better compromise than she expected. Letting out a breath, she said, "Yes."

Silently, Ormric offered her the walking sticks and supported her as best they could while she levered herself up to stand. In the cafeteria, Halla was not surprised to find Kim already present and pacing between the tables. The room was beginning to fill, with staff arriving in small groups as the middle of station day and the time for "lunch" approached. She rolled the English word for the midday meal around her head and waved Ormric toward the food as Kim came to take her arm.

"My grandparents think I should leave here and be about my work," he said in a pained voice, as he led her toward a nearby empty table. "I told them we cannot leave before you have recovered from your injury."

He had spoken Suralian, she realized.

"What did they say to that?" she asked, in slow English, as she eased herself into a chair that was too small and too low for a person of her height.

He smiled luminously, but some chagrin lit his presence. He leaned a hip against the table. "How do you feel?" he responded, speaking English now.

"Good. My head is not painful. How do *you* feel?"

He sighed. "I wish I'd met my grandparents sooner. My grandmother is, well, the way we put it is that her age is catching up with her. She could live longer if she would just let the apothecaries take care of her."

"Ormric told me."

"I know that I'm lucky to have any time at all with them. I can never thank Bertie enough for that." He puffed out a breath and shook his head. A small smile, a mix of delight and disbelief, lit his face. "I have a family. A *family*."

Ormric returned with an overflowing tray in one hand and a steaming mug in the other, and placed both on the table before her.

"Will you ensure that she eats?" they asked Kim, whose reply was a firm nod.

Halla felt no hunger, not yet, but resolve was forming in her lover and determination colored her aide and, after all, she *had* agreed to eat. She sighed lightly and reached for a roll. Ormric offered them both a bow, then strode away.

"I didn't want to eat either, right after my implant," Kim said, who remained standing, one hip against the edge of the table. "But I felt better for it after I did."

She nodded, chewing, and their gazes locked. Then he flared with

251

delight and looked behind her, the smile beaming now, and she needed no empathy to realize his grandparents had arrived. She turned to see them once more on Aran's arms, making their way across the room at Sadira's shuffling pace. As before, Kim rushed over to take his grandmother from Aran, this time settling her in the chair next to Halla. Hassan took a seat across the table, while Aran and Kim headed off for another round at the food.

"Good afternoon," Halla said.

Sadira smiled brightly. Hassan started.

"You speak English?" he asked.

"I received an implant today in the morning."

"How wonderful!" Sadira said. "That will make it easier for Kim to teach English to your children."

Halla took a breath, and bit down on her lip as she let it out.

Sadira's wrinkles deepened, and dismay filled her emotional landscape. "You do not plan children?" she asked, her voice neutral but enunciating each word carefully.

"No, grandmother," Halla replied. "It would be—" She hesitated. This was not the time or the place to explain, in a public room that was loud and growing louder. "No. I regret."

Sadira patted her hand, imparting sharp disappointment through the touch, but whatever the elder had been about to say was interrupted by the return of Kim and Aran with steaming mugs and trays of food, and then eating overrode conversation for a time. Halla watched, and noticed Hassan and Sadira exchanging frequent looks, but what those meant, she could not guess.

After the meal, the elders pled exhaustion and bade Kim to remain with Halla while Aran took them to their sleeping place. Kim seemed to take it as an opportunity and led her to his quarters, where her injury was no impediment to proving what the Sural had said about the more intimate aspects of a triggered Grandchild's life.

And, she reflected as they lay in mutual contentment, a sleeping mat was a far more comfortable place to find joy than a chair. Or a floor. They had tried both, the first time. And other things as well. For most of the afternoon.

Kim chuckled, as if he knew where her thoughts had gone. She touched his lips with the tip of a forefinger.

"Kim?"

"Hm?"

"What did you say before you kissed me the first time?"

He kissed the finger and smiled. Then he said, slowly, "You are magnificent."

She smiled back, but he frowned, and swiveled his face toward the hall outside his quarters, and then she sensed it too: an urgent presence, unfamiliar to her. No, two presences, and one was Ormric, and there was an emergency looming, from the feel of them. Kim jumped up from the sleeping mat and threw on a robe, casting a worried look back and a quick, "Sorry!" as he hurried out of the sleeping room.

A soft whoosh of the door to the hall opening, and Ormric's voice. "Your grandparents are in Medical. You need to go there. Now."

She sensed something close to panic grip Kim.

"I will assist Halla," Ormric added. "Go."

Kim rushed away with the other presence. Ormric appeared in the sleeping room doorway.

"What happened?" she asked.

"Aafreen found both Kim's grandparents unconscious in their sleeping place," they said. "That is all I know."

* * *

"How the hell did my grandparents get hold of the blessing?" Kim demanded. *How could this happen?* "I thought you didn't have enough to spare!"

Kim took a deep breath, trying to get a grip on his temper, and stared down at Hassan and Sadira lying on adjacent treatment beds. By all appearances, they were sound asleep.

"We do not, in fact, have enough to spare," the head apothecary said. Truth rang in his voice. "*We* did not give it to them, and we do not know who did."

"Will they survive?" asked a grim Aafreen.

The apothecary blew out a breath. "Hassan, yes. He is progressing normally. Sadira—" he grimaced.

"What?" Kim said. "What about my grandmother?"

"Scholar, we know little of this process. In Suralia or Parania they might know more."

"What. About. Sadira."

The man pressed his lips together. "You can see for yourself. Her glow has dimmed substantially. It is my understanding that this also happened to the beloved of Parania. We communicated with the Paran's apothecaries, but the records they sent were a mere outline, a scholar's notes. They say that we can expect her glow to continue dimming and can only hope that it flares back to normal, as did that of the Paran's beloved before she woke. Until then, all we can do is provide support to her somatic processes and monitor her condition."

Kim closed his eyes. The difference between his grandparents was stark. His grandfather was, if anything, a little brighter than he had been. His grandmother was significantly less luminous. Nothing stirred in either of them.

"Damn," he said, as he opened his eyes. "Why do you know so little?"

"Of a normal conversion, we know more. Our apothecaries in Monralar monitored two closely—those of the guard Bertie and the farmer Neera. Your conversion to a sensitive was also closely observed, and while you slept overlong, our Monral's apothecary reported no dimming. But the Jorann herself gave the blessing to the Paran's beloved. We have only the observations of a scholar who was present."

Kim grunted. "I'll keep watch, then."

"Kim, it could be hours," Aafreen said. "We have no information on when they took it. It could have been right after lunch. It could have been just before I found them."

"Then I'll read to them. I'm sure I have your holy book somewhere in my tablet."

She sighed. "I can stay with you for a short time. Aishyn, let us have the room, please. For just a few minutes."

The Tolari apothecary grumbled, but left, motioning the nurse and his aide to follow.

After the door shut behind them, Kim asked, "How did they get it? I assume that's why you cleared the room. So tell me."

"You're one of us," she said. "You were raised by the government, but you're one of us. And you've begun to act the way the outcastes do toward provincials."

Kim peered at her sidelong. "What does that have to do with anything?"

"Do you feel it, the same irritation that they do?"

"Why is that important?"

"Because I need to know if I can trust you."

"You can trust me."

"Then tell me if provincials irritate you as they do the outcastes."

"*Why?*"

"Because if you're one of them *and* one of us, even if only partially in both cases, maybe I really can trust you."

"You can trust me, but not for any of those reasons," he said. He stood between the beds and placed each hand on a thin shoulder. "These are my *grandparents*, Aafreen. Do you understand what that means to an orphan? What it means to see the way they glow with love when they look at me?"

Aafreen nodded. "I can guess."

"No matter what they've done, I won't do anything to harm them. Or your people, either."

She fell silent for a few moments.

"We have an understanding with the Den," she said, slowly. "We Sayyar."

An *understanding*. With the race that built a majority of the Trade Alliance orbital stations. He wasn't sure he liked where this might be going.

"I know you have bolt holes," he said. "Everyone knows that."

Her niqab puffed. She continued, more softly, "Every station the Den build also has access points, and we know how to find them. Every deck, every section. I checked the accesses into Medical. Your grandfather must have used one to take some of the blessing they have here. Two pieces of it."

"Damn."

"Kim, what I need to know is, how did he know where to look for it, and how did he know what it does?"

Kim clamped his jaw. *My fault.* "He asked me what the gen mod does. I told him. But I didn't tell him where to find it, because I don't know, and I didn't encourage him to steal any, either."

"That explains this then." She pulled a folded sheet of official stationery from a pocket and handed it to him.

He unfolded the paper to find it covered in spidery handwriting.

Karim, our beloved grandson,

How wonderful it is to write such words as we had given up all hope of writing! But God is merciful and gave you back to us as a comfort for our remaining years. We dared to hope also that we would live to see your children in such time as we have left, but now we know there will be none.

So we have begged Allah's forgiveness. Not for taking the little cubes of the genetic change, for what does not belong to our God? And what will Allah not give to faithful pilgrims? No, we beg forgiveness for wishing to live longer than our allotted time and to seek healing that our own medicines cannot give. For perhaps if this Tolari healing does not kill us, God will give your grandmother fecundity in a second youth and we may keep our family line from ending. That will be our last prayer before we put the little cubes in our mouths.

We know you do not pray, beloved grandson, but we

beg you, do pray for this one thing, this one time: for our family.

Hassan, sayyar

"Oh babayi," Kim murmured as he lowered the paper. He met Aafreen's worried eyes. "How is it the apothecaries didn't sense him?"

"Station security puts guards on the outside of Medical, not the inside," she replied. "The accesses are in the supply rooms, well away from the labs and treatment areas. I will seal them so this cannot happen again, but if the apothecaries find out how your grandfather obtained the blessing, Tolar will ban Sayyar from the station and send your grandparents back to Satendra."

"Like hell they will—!" He took a deep breath. "I won't say a word."

"Thank you. Good." She planted her hands on her knees and pushed herself to her feet, all business once more. "I have to get back to work. I'll have a tray and some tea sent in. You're missing the evening meal."

* * *

KIM HAD BEEN READING to his sleeping grandparents for fifty-eight minutes and forty-two seconds when a nurse came in, leaving the door open behind her. He bookmarked his place. The nurse bent over his grandmother now, scanning her. Her glow was feeble and still growing dimmer.

He reached for her hand. It was dry and papery in his clasp, and when he looked up, she was there, standing at the head of her bed, out of her body the way he had been after taking the blessing in Monralar. He must be seeing her now as Jeryneth had once seen him.

"Mamani!" he exclaimed.

The nurse straightened and looked around. "Scholar?"

"She's here, can't you see her? Standing right *there*." He pointed.

Sadira smiled. "My beloved grandson. I am so happy to have known you."

"Mamani, open your eyes. Get back in your body. Just open your eyes. Please."

"It is time for me to go, Karim. Tell your grandfather," and she smiled down at Hassan, "that I want him to give you aunts and uncles so you can have cousins."

"No!"

A blinding flash filled the room, and even the nurse ran a hand across her eyes. His grandfather jerked and stirred. Then his grandmother was gone.

Her glow was extinguished.

Hassan opened his eyes and coughed a little. Then he sat up, easily. He smiled and looked toward Sadira, and the smile fell from his face.

"No," he whispered.

Kim went to him.

"I tried," he said, putting his arms around his grandfather, shielding him from the sight of his wife on the other side. "I told her to open her eyes. She refused. She said it was time for her to go. And then she was," he swallowed, "and then she was gone."

Hassan's shoulders began to shake. He wept softly, holding onto Kim while Kim's own eyes streamed.

"I'm so sorry, babayi. I'm so, so sorry. I couldn't convince her to stay."

CHAPTER 30

*T*he arrangements for his grandmother felt rushed to Kim's sensibilities, but Sayyar custom dictated that her funeral take place the following day, even if the station lacked one of their holy men to lead it. The service itself was short, and by his grandfather's choice, sparsely attended, but Hassan permitted Halla into the hidden Sayyar areas with Kim and Aafreen. They sat quietly on their heels next to the bier on which Sadira lay swaddled in white sheeting, while Hassan, too early in the rejuvenation to have changed much in appearance, murmured prayers in the language of his people.

After the prayers, Aran received the body and took it to the station's fusion reactor, aided by a stretcher from Medical. There, a brown-robed Monrali engineer reduced it to dust and gathered the dust into a red crystal jar the station apothecaries had provided. They called it a *sending jar*, and a Sayyar symbol, a circle of nine mandorlas enclosing a stylized star, had been etched into its surface. Hassan received it in silence and led the small procession from the core of the station all the way to the restricted docks, where a Tolari tradeship waited for them. The jar's final destination, as Kim understood it, was a place the Sayyar called the Heart of God, said to be about one week's travel away in a direction neither Hassan nor Aafreen would reveal.

Aafreen had allowed as how outsiders were permitted to attend the disposition of Sadira's remains, though it was rare and unusual, but Halla couldn't spend so much time away from her therapies. She also couldn't manage the procession to the dock and dropped out early along the way, using her call-bracelet to send for Ormric. Kim felt her absence keenly as he continued on, trailing a pace behind his grandfather, with only Aafreen at his side. As they reached the dock, she too dropped back with a murmur and a bow. The two-week journey was longer than the stationmaster felt comfortable leaving the station.

The ship was, Kim had been told, one of the smallest in the fleet. It was milky white, jellyfish-shaped, and dotted with translucent patches that resembled portholes. A solemn mood soaked the air as he and Hassan approached the airlock. His grandfather didn't seem to notice it and walked straight inside. Kim's stride hitched as his foot touched the vessel's—deck?—and the enormity of the creature over-whelmed his senses. The solemn mood, it seemed, emanated from the *ship*.

Before he could gasp, his awareness of the entity faded to a more tolerable level and became grave but welcoming. He had wondered what it would be like to board a living ship. He had never imagined what it could be like to do so as an empathic sensitive. It had wrapped a sort of shield around him, to protect him, but whether that was out of consideration or from a desire not to crush him senseless, Kim didn't know.

As he stepped fully into the open area just inside the airlock, the inner door sealed like skin, leaving no trace of an opening behind. Surprisingly, or perhaps he shouldn't have been surprised, the air within the ship was fresh and clean-smelling. Ahead of him, Hassan had stopped, clutching the jar close and glancing about with small sparks of curiosity peeking through the ravaged grief. Two outcastes stood to one side, a very young man and a greying one, representing the crew of six.

The greying man, a sensitive with sharp features, hair trimmed to chin length, and an air of authority, stepped forward and bowed. "I am

Ofek, guide to this vessel," he said in English. "Tuvyn will show you to a place where you may rest."

"This way, grandfather," said the younger outcaste, gently.

Hassan turned slightly. "Karim?"

"Rest, babayi. I'll join you later."

Ofek eyed Kim with a lifted brow, but said nothing until after Hassan left with the younger man.

"Do you have a concern, scholar?" Ofek asked.

At the sound of the title, Kim flicked a glance at himself, but no, he wore an outcaste's grey robe over his usual clothes.

The guide chuckled ruefully. "Forgive me. You were made known to us as a scholar from among the humans. Does it offend you to be called so?"

Did it? Kim rubbed the back of his neck. "Not...exactly. But I've become one of you. Perhaps it's best not to call me that. I have no caste to speak of, and my hair will grow no longer than it is today."

"Of course, Karim."

"Kim."

"Kim?" Ofek nodded. "Yes, I was told this name. I make no end of missteps today! So I will inform you straightaway that my ship likes you, but also that it is time for us to depart. Your grandfather, as the vessel shows me, is exhausted and already begins a journey to the far shores of sleep. As an apology for my stumbling, would you care to come with me to the control room to witness the drop into K-space from there?"

Kim sucked in a breath. "Oh yes. I'd like that very much."

* * *

KIM DIDN'T KNOW where the Heart of God might be located. No one had said, and he'd not asked since he had the feeling he shouldn't. Tuvyn remarked, on their second "day" in K-space, that other than Hassan, only Ofek knew where they were headed, but that Ofek could be trusted not to risk ship or crew. He was, the young man said, a very careful guide.

Hassan avoided any mention of their intended destination, and when he spoke at all talked mainly of his life growing up on Al-Kindi Station in the Epsilon Eridani system. Coming from the most conservative station in human space made sense of his plain-colored clothing, which contrasted sharply with the vibrant Swan Hindi fabrics Sadira had worn. Hassan had traveled to Far India's Satendra Platform for work, just as Kim's mother had traveled from Satendra to Liaonang. Was it clan exogamy? Or merely nomadic wandering? He didn't know enough to even speculate, but he discovered through the stories that his grandfather had been something of a troublemaker as a young man, once using the secret access points to prank Al-Kindi stationers so thoroughly that some still believed one of the docks to be haunted by a mischievous djinn. A few times Hassan smiled as he told the stories, or even chuckled, but he cradled the precious jar at all times, even when he slept. Kim refrained from remarking on it. His grandfather's senses were so tightly wrapped around his grandmother's dust that it was probably a futile gesture to prise it away from him before he relinquished it to the Heart of God.

And meanwhile, Hassan slowly grew younger in appearance. The second day, his deep wrinkles were less pronounced. He walked like a young man by the third day, when they came out of K-space for a few hours to rest at an unspecified star so that the ship could feed. By the fourth, Hassan's bald head showed the dark roots of new hair and his beard was no longer white but smoky grey. How *that* was possible, when human hair wasn't even composed of living cells, Kim couldn't begin to understand. It was all frankly impossible.

And to think that when he arrived at Tolar Trade Station, he'd thought that ship-creatures living in hard vacuum didn't make sense. The living ships were easy to understand compared to the blessing, which did things that defied not only reason, but physics itself.

Well, and perhaps that was why the Tolari called this gift of their equally impossible Jorann her *blessing*. They were the ones who knew, after all. Whether she was one of the original Tolari or not, he owed the purportedly ancient woman a debt of gratitude for saving Halla's life.

On the seventh day, Ofek came to Hassan to tell him, and Kim with him, that they had arrived at their destination.

"Will you wish to go now, how do you say, to the observation dome?" the guide asked, from the door of the small space assigned to them for a sleeping room.

Hassan's presence, still sharp and spiky with grief, filled with longing. "Yes," he said, and that was sufficient.

Kim had learned enough from his grandfather's stories to scoop up the neat roll of Hassan's prayer rug before following Ofek. The three of them made their way up through the ship's compartmented levels, from the lowest, where they were quartered with the crew, to the highest, where a dome crowned the ship's jellyfish-like bell. As they entered the arched, open space, the ship's skin cleared from opaque to nearly as transparent as glass, revealing the intense black void of K-space.

It wasn't entirely black, not to Kim's senses. Rather, it was layered, and the layers glowed enough to overlay his physical vision, as if space itself were alive.

Hassan approached the bulkhead and stopped, head bowed over the crystal jar. Kim unrolled the prayer rug and smoothed it on the deck beside him.

Ofek remained in the center of the room. "Will you wish to keep the sending jar?" he asked, in a quiet voice.

Hassan shook his head. His cheeks were wet. So were Kim's.

"Touch it to the skin of my vessel, when you are ready."

Hassan murmured something in a reverent tone, in his antique Persian. Then he bowed deeply. Kim copied him, uncertain what he was bowing *to*, as his grandfather shifted the jar from its clutch against his chest into cupped hands and offered it to the ship.

The transparent bulkhead...sucked in the jar, slowly. The crystal dissolved as it went, or at least, that was how it looked to Kim. When the last of the red vanished into the ship's translucence, a puff of dust appeared in the vacuum outside. Seconds later, the bulkheads and dome clouded to white.

Hassan dropped to his knees on the prayer rug and bowed down until his head touched its soft weave. Lacking a prayer rug of his own, Kim remained standing, hoping it was enough just to be there while his grandfather quietly wept his prayers and Kim's own eyes streamed. Behind them, Ofek hadn't moved from his spot, silent and, Kim suspected, communicating with his vessel. The ship still shielded Kim from itself, allowing him only a sense of its grave mood, and that led him to wonder if these creatures were more intelligent than their Tolari pilots thought.

Finally, Hassan finished his prayers and sat back on his heels, pulling a cloth from a pocket and using it to wipe his face. Kim offered a hand. His grandfather took it.

"Navam," he said as he rose to his feet. "It is time to go home."

* * *

HALLA BOUNCED ON HER HEELS—ONCE, twice, a third time, before the muscles in her lower legs complained. That she *could* perform even so small an act as this was nevertheless cause for delight. That she had shed her walking sticks and now needed only a staff for support was a source of amazement even to Jeddin. Her recovery had outpaced his every prediction.

She bounced again. Through the disappointingly small viewports of the restricted dock where she stood, white eclipsed the view of Tolar as the living ship bearing Kim and his grandfather crept toward the airlock. Beside her, Finnic flared with amusement.

"Patience," he murmured, in the language of Sacaea.

She muttered a Sacaean aphorism about children who admonish their elders. Finnic grinned up at her, all teeth and sparkles.

A gentle sound like a bolster falling to the floor came from the airlock, and now Halla could sense presences on the other side of it. One was Hassan, grief-laden and bereft in a way she recognized all too well. Another was Kim, whose bereavement was overlain with scintillating anticipation. Her own heart lifted at the feel of it. *He still wants me.*

Finnic made a sound that might have been a hiccough, but too much happiness sang through her now to spare him another frown, and besides that, an almost painfully wide smile had taken over her face. She could not have frowned had she wished it.

The airlock spun open.

Hassan stepped out first, his appearance greatly changed by the black stubble on his head and the thick grey hair adorning a less wrinkled face, his gait marked by both the ease of youth and the dignity of age. As he cleared the opening, Kim slipped around his grandfather, dropped the bags he was carrying, and rushed into her arms—or rather, her extended free arm. His presence bubbled with joy and his heart's song hummed through her senses. She gave herself up to the beauty of it, eyes closed, as they held each other. *His heart is still mine!*

Finnic coughed.

She opened her eyes. Kim sighed lightly and drew back from her embrace.

"Finnic," he said, and offered as easy an outcaste's bow as if he had practiced it all his life. Halla's heart swelled.

"You do well to be proud of our Karim," Hassan said, his voice resonant and lacking any sign of its former quaver.

"Babayi." She bowed, although that was still a challenge, even holding firmly to her staff. "Aafreen sends regrets for her absence. She is consumed by urgent matters of the station."

He smiled gently. "Navam." He glanced around the dock. "Have my people begun to arrive yet?"

"Yes," Finnic replied. "Only a few, so far, but they arrived saying the call has gone out. Some came from a place called Satendra, some from another place called Al-Kindi, and some from..." He paused, then continued, "Capella Free Station. Those just arrived yesterday. Aafreen told me to let you know she saved your sleeping place."

Halla sensed a pang shoot through Hassan, and Kim laid a gentle hand on his shoulder.

"Ah. I shall have to think on that. Perhaps I will choose another place to sleep."

* * *

A MONTH after their return from the Heart of God—or three tens of days, as the Tolari would have it—the project was finally a go.

Kim planted his hands on his hips and glanced through the sparkling safety field at the departing supply shuttle. It had left the bay littered, and in some cases smeared, with bits of organic material, mainly escaped from the open crates of food that had gone into it. By comparison, the space around Monralar's A'aan' vehicle was a marvel of cleanliness, despite the disorder of medical supply boxes outside its back hatch. Pack those in, and they were ready to go. Finnic was already handing the first box in to Halla.

The three of them were as fully briefed as had been practical, considering the breadth of Halla's globetrotting experience. She had spent a year, usually two, and sometimes three, in each of the seventeen sanctuaries, and those were Tolar years. It added up to something on the order of seventy standard years, which impressed Kim's grandfather. It made her not much younger than he was.

Then, astonishingly, the station's head apothecary cleared her for travel, before she'd managed to impart more than a general idea of a mere half dozen sanctuaries, and regardless of the Sural's preference for nearby Sanctuary Triss, their starting point was Sacaea.

Guilt pricked at Kim as he joined Finnic and picked up a box. He still hadn't told Hassan of Sadira's last words.

The cleaning crew bustled in, carrying general cleaning equipment along with decontamination supplies to remove the organic debris. Near the back of the pack of grey robes was a cream-colored tunic.

"Babayi!" Kim called.

His grandfather changed course, shaking a finger. "Now Karim," he said, in a scolding tone of voice, "I have told you that you cannot call me that anymore. We look the same age."

"I will never call you anything else." Kim wrapped him in a warm hug, then stepped back. "And your beard gives you ten years on me, at least."

"No excuses!" Hassan tried to give him a stern look through the glow of pride.

Kim grinned, then sobered. "Babayi. Will you be all right up here by yourself? I don't like leaving you alone so soon."

"We talked about this, navam. I am not alone since the new ones arrived."

"All right, but you don't have to stay so busy. You can take some time."

"Since I can work, I will work," Hassan said. "It helps to pass the time. Today I will clean the shuttle bay after you heathen world-walkers finish dirtying it up."

Kim shook his head. Halla stuck hers out the hatch. The rest of her followed.

"Babayi!" she called.

"Merciful Allah, the pair of you. Call me *brother,* not *grandfather!*"

"Babayi," Finnic said, laughing. "The others think we make fun of you for being so old-fashioned."

"Old-fashioned? Is that what the new ones say about me behind my back?"

Kim snorted. "It's the *first* thing they say about you behind your back."

Hassan grumbled. "Well, perhaps they need an example of good manners then."

"There you go," said Bertie, as he climbed out of the shuttle. "The perfect job for you, sir. The rest of you hurry up or I will never get home in time for supper."

Halla snickered. Bertie aimed a swat at her, and suddenly she was on the other side of him. He whirled.

"You're a menace," he said. "But I'd love to teach you a few moves—"

"No!" Halla, Kim, and Finnic shouted, in unison.

"The last thing she needs is to move the way a provincial guard does," Kim added.

Bertie shook his head regretfully. "Good point. But *my* point still stands. The journey of a thousand kilometers—or 400 straight down, anyway—begins by getting out of this shuttle bay. Back to work! Vai-vai!"

"Sir, yes sir!" Kim saluted and picked up the box containing Halla's medical mesh, which she no longer needed, although she clung to using her staff, intricately carved and as tall as she was. The box, surprisingly light, would go back to Monralar with Bertie. He handed it in to Finnic, and turned for the next box—and there was no next box.

"We're packed!" he called out.

Slow claps greeted him. He'd once seen a social history of *that* gesture—hard to believe, but the sourcework looked sound.

"Everyone's a comedian," he muttered. He shook his head and rejoined Hassan at the wall, where the cleaning crew waited. "Babayi," he said, when he caught up.

Hassan put his hands over his own heart. "I will miss you, navam."

"I'll miss you too, babayi." Kim squared his shoulders in an attempt to firm his resolve. His grandfather was still deep in mourning. *It's too soon to speak of such things*, he thought, but this was his last opportunity to speak with his grandfather face-to-face for months to come. He'd procrastinated long enough.

"There was one more thing that mamani said before she left that you should know, even if you don't like it."

"Very well. Tell me."

Kim drew a deep breath and said it all in a rush. "She wants you to give me aunts and uncles so that I can have cousins."

Hassan sputtered.

"I'm sorry, but that *is* what she—"

The laugh cracked the air, startling Kim.

After taking a few breaths to calm himself, Hassan said, "She gave me *permission?*"

"Uh," Kim replied. "Yes?"

"Merciful Allah. I will *miss* that woman. Come here." Hassan pulled him into a bear hug. "Ah Karim. I will miss you so very much too. Go, do your work well, and remember us."

"All a-*board!*" Bertie shouted from the back of the shuttle.

"I will," Kim said, pulling back from the hug. "I had better go. He'll turn into a carnival barker next."

Hassan smiled, eyes shining. "Farewell, navam. May God protect you down there."

"Next stop, *Sanctuary Sacaea!*" Bertie bellowed.

Kim sprinted for the shuttle, waving to his grandfather and laughing. Halla reached out to pull him in with a warm hand and a warmer smile.

"Let's go," she said.

The End

ALSO BY CHRISTIE MEIERZ

The Marann

Daughters of Suralia

The Fall

Farryn's War

Rembrandt's Station

For news about upcoming releases, advance copies, extras, AND a free ebook, sign up for Christie's newsletter at ChristieMeierz.com.

ABOUT THE AUTHOR

Award-winning author Christie Meierz writes space opera and science fiction romance set on a world of empaths at the edge of an advancing human empire. Her published works include her PRISM award-winning debut novel, **The Marann**, four more novels set in Tolari space, and several short stories. She is a member of the Science Fiction & Fantasy Writers Association (SFWA), spent 10 years raising sheep in Broome County, New York, and has been declared capable of learning Yup'ik.

Christie now lives in Rochester, NY, where she and her mathematician husband serve as full-time staff to two parlor panthers known to humans as Banichi the Assassin and Miss Myrtle the Hurricane Cat. (Their true names remain a mystery). Find out more at christiemeierz.com.

ACKNOWLEDGMENTS

No book is written in isolation. As an independent author, I organized an ever-changing team of helpers who edited and beta-read my words, designed my covers, and formatted my novels for both ebook and paper.

Outcaste wouldn't have been possible without the alpha reading and sometime steadying hand of Jeff, the incredible person I met more than 40 years ago who then proceeded to marry me; without the editing talent of Laura Anne Gilman; or without the feedback and enthusiasm of my intrepid beta readers, Lauretta Nagel and Kay Theriault. Ya done good, team.

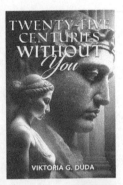